Ilahara

The Last Myrassar

C. M. Karys

Literary Wanderlust | Denver, Colorado

Published in the United States by Literary Wanderlust LLC, Denver, Colorado.

https//www.LiteraryWanderlust.com

Hardback available through FaeCrate
https://faecrate.com

ISBN Hardback: 978-1-942856-96-2
ISBN Paperback: 978-1-942856-83-2
ISBN Digital: 978-1-942856-95-5

Cover design: Gabriella Bujdóso

Interior illustrations: Kim Carlika
Map: Aleksandra Dimoska-Acedimski

Printed in the United States of America

Dedication

To Ren and Aleksandra—
Our first readers and harbingers of magic.

FROSTHEAD HALL

DAGANVER

TEIRAK'S MAW

VOLARIA

MAKKAN

THE'ILAH

THE HALL OF KINGS

HEARTSTAR

THE ARTERY

TYRRA

LUR

ADARA

EMBERNEST

ARA

Prologue

Maenar Elvik had never been a brave man, but he was loyal.

The scholar hastened down the Embernest's familiar hallways. Each step echoed against the polished marble floor as loud and hollow as his heartbeat. Once, the castle teemed with life. Music spilled from open doorways and dragonsong wafted from the courtyard. Poets and bards entertained guests at receptions. A beautiful queen commissioned frescoes, which embellished the walls from the skirting to the high ceiling. Art was a passion she passed on to both of her children. Their laughter filled each corner of the castle.

Once.

Now, their home was a tomb. The frescoes were painted over with white. Blue and silver replaced the red carpets and golden curtains. The proud dragon statues atop the pillars were cast down. No more music, no more laughter. Only memories remained.

The maenar climbed the stone stairs of the eastern tower, feigning a steady gait. The incessant hammer of his heart could betray him at any moment. As he approached the guards stationed in the hallway, he acknowledged them with a nod none returned. He held his breath, waiting for the command to stop and the whisper of an unsheathed sword.

Seconds passed, and the guards remained at their post.

They hadn't heard what happened with the queen's seer.

The maenar's thoughts drifted to the past. He'd been a young man when the Maenari sent him to Adara to serve at the Embernest, the seat of the Dragon-Blessed, a position coveted by many scholars.

The faces of the Myrassar he'd served faded under the hands of time. He couldn't remember King Gailen's voice or how Queen Jaemys's amber skin shimmered under the sun. One Myrassar, however, was indelible in the maenar's memories, a bright light time couldn't dim.

Asharaya.

Fourteen years had passed since Maenar Elvik last saw her. The night annals would later describe as the Coup of Fire. Men and women he cared for fell to traitors' blades and dragons fought and died. Aerella Argarys led the attack that felled the king and won her the throne. The morning after, the Myrassar had been lined up for the new queen's inspection. Her skin had been red with the blood of the family he'd loved.

A maenar does not interfere in the wars of men. Kings change, but a maenar's loyalty is to his post. His duty is to serve and offer counsel. The words of his oath often haunted him, but his heart refused to heed their hidden warning. How could he be loyal to a woman who stained her hands with the blood of the innocent? How could he love the children who replaced those who still lived in his heart?

Maenar Elvik had been powerless the night of the Coup of Fire, but tonight he was not.

Voices echoed up from the foot of the stairs. He hurried up the last steps and barged into the rookery. Ravens cawed and thrashed within their cages as he locked the door.

Shouts and footsteps rang out on the other side.

A raven struggled in his hold.

A few moments more.

His fingers trembled as he secured a note to the bird's leg. The door groaned with the weight of the guards barreling into it. "Let us in, by order of the queen."

The maenar released the raven as the door flew off its hinges. Two guards burst inside, eyes wide as a dark shadow took to the sky. "What have you done?" one shouted as his comrade rushed to the window.

"What had to be done."

The guard fired an arrow at the raven, missing it by a single breadth. By the time he notched a second arrow, it was already too late.

Every flap of the raven's wings was a weight lifting off the maenar's heart.

Maenar Elvik didn't fear death, and when the sword pierced him, he accepted the pain like a long-lost friend. Blood poured from the mortal wound, and the guards stood by as he fell to his knees and then to the ground.

His mind drifted to the moment the old crone's eyes glazed over and she'd spoken the words that stopped time and made a loyal man brave. As he walked away unnoticed, the seer's gaze turned to him amid the queen's bellowed order to have her seized.

Two survivors of a different Ilahara saying farewell.

Taking labored breaths as his lids grew heavy, Maenar Elvik could make out only muffled sounds, but the crone's words lingered. The maenar breathed his last with a smile.

Asharaya Myrassar is alive.

1

Princess Cassia Argarys strolled the Embernest's rose gardens with her friend and had the unmistakable feeling something terrible would happen. Courtiers loitered beneath shadows of fronds, seeking refuge from the heat. Autumn was fast approaching, but it would be some time before fresh winds reached them here in the south. She couldn't ignore the glances thrown her way or the whispers that followed. Her thoughts went to Korban. She hadn't seen him all day.

"Is everything all right, Cassia? You seem thoughtful."

The smell of roses was strong enough to taste. The scent brought with it happy memories, and a small smile soon bloomed on Cassia's rosy lips. "It's nothing." She patted her friend's arm, but the concerned expression remained. "Stop worrying, Eileen. You're too young to have wrinkles."

They walked in amicable silence, Cassia looking down at her feet as they crunched the gravel pathway, Eileen glancing sideways at her friend. Despite having spent most of her life in Adara, Eileen Todrak was a northerner in her bones and too serious for her own good. Cassia knew Eileen was biding her time, waiting for the moment the princess would erupt.

"We should choose our dresses for tomorrow's dinner," Cassia said, veering Eileen's attention elsewhere. "High Keeper Baramun has confirmed he'll join us."

"He's been visiting often lately."

"The Crown and the Faith are the pillars of Ilahara."

"Spoken like a true royal." Eileen heaved a sigh. "We wouldn't want to upset his Holiness with common clothes."

"You should wear the pink gown with the pearl bodice. It favors your complexion."

"I'm not sure..."

"Derron couldn't take his eyes off you." A small lie, but not completely untrue. Derron had been staring quite a lot at Eileen that night since he'd discovered the queen would have him marry their northern ward. Derron loved Eileen and they made an excellent match—Fire and Ice, light and dark.

Cassia's brother, however, was complicated.

Eileen blushed, a red glow spreading on her umber cheeks. It was no secret she fancied Derron. "Do you think he'll wear rings on all ten fingers, or will he stick with the usual seven?" Cassia required a moment to understand they were talking about the high keeper again. "I wonder how he manages to move his fingers."

The young women's laughter died down when a dozen royal guards crossed the far end of the gardens, silver armor clanging and shining as they marched. Cassia recognized the young man leading them by the way he moved alone, but the silver-blond hair tied back with a strap of leather confirmed it.

What business did Derron have with those guards?

"They must be headed to see the queen," Eileen said.

"Your brother mentioned he's been summoned."

Cassia spun to look at her, freeing her arm from her friend's. "When were you planning on telling me?"

"It slipped my mind."

"Slipped your mind? As if you ever forget anything, Eileen. Don't insult my intelligence."

Eileen sighed. "He didn't want you to worry."

"Mother summoned him. Why should I worry?"

At Eileen's silence, uncertainty wedged itself in Cassia's mind. These were strange times to be keeping secrets and Cassia hated being left in the dark. She had no choice but to hurry after her brother.

The princess wasn't allowed to enter the throne room. The guards were under direct orders from the queen to keep everyone out, including Cassia. If her mother was determined to avoid Cassia's presence, she and Derron must be discussing something Cassia would strongly oppose.

One way or another, Cassia would find out what was happening. If she couldn't see Derron in the throne room, then she would wait in his chambers.

Derron's rooms weren't far from her own. The twins couldn't stomach staying away from one another in their early years. They did most of their schooling together and played games together, too. For a while, they even slept in the same room.

Derron's quarters were exceptionally chaotic. The exquisite craftsmanship of the minimal furniture was the only sign the space belonged to a prince. A small bookcase and a low divan furnished the living area. Portraits and paintings gifted by the derelicts he called friends either hung on the walls or rested against them. A piano occupied most of the bedroom's large space, making the bed, armoire, and long mirror look out of place. The curtains were silver and dark blue like the coverlet on his bed, which was cluttered with Derron's music sheets. Cassia slid some aside to make room for herself as she waited.

An hour passed before the door opened and her brother stepped inside the room.

"Forcing your sister to wait is not princely."

"I thought you'd be here." Fire from the hearth cast golden light on Derron's fair skin, highlighting the haggard lines of his face. He shook his hair loose with slow movements.

"You told Eileen and not me?"

"She'll be my wife in case you've forgotten."

"Yet I'm the one who had a bath prepared for you."

"I'd be lost without you," Derron said with a saccharine smile.

"I don't appreciate sarcasm." Cassia placed her hands on her hips. "What did Mother say that you didn't want me to know?"

Derron removed his clothes and shuffled into the adjacent bathing chamber. Cassia followed, unperturbed by her brother's nudity. Watching Derron was as unsurprising as looking at her own reflection, albeit with fewer curves. Nevertheless, she averted her eyes from his bare back as he settled into the warm bath. She sat on the marbled edge. Waiting.

Eventually, he let out a long, defeated breath. "Honestly, sister, I thought you would have guessed by now."

She had.

It wasn't uncommon for Aerella Argarys to request an audience with the seer. The Sight was a rare gift and one her mother liked to keep close. Unrest in the North, a rainless summer—these were the visions the Argarys anticipated. They'd always proven true. Yet the future was never set in stone. The smallest event held the power to alter its course.

Asharaya Myrassar is alive, and she shall return to reclaim what was stolen.

A wicked sort of delight had sparked in the old woman's eyes at the chaos she unleashed in the throne room. Her words had been like a stone in a well, taking their time to sink in. Her mother, regal upon her throne, went rigid. Her father, Vaemor, denied their truthfulness. Derron stared unblinkingly and Cassia clutched his fingers, her heartbeat steadying at the touch.

The courtiers, who had silently waited to hear the latest vision, murmured the name until it became a pounding in her ears, striking like a cudgel.

Asharaya.

"Seize her," Aerella ordered, standing so fast it was a wonder her legs hadn't snapped in two. The crone smiled as the guards took her. Had she known that was going to be her last vision?

"So, it took three days with Semal to break the hag?" Cassia asked now.

"Everyone breaks eventually. We've lost precious time. The raven has no doubt reached its intended target."

"I wouldn't be surprised if it caught a slight chill."

Derron nodded, looking grim. "Princess Asharaya has to be dealt with."

"She's no princess. I am."

The prince looked down at his finger trailing the still surface of the water. "Semantics."

"Who is she sending?" When Derron set his jaw, Cassia had her answer. "You?" she exclaimed. "Why not a more seasoned warrior?"

"An Argarys blade earned us the throne. An Argarys blade will keep it." It was Derron's voice but their mother's words.

"You're needed here."

"I must do this for our family." He avoided looking at her. There were things he wasn't saying.

"You'll have to kill her in cold blood."

His throat bobbed. "I know."

"The past is the past. She's the enemy."

Derron punched the water and some splashed over the sides, drenching a part of Cassia's gown. "I know."

She didn't press him further, choosing to let the silence linger as he sank into the water.

Cassia walked to the head of the tub. Derron relaxed as she gathered his hair and brushed it back with her fingers. "What's the plan?"

"Semal will arrange passage on a ship in Tyrra. He knows a captain who won't ask questions. I'll have to give him a letter, and he'll take me where I need to go. Only a handful of men will come with me to avoid drawing too much attention."

"You'll draw attention. You're an Argarys. One look at your hair and people will know who you are."

"That's what glamours are for, sister." Despite the tension, Cassia held on to the hint of levity in her brother's tone, seeking comfort in their familiar teasing. "It will hold long enough to get me on a ship."

"How long will you be gone?"

"It'll take me a week on land to reach Tyrra, and then a fortnight at sea. Gods willing, I'll be back in two months. I'll send word once I'm back in Ilahara."

Cassia nodded, releasing her brother's hair. Her hands trembled at the thought of Derron being gone for so long, and she tucked them between her legs to hide them. It was more time than they'd ever spent apart. "Where will you find her?"

Derron paused before he answered. "Havanya."

The Human Continent.

2

"You're tempting fate these days."

Mykal Todrak watched his little sister run toward the great iron doors of Frosthead Hall. Her small feet left imprints in the thin layer of snow dusting the courtyard. A brisk wind blew from the north, ruffling the fur collar of Mykal's cloak. Autumn neared, and Daganver would be the first Ilahein region to hail the upcoming winter.

He turned his attention to his companion. An amused twinkle lingered in Kael's blue eyes, a consequence of being caught red-handed breaking the rules. It hadn't been hard for Mykal to find his friend. He needed only to follow the sound of his mother's rules being broken, and there he found Kael guiding Luna through a series of fighting stances.

"Is that so?" Kael asked.

"You know my mother doesn't want Luna anywhere near a weapon." It wasn't simply that Lady Alissa considered it improper for a lady to wield one. She'd already lost her eldest son to a sword and wouldn't risk the same fate befalling her eight-year-old daughter.

"You know it's in her best interest to learn."

"Mother disagrees."

"Will you tell on me?"

Mykal held Kael's gaze for a long, silent moment. A smile bloomed on Kael's lips, helplessly mirrored on Mykal's. Mykal would never tell on Kael. He'd sooner cut off his right hand. They were more than friends, closer than blood.

They were Do'strath.

The two young men grinned as they started toward the stables, snow crunching beneath their boots. They hadn't agreed to a ride, but between them, it was never necessary to make plans.

"You could at least choose a more inconspicuous place to practice."

"You'd have to stress too much to find us." Mykal's smile widened at the subtle lilt in Kael's voice. When Kael teased, it didn't always sound like it. Most times what came out of Kael's mouth sounded serious. Understanding the subtlety was the key to understanding Kael.

For Mykal, nothing was easier.

He and Kael had been friends since childhood. There wasn't a day in memory when the names Mykal Todrak and Arkael hadn't been pronounced together. Mykal didn't have friends—only acquaintances and Kael. Friendship was too simple a word to describe what passed between them, so when Kael had asked the Soul Binding of him, Mykal said yes, unflinching where others might have pondered the risks. Together they survived and endured the union of souls, a sacred rite performed by one of the few surviving ministers of the Dragon Faith. The fire turned blue, and the Dragon had two more Do'strath.

The slide of leather was the only sound as they saddled

their horses. Because the ride was unplanned, they had neither food nor water to carry. No matter, since theirs would be a quick excursion into the nearby forest.

A gust of wind carried the strong aroma of pine trees, and Mykal breathed in deep, relishing in the familiar scent. His heart thrummed with the anticipation of exploring the forest paths. During the colder months, he and Kael often rode north toward the mountains. Now, the weather was too warm to attempt the trip, and the risk of avalanches too great.

Under both heavy winter snowfalls and light summer flurries, Daganver's forest was beautiful. It embodied the freedom to pursue an adventure and an escape from responsibilities. It was home as much as the gray stone towers of Frosthead Hall.

Mykal heard Kael's name called out, and then a figure ran past the stables and turned back. The woman leaned against the threshold, chest heaving. A fragile human heart thundered in her chest. Despite his longer fae limbs and pale blond hair, one couldn't mistake the woman as anything but Kael's mother. The same straight nose specked with light freckles, the same blue eyes, and the same full lips, the lower one fuller than the upper.

"Ma?" Kael released his horse's bridle and took a step toward his mother.

"Good, I caught you before you left," she said, panting. The smile she reserved Mykal was as sweet as the one she gave her son. "Good morning, my lord." Seven years had come and gone, but the human persisted in calling her son's Do'strath by his title.

"Is something wrong?"

"Lord Darrok wants to see you. Both of you."

If Mykal's father called, then it had to be an urgent matter.

Mykal and Kael hurried through the dark hallways, a perpetual chill seeping through the stones of the Todrak's stronghold. Indeed, the lord waited in his private study, where he only received to discuss delicate matters.

The minimalist space was a perfect reflection of Darrok Todrak. No rug embellished the gray stone floor. No adornments sat on the top shelves of the floor-to-ceiling library. Old tomes were neatly organized in alphabetical order, their brown leather covers enveloping pages upon pages of Ilahein history, war records, and philosophical and medical treatises.

Those who knew him considered Darrok Todrak a quiet man, good lord, and proud Head of Daganver like his father and grandfather before him. Lord Todrak was a loyal man, they said, none more trustworthy. Those who didn't know him perceived him as a powerful fae—powerful enough to maintain a position as Head despite the wheelchair that confined him for the past fourteen years.

Mykal saw his father's loyalty whenever a guest noticed the lack of effigies representing Borethes, the god who, according to the New Faith, they were to worship in the North. Loyalty to the Dragon Faith, despite it no longer being tolerated, made it possible for him and Kael to be Do'strath. Loyalty to a name long since gone.

"Father," Mykal said, as Kael closed the door behind them. He started at the familiar figure in the chair. "Mother."

"Son, Kael. Come." Lord Darrok gestured them closer to the desk. Mykal sat beside his mother while Kael stood behind him. "A raven arrived from Maenar Elvik."

The lord leaned forward on his chair and handed over a scroll to his son. Mykal's stomach sank at the smear of blood on the paper. Ravens had sharp claws, but the Maenari were careful. Maenar Elvik must have been in a rush.

He held the note up so Kael could read over his shoulder.

A shiver raced down the length of his spine, and his fingers tensed around the parchment. Mykal didn't know how to react to the words—one sentence, but it could change Ilahara, spread courage, and raise armies.

"It was Seen. Asharaya Myrassar," Kael read aloud. "She's alive?"

"And she shall return to reclaim what was stolen," Mykal finished.

Darrok Todrak nodded. Candlelight cast shadows on his onyx skin. "The Dragon couldn't let the Dragon-Blessed die so easily." He spoke as if he'd always known there was hope.

Mykal's loyalty to the Myrassar reflected his father's devotion. He'd been seven years old when the Argarys staged the Coup of Fire, but he remembered enough. Grief drove his father to take up arms in the Uprisings against the usurper queen. Men died in name of that loyalty, and still they'd lost. Every Myrassar in the kingdom was seized, slaughtered, and their supporters either killed or subdued.

"Father, you saw the bodies," Mykal reasoned. Aerella Argarys had kept the corpses hanging from the battlements of the Embernest when the Heads of Ilahara gathered in the capitol to swear fealty. "The Myrassar are dead."

"Aerella must have replaced Asharaya with someone else."

"You deduce this from the scribbled words of a maenar in Aerella's service?" Mykal waved the parchment before his face. "Father, this is madness."

"I have known Maenar Elvik since before you were born." Lord Darrok didn't raise his voice, but Mykal recoiled nonetheless. "He wouldn't lie, especially about this."

"What do we do now?" Kael's whispered question broke through the heavy silence.

Mykal turned to his Do'strath, bewildered.

"We do what we must." Darrok's solemn tone would normally quiet a room and pin the eyes of the gathered on the lord. "The Argarys have usurped the throne long enough. We must send word to the other regions."

Mykal gave a mirthless laugh. "The other regions?" He leaned forward, meeting his father's gaze. "The Vynatis in Tyrra turned their backs on you during the Uprisings. The Farwynd in Makkan are Aerella's strongest allies. The Nahar in Merania serve no interest but their own. Are we to send word to the farmers in Adara?"

"The Myrassar name still means something to loyal men."

"Have you considered Aerella's hand may be behind this message? It's no secret you despise her. Don't give her an excuse to execute you."

"I trust Maenar Elvik." He gestured for the note, which Mykal placed on the desk.

Lady Alissa glared at her husband. "You forget we've lost a son to the Argarys, and they hold our daughter, our Eileen."

"It's also for them that we must do this."

"Your obsession with the Dragon-Blessed has brought our family nothing but woe. You were crippled, we've lost two children, and Daganver suffers. I will not—cannot—stand by and let you risk another of my sons for the Myrassar."

Mykal straightened. *Another of my sons.*

"What is it you ask of me, Father?"

"Mykal," his mother pleaded.

"You and Kael are Do'strath," Lord Darrok said with pride. Even before the Soul Binding was outlawed, not many chose to undergo the ritual, for not all who did survived. To be Do'strath was a mark of strength and nobility in the eye of the Dragon and gave the soulbound the ability to combine their elements, making them hard to defeat. "I believe your tracking spell could find Princess Asharaya, wherever she is. Maenar Elvik's information came from Aerella's seer. Aerella may already know the princess's location."

"And the queen has the advantage," Kael added. "A raven from the Embernest would have taken at least a week to reach us."

Lord Darrok nodded, looking grim.

"If Princess Asharaya is alive, how will we find her?" Mykal asked.

Lord Darrok produced a golden pendant from a drawer. Mykal had a vague memory of it catching the light around a lovely golden neck. "This belonged to Queen Jaemys Myrassar." Mykal could picture his father fighting in the Uprisings and breaching the castle with his eldest son, Rendal, in tow. He must have found the necklace between one conflict and the next before a dozen guards and a sword to the spine stopped him from killing Aerella. "This would have been Princess Asharaya's for her Rite of Passage once she came of age. You'll find her with this."

A hesitant moment passed before Mykal reached for the necklace. The heirloom was one of the last relics of a lost family. The golden pendant appeared fragile when one thought of it that way. His fingers barely tightened around the gemstones composing the dragon's body.

"And when we find her?" Kael asked although they both knew the answer.

The lord took up the maenar's note from the desk. His eyes skittered along the words one last time before he held the parchment over a lit candle. Mykal followed the flame as it devoured the paper. "I want you to bring her home."

3

Heat filtered through the Establishment's open windows. Red and golden drapes swayed as young men and women wiped sweat from their foreheads, cooling down before the night's work began.

Shara was at ease in the stifling warmth. Sultry air parted around her amber skin and caressed her exposed arms and waist like a friend's intimate touch. Curious glances prickled her skin as the prostitutes took in the generous curves, the waterfall of brown hair, and the black dragon tattoo on her right leg. Anyone who looked her way would know she was like no other in the Lioness's Establishment. The expensive gossamer dress told them she wasn't up for grabs like the rest, her rare beauty one only select patrons could afford.

A young girl approached Shara with a tray of pastries, her brown eyes downcast to avoid the stares of those she addressed. Like the other child workers, Lily was an orphan taken off the streets by the Lioness only to have one nightmare exchanged for another. Lily served refreshments to the clients, but soon that would change. The first signs of womanhood appeared on the girl's face. Beneath her dress, breasts swelled, and she was taller than the last time Shara saw her.

Shara plastered on a smile to hide a surge of pity. She'd once had the right title to help girls like Lily, but here in Havanya, the strong preyed on the weak. Shara no longer had the power to change the world. She could only try to make it better. "Thank you, Lily," she murmured as she took a pastry. She was never hungry before a job, but she knew it would please the child to be of service.

Indeed, the girl smiled and peeked at Shara beneath dark lashes. "Will you be staying with us long, Lady Shara?"

"Not long."

If Lily was saddened or relieved, she didn't get the chance to say. The Lioness prowled into the main room and clapped her hands to capture the attention of her cubs, causing Lily to scurry away. The Lioness's rings of gold, rubies, and sapphires, gifts from rich patrons, gleamed as they caught the candlelight.

Shara had never learned the Lioness's real name, but she'd heard stories of the woman who clawed her way from the darkest corners of Havanya to the riches of her Establishment. She'd been a rare beauty, with skin fair as snow and hair golden as a ray of sunshine. Men would have gone to war for her if only she'd been born a princess. Even now, in her late fifties, the Lioness moved with a feline's grace. Only the marks cornering her eyes betrayed her age.

"My cubs," the woman said, sighing. Her gaze raked across the receiving room's wide space, meeting every youth sprawled on the plush, low divans and intricately designed golden rugs. "I want our guests to leave our humble home with featherlight pockets and a smile on their faces."

Two men heaved open the golden doors, pouring more heat inside the lavish space. As if summoned by the warm wind, scents of jasmine and lavender lifted from the burning candles in sconces placed at intervals along the burgundy walls. The fragrance blended with an exotic smell Shara couldn't place, filling her lungs and warming her skin.

The Lioness stood beside Shara, masking her tension with a smile. "Don't make a scene."

"I know my craft, Lioness," Shara whispered. "For your sake, I hope you do, too."

Soon, a flow of clientele filled the Establishment. In a way, the Lioness was a lovely host. She greeted clients with a full smile and small talk before directing them to the right kind of fantasy. Be it experience or natural talent, the Lioness had a way of sizing up a person with a glance and few words. No one ever left her Establishment unsatisfied.

The main room resonated with soft murmurs, moans, and giggles. Girls sat across men's laps, feeding them grapes and sweet tarts from silver platters. Curious hands roamed over warm skin. Like any slow dance, seduction required time. Haste could sever attraction's thrall and spoil the pleasure. Still, some newly formed couples were already lost in slow, lustful kisses. A young man led a woman to the private rooms in the back.

Shara observed with hungry eyes and waited. Tension warred with training-induced calm until her mark swaggered into the Establishment.

Master Crane was a middle-aged man, tall, polished, and clad in a black suit. A limp forced him to carry a cane, which was adorned with a silver crow's head, and his black hair grayed at the temples. He was one of the wealthiest men on the continent thanks to trade with the Magical Lands, as they called them in Havanya.

Ilahara.

The Lioness greeted him with the same flourish reserved for royalty. After all, he was one of her best clients, and tonight he'd paid in advance for something unique. His dark gaze drifted past the Lioness as he kissed her knuckles and locked onto Shara like a moth drawn to a flame. Shara smiled, dipping her head in greeting.

Master Crane wasn't the only new arrival.

A man sauntered in, attracting all attention in a matter of moments. He wasn't wearing fine suits like the other patrons but light fighting leathers in polished shades of blue and silver. Twin blades were sheathed at his back, the blue jay pommels setting them off as the work of a skilled blacksmith. His warrior's build highlighted a natural beauty, yet it wasn't the reason everyone stilled. A strap of leather held back the man's silver-blond hair, revealing the pointed tips of his ears.

The man seemed unburdened by the fearful stares and whispers as he looked around the room.

Shara's heart raced. Training pinned her in place, but she couldn't silence the small voice inside begging her to run. She'd been a girl the last time she saw a fae. Men and women who she knew and loved screamed as they died, devoured by furious flames. Those memories swarmed to the surface. Walls burned around her. Moans turned to pained screams. Sighs morphed into sounds of dying creatures. All of that narrowed into the pointed tips of the stranger's ears.

He's here for me, a primordial instinct screamed. She wanted to run into the humid Havanian night, away from this stranger and the things he evoked.

She remained frozen in her seat.

For once, the Lioness wasn't smiling. Her face was ashen and her eyes wide. Shara doubted she'd ever seen a fae in her life, although the Lioness knew of the powerful beings to the east and separated from them by a large expanse of sea. Any human with an ounce of self-preservation stayed away from the Magical Lands. Those who didn't—or couldn't—lived to regret it.

"H-hello," the Lioness stuttered in Havanian. The fae turned, a furrow on his brow. The Lioness gestured one of the girls pressed against the far wall to come forward.

"You have come to the right place, friend," Master Crane said in fluent Ilahein, clearly the only one at ease with the fae's presence. "Trust the Lioness to make a fae return to our shores."

Shara fisted the thin fabric of her gown. *He's not here for you.* She sucked in a breath. *Remember your mission.* She released it.

The girl, shaking like a leaf, took the fae's hand. Instead of letting himself be led out the main room, he drew her close and cupped her face. The girl's shaking ceased. A chunky ring on his index finger prodded Shara's memory. "You are lovely," he said in surprisingly fluent Havanian. His voice was like a song and as soft as velvet. The girl sighed. "Unfortunately, you are not the one I seek."

The fae looked straight at Shara.

Her blood curdled and her hand drifted to her back.

"That one is taken." Master Crane's amicable tone held an undercurrent of threat. Had he been less arrogant, he might have practiced caution. If the fae chose to resort to a physical challenge, then he would hold the advantage.

Tension thrummed in every sinew of Shara's body as she stood. She kept her gaze downcast, meek, and obedient and dared to glance upward only when Master Crane extended a hand.

The fae stepped between them, ignoring Master Crane's low string of curses. Shara recoiled before they could touch. "Is there no way I might change your mind?"

Up close, she couldn't miss the obsidian ring's dark shine. A dragon's head rested regally against the fae's pale finger. A red gem in its eye winked as if enlivened by flames. Something about the ring was familiar, although she couldn't place why. Her eyes lingered on the dragon's masterfully rendered features. *Black like his scales. Red like his eyes.* Though her heart constricted, she itched with the curiosity to examine it. Instead, she met the fae's expectant silver gaze.

"You cannot afford me."

"Is that so?" Amusement coated each word. "I could offer more than gold."

"Like?"

"A story."

Shara laughed, hoping the fae wouldn't catch the hint of tension hidden within its depths. His eyes roamed her face, never straying to the generous neckline of her dress. Shara flushed at his scrutiny. Up close, he was even more handsome. The combination of pale skin and hair, silver eyes, and the perfect cut of his jaw made him resemble a storybook prince. In another life, she'd known someone with that same striking combination, and he'd loved stories as much as she did.

She had to get away.

"Stories don't keep bellies full." Shara sidestepped him and grasped Crane's hand in hopes the fae would direct his attention elsewhere. "Besides, the Lioness only accepts payments in gold."

"I would make a far better companion than my friend." The fae's emphasis on the last word made Crane freeze, face going red.

Shara offered him an apologetic smile before looking back at the fae. "Perhaps, but not tonight." She saluted him with a courteous nod. "Come and find me with that story."

She didn't plan to be in the Establishment to hear it.

"Please, make yourself comfortable."

Shara unlaced her fingers from Master Crane's, closing the door behind them. Master Crane moved with the familiarity of one who spent many nights in these rooms. He sat on the bed as Shara headed to the refreshment table. She sensed his greedy ogling of her body as she poured the wine. At least he couldn't see the slight tremor of her hands. Her thoughts conjured the red glow of the dragon's eye and the fae's steady silver gaze. *What is a fae doing in Havanya?*

"I've never seen you before." Master Crane's voice dragged her back to the present.

"You couldn't have, Master. I'm new."

As they drank, Shara didn't miss the lust darkening his gaze or the rising bulge between his legs, courtesy of the aphrodisiac wafting from the main room.

"I asked for the best, not some novice."

"I am the best."

The master took the chalice from her and placed it on the bedside table along with his own. "Let's see what I paid for, then."

Shara's stomach churned in distaste, but she wore a fake smile. She flexed her finger, beckoning him closer. "Come."

"Master," he reminded.

"Master." Shara led his hands to her hips. The master leaned in to kiss the skin around her navel. Shara's left hand tangled into the master's hair.

Her right hand drifted to her back. A cool kiss to her fingers steeled her resolve and cleared her mind of the turmoil brought by the fae.

"Look at me," she whispered.

The master looked up.

Shara plunged the dagger into his eye.

She relished in the sound of the master's anguished

screams. As he pressed a hand to his bleeding eye, Shara cleansed her dagger with the fold of her gown. "I was going to wait, but you were getting far too greedy."

The master fixed his good eye on Shara, whimpering with fear. He assessed the distance between himself and the door. Shara blocked his path to freedom. If he tried to run, she would intercept him. "Help!" he cried, scampering away from the assassin.

"No one will come, master. Save your breath."

"The Lioness—"

"Couldn't stop me even if she wanted." She took a step forward with a cunning smile. The master slithered back. A dark stain spread on the front of his breeches.

"Please..." he whimpered. "I'll pay you. I'll give you anything."

"Do you remember Thalina?"

"N-no."

"You wouldn't, would you?" Shara grimaced. She twisted the dagger in her grip. "But Thalina remembers you. Your raiders broke into her village and took her only son."

"No...I...p-please..."

"You sold him to the fae."

When Thalina sought the vrah's justice, afraid and broken by grief, Shara had been there. Listening to the woman's story reminded Shara of another place, another time, and another girl who lost everything in the span of one night.

"I'm sorry," Master Crane lied. "I'll pay her for the boy she lost."

Shara grabbed his hair and the man cried out. Her blade grazed the skin of his exposed neck.

"Even if you kill me, it won't bring back the boy. It won't change anything. This will happen again, to another boy, to another mother. What will you gain from my death?"

"Nothing." A drop of blood trickled along his neck. Darkness seeped into the room from the slit beneath the door and the balcony. The sounds of laughter and frolicking from the other rooms faded. A brisk wind snuffed out the candles. "But you'll be dead."

4

Compared to the vastness of the Magical Lands, Havanya wasn't a large continent. Villages extended from the base of one of its tallest mountains, which made up the majority of the terrain. The fishmongers' village was the closest to the port, where ships made anchor and men sold the result of late-night ventures at sea. The catch was mostly common fish, but among the shrimps, codfish, oysters, and clams one could often find extraordinary creatures with peculiar shapes and vibrant colors. Havanians knew better than to eat something from Ilahara's waters, but those rich enough to afford such a relic proudly kept the fish as trophies of adventures they'd never lived.

Havanya's colors concentrated in the village. They dimmed the higher up one walked the mountain's narrow paths. Onyx slates made up the roads and houses. Rooftops and wooden tavern signs alone broke the monotony. Gray smoke rose from chimneys and a veil descended from the mountaintop like a misty waterfall. Shara had never been able to glimpse the highest peak of Havanya's mountains, so dense was the fog surrounding them.

Small markets lined the streets, and vendors shouted over the crowd's chatter to attract attention to their wares.

"The softest silks from the Magical Lands."

"The best spices on this side of the sea."

"Pearls from the Siren Coves."

"Look yourselves, friends, 'tis a true dragon's skull, on my mother's honor."

Havanya had no king. Gold was its only ruler. Those who had it thrived, while those who didn't became thieves, liars, and killers to acquire it. There was no honest trade between Havanya and Ilahara. The silks were spun by housewives, the pearls had never seen the ocean, and the dragon's skull was nothing but the remains of a dead house cat. Still, Shara smiled as she made her way uphill. These thieves, liars, and killers were her people and Havanya was her home.

Along the way, Shara stopped by The Little Loot. She loved spending her free time cooped up in the bookshop, and Master Rocke, the elderly shopkeeper, had recommended to her the best titles. Tomes of various genres lined the shelves, but Shara's favorites were stories of epic battles and great evils to defeat. Master Rocke made it his mission to provide her with new titles every few months.

Shara peeked through the window. Master Rocke balanced on his wooden ladder, gentle as he placed new volumes onto the higher shelves before closing hour. The temptation to enter nagged at her but the weight of her satchel gave her pause.

Drip, drip, drip, drip.

She would have to visit The Little Loot come morning.

The Vrah's Keep resided halfway up the mountain, crammed between houses and taverns and yet impossible to miss. Several levels formed the structure, built entirely of red stone. A golden flag with crossed black daggers jutted from the watchtower on its right. The Keep was the single splash of color in a world of gray.

Shara had first seen it as a child. Covered head to toe in dried blood, she had smelled fouler than the fish in the market after a fortnight at sea. Grief weighed down every unsteady step. Her family, her home, and her dragon were all lost in the span of a night at the hands of a woman who should have been a friend. If Shara stopped moving, she never would have taken another step, so she kept walking and found the Keep.

The somber tones of Havanya's streets reminded her of ashes and death, but the red of the Keep was fire, life. She drifted to its doors as if guided by a phantom hand. A voice in her head told her she'd survive if she reached the great black doors.

I want to be strong.

Now, Shara stepped into the Keep. Blood dripping from the satchel traced a red line on the black marble. The hall was vast and dark. Low light diffused from wrought iron chandeliers, which were fashioned into blades and arrows. An intense smell of incense tickled Shara's nose. During the day, those who hadn't worked the night before would train, filling the halls with the sound of steel. Tonight, the Keep was silent as a tomb and the only sound came from the crackling wood and the *drip, drip, drip* following Shara's steps.

Douglas Spirre stood before the hearth, dressed in a white suit with golden embroidery, which set off the rich brown of his skin. Only the Vrahiid wore the color. His dimpled smile made it easy to forget he was the most skilled killer Shara ever met, but the scar on his exposed chest served as a reminder that the Vrahiid was not to be crossed. The only man who'd tried now rotted in the ground.

"You're early." Dougas's voice rumbled in the vast hall.

Before Shara could turn for the stairs, the Vrahiid blocked her path. She clenched her teeth hard enough to hurt, avoiding the man's gaze. Disapproval rolled off him in waves. Though she had no regrets, his judgment stung. "What do you have there?"

"A gift for the Maiden."

When he reached for the satchel, Shara tightened her grip, a challenging look in her eyes. Dougas didn't shout or strike. He did nothing but stare, and it was enough. Shara's resolve crumbled like fragile ruins before the man who'd been a father to her for the past fourteen years. With a resigned sigh, she released the satchel.

A bloody eye and a glazed one stared lifelessly at Dougas from a severed head.

"This is Master Crane."

"Yes."

"You didn't give him a painless death," he observed.

"He didn't deserve one."

"That's not for us to decide."

"It's for the Maiden to decide." Shara recited the words she'd heard many times before. "And she moved my hand."

"Has she?" Shara was the first to look away. "I seem to recall the woman could not pay for the Maiden's justice."

"The Maiden has no need for gold, only blood. The boy Crane stole was Thalina's only family. It wasn't right to let him go unpunished because she couldn't afford your justice." Shara lifted her chin in defiance. As a vrah, she owed her obedience to the Vrahiid. Going against his orders went against everything she'd been taught, but she couldn't bring herself to regret it. One less slaver tainted Havanya's soil. Perhaps one less child would suffer because of it. She would do it again if given the choice. Whatever punishment awaited her would be worth it.

Dougas's eyes flickered in the dark. "Is it for justice, then, that you disobeyed your Vrahiid?"

The truth was a living presence in the room. Thalina's grief touched Shara more than she cared to show. Her shoulders slumped as the night's events caught up to her.

The Vrahiid brought his hands around her face. "I know why you did it," he whispered against her brow before placing a soft kiss there. She couldn't help but smile at the tenderness. "Get some rest."

Shara stifled a yawn. Hot tears of exhaustion dampened her lashes. She couldn't wait to surrender to a deep and restorative sleep. Hopefully, in the morning she would forget about both the fae and Thalina's child. Blood was spilled, and her debt was paid. Life could go on.

First, she needed a bath.

Shara threw open the door to her room. Her heart lurched, and she snatched the dagger at her hip. A figure lounged on her bed with her sketchbook in hand. Rami grinned, but she grimaced as he gracelessly set it aside. "Nice to see you, too."

She slammed the door shut. Though months had passed since she surrendered to Rami's flirtations, she was no closer to expecting anyone who wasn't Solana in her room. With everything that happened tonight, Shara's self-preservation instincts multiplied tenfold. To his credit, Rami didn't seem concerned that Shara nearly lodged a dagger between his eyes. He prowled to her, all slim muscles and unruly black curls. "One of these days I'm going to kill you and I won't hold myself responsible."

"Did the old man make a scene?" His green eyes gleamed with mischief.

"Don't speak of your Vrahiid that way."

Rami hummed in amusement, but when he was close

enough to look into her face, his eyes darkened. "What happened?"

Shara shook her head. "It's nothing."

"Shara."

Like many Havanians, Rami's path crossed with raiders as a young boy. While he escaped, his brothers hadn't been as lucky. Rather than deal with those memories, Rami liked to smile and pretend the past had never been. Shara saw through the ruse. She recognized a haunted look.

Shara brought her hands to his, the past he'd shared and the one she hadn't lodged in the space between their bodies. "There was a fae in the Establishment."

Concern crossed Rami's face as he searched hers. "Did it hurt you?"

"I can protect myself." Although the words were true, nerves coiled in her stomach like a pit of vipers ready to strike. *They think I'm dead.* Yet the scrutinizing silver gaze of the fae rattled her. *He couldn't know.* Yet her eyes were golden like her father's. Even if the fae hadn't guessed her identity, would he start to suspect?

"Perhaps it's still in the Establishment."

Shara grasped Rami's arm before he could take another step, fingers digging deep, causing him to wince. "Where do you think you're going?"

"To kill it." Bile coated her tongue as the full might of his hatred for the fae contorted his face and hardened his features. While the raiders had taken his family, he despised the fae who paid for them in gold even more. *If he knew the truth, would he hate me, too?* Fae were the enemy. Rami didn't know any better.

"Or maybe it'll kill you." Her words met deaf ears. Rami pulled back, but Shara's grip tightened. The remnants of her fae strength, a secret she kept from him, aided her in keeping her lover from his destructive course of action.

"Let go of me."

"Killing the fae won't bring back your family."

He laughed, but there was no humor in the sound. "You're one to talk about caution."

"Let the fae be." Shara caressed his cheek and leaned forward. Her heart fluttered at the suggestion of his warm lips. "Stay."

Rami's lashes brushed against her amber skin. His body relaxed beneath her touch. The arm he'd so stubbornly worked to pry away from her locked around her middle.

"Yes."

5

Amethyst clouds glided across a midnight blue sky when the *Silent Merchant* docked in the Havanian harbor after a fortnight at sea. The ship was neither the biggest nor the fastest, but it was sturdy and discreet. While sailors unloaded cargo, two men disembarked. The captain, a fae glamoured as a human, would wait no more than three days for them. It was a kindness to Lord Darrok, who showed mercy to a former pirate many years before.

Three days for the Do'strath to find a lost princess.

Kael took in a deep breath. Wind ruffled his hair and carried smells of the sea and the nearby market. Familiarity and novelty coalesced in the stench of fish and the scent of humans. His mother's family hailed from the Human Continent. These were her people—his people. In part, at least.

Behind him, Mykal groaned. "This place reeks." His dark complexion was unusually pale. Kael had felt and seen his Do'strath's seasickness, and he sensed his distress now down the soulbond. "No wonder our ancestors took a rowboat and chanced the waters."

"I don't think they used a rowboat." It was true, however, that the first fae had been human settlers changed by the Ilah's waters.

Havanya wasn't as vast as Ilahara, but finding Princess Asharaya would still prove difficult without the use of magic. All they knew was that the princess had inherited the traits typical to the Myrassar: her father's golden eyes and her mother's amber skin. As Mykal had graciously stated, she could be anyone on this overpopulated speck of shit.

Kael thumbed the Myrassar pendant beneath his shirt, a gesture he'd caught himself doing often during the voyage. The tracking spell had led them west to the shoreline. As the only known land west of Ilahara, Havanya was an educated guess.

"Can you feel her?" Mykal's loud Ilahein rang like a warning bell for every Havanian in earshot. Kael silenced him with a glare. Mykal flinched. "Sorry."

"What's the point of a glamour if you can't shut up?"

Mykal was a purebred fae. The only Havanian he knew were a few words and phrases Kael taught him over the years, which was enough to follow a simple conversation but not to pass as human. Kael would have to do most of the talking, and keeping Mykal quiet would be his first challenge.

He concentrated on the spell's steady thrum against his chest, warmer now that they were closer to the object of their search. "Yes, I can feel her."

Mykal stretched out his arm. "Lead the way."

Kael gave his friend an assessing look. "It wouldn't hurt to look for a room while we search."

"I'm fine."

"Tell that to someone who doesn't have his soul cross-stitched to yours."

"You're insufferable." Mykal huffed. "We'll look for a room, but the princess has priority. If we find her first, I'll hear no complaints about my well-being. That's my compromise, so don't try to argue."

Mykal walked ahead and Kael bit the inside of his lip to suppress a laugh.

"If only we could glamour this stink." Mykal sniffed himself and cringed. "And ours."

Unable to hold it back any longer, Kael laughed. "Myk." He pointed left. "This way."

The Do'strath made their way through the market and removed their cloaks when it became evident their Daganveran clothing was too heavy for the Havanian weather. In Ilahara, all activity ceased after sundown, but here the market was still swarming with people despite the late hour.

Being around this many humans earning their keep, unbothered and unafraid, was both beautiful and unsettling. Humans in Daganver were lucky. They received fair pay for their work and could own humble homes, though they couldn't run businesses. That was a higher practice meant for fae alone. Kael was luckier still. Though he was the half-breed son of a servant, Lord Darrok allowed him to study and train beside the lord's son. In a world where people like him were hardly considered fae, it meant something that the Head of Daganver had led a nameless bastard to the Stone Altar for the Soul Binding. Elsewhere, humans were enslaved in all but name. They were property, pets at best, meant to satisfy a fae's every whim and need. That mind frame had fathered him.

Most of these humans lied about their merchandise, but they were free to do so. Wouldn't it be nice if his mother could enjoy that same freedom?

Mykal gaped at the wares on display. More than once,

Kael had to stop his friend from calling out the lies and drag him along. "That's not from Ilahara," Mykal protested, but Kael reminded him that it didn't matter and that for as much as he tried, Mykal couldn't fix every wrong in the world.

Though he'd never stop trying.

They walked past a woman and a man settling on a price for a pearl necklace said to come from the Siren Coves. Neither Kael nor Mykal had ever seen the Siren Coves—even the *Silent Merchant* had taken a longer route to avoid them—but these pearls had an ordinary luster, not the otherworldly luminescence of those born in magical waters.

Mykal's outcry rose before Kael could stop him. "Those are not magical," he accused in rudimentary Havanian. The man and the woman turned to him, one in outrage, the other in surprise. "You, man,"—Kael guessed he'd meant *sir*—"are a liar."

The man's face turned purple. "How dare you call me a liar?"

Kael pulled his friend along. "You're going to get us killed," he muttered, but Mykal understood the human and said, "That is what you are."

"How do you know these are fake?" the woman asked instead. Kael noticed the wary look she threw Mykal. She saw a human and not the long limbs, the grace, or the casual tip of an ear poking through Mykal's mop of dark hair, but his accent gave him away as something *other*. The man didn't notice those things since he was too busy steaming and trying to close the deal, but the woman had eyes only for Mykal. Because he was strange and different.

Honest.

Mykal disentangled from Kael, who swore under his breath. "Mermaid pearls glow."

With that, Kael scurried them both away. They looked

back only once and found a small crowd gathered to witness the woman's accusations and the foul list of names she concocted in seconds. Despite himself, Kael laughed.

"Serves him right," Mykal said.

"Next time, try not to start a riot."

Mykal flashed a lopsided grin. "I won't make promises." He gestured to himself, implying his appearance alone could stir trouble.

Kael flushed and rubbed the nape of his neck. He should have countered with a smart remark, but Mykal hauled him into a nearby alley before he could. Kael peered over Mykal's shoulder to see what he'd missed that his Do'strath hadn't.

A fae patrolled the street.

"That doesn't look like a princess." Mykal paused. "It could be one of Aerella's agents. I say we follow him."

"And risk being seen? Our priority is the princess. If we get caught, we're of no use to her."

"He's just one man."

"You're assuming he's alone."

"And what if he's not and his accomplices already found her?" Mykal grasped his Do'strath's shoulder, a fervent light in his brown eyes. "My father could have sent an army, yet he chose us. Why do you think he did?"

"Because this is a covert mission?"

"Because we are Do'strath. There's nothing we can't accomplish together." His grip tightened. "We can take on whatever scum Aerella has sent to this foul place. We'll save the princess and bring her home."

Kael smiled. If only Mykal realized how much he sounded like Lord Darrok. At that moment, Kael would have fought the entire Argarys army if Mykal asked.

A door opened, light spilling onto the street along with laughter and far more indecent sounds. The Do'strath shared a long look. Kael's cheeks warmed while Mykal's eyes widened a fraction.

"What in the Dragon's name is this place?" Mykal muttered, dismayed.

A long shadow etched against the pavement. Kael chanced a peek at the street, and his heart nearly stopped. Maybe Mykal sensed his alarm down their bond or saw the way Kael's body froze. He glanced around the wall, stifling a curse.

The shadow's owner was definitely fae. He hid it neither with a glamour nor with the spill of his silver-blond hair— hair similar to his own. This was the queen's agent.

"Derron Argarys." Mykal spat the name, hatred prevailing on stupor.

The prince.

Kael's half-brother.

6

"**M**other?"

Young Asharaya dropped beside the queen's body. The golden silk of her mother's nightgown was drenched through with blood. Her small fists closed around the fabric. Red stained her hands, warm and unwelcome. No matter how much she screamed and begged, her mother didn't stir. Her amber skin dulled. Her warmth faded fast. "Mother, please." Shards of glass replaced the heart inside her chest. "Mother, I'm scared. Don't leave me."

The queen was already gone.

An anguished sob ravaged her throat and she clung to her mother's body. Blood mingled with tears. It coated her tongue with its metallic taste and filled her nostrils. The splintered remains of her heart shredded her chest, cleaving it open.

Outside, men screamed. Dragons roared.

They were all dying.

Asharaya!

Shara startled awake, hands fisted around the sheets. The dragon's voice echoed through her, a whisper drowned out by her galloping heart. Her eyes fixed on the solitary painting of the black dragon hanging on the burgundy wall across the room. Slowly, her breathing steadied.

Rami's arm was around her waist and his gentle breath rustled her hair. The serenity of the long hours wrapped up in her lover had been short-lived. Her dreams had known no rest—fire burning down walls, swords clashing, smoke and copper filling her lungs. She woke often drenched in sweat and pawing her throat. In one dream, a stranger cut her mother's throat and then hers. She was choking, dying.

Another dream dragged her through a memory. This time, her mother was dead, but Shara was flying. Her dragon's roars shook the earth. Rage and grief mingled in the sound, a mirror to the pain that summoned fresh tears and crippled her tiny heart. His body felt so warm, so real, but it wasn't. Her Deimok was dead, and his loss left a void inside her, a space once filled with his booming voice, which only she could hear. No amount of kisses in the dark could ever fill that emptiness.

Rami slept through it. A vrah with such a heavy sleep was rare, and most times Shara found it endearing. Despite the lives they'd chosen, being with Rami never made her restless. Theirs wasn't a consuming love like the ones she read of in books, devastating like the rushing of a river. It was calm, safe. *Unless he learns the truth.*

Shara examined her index finger where the fae had worn the obsidian dragon ring, triggering memories of Deimok. Her dragon had been a mighty beast, with black scales like a starless midnight sky and red eyes as bright as dragonfire. She was standing at the edge of a precipice, jagged rocks waiting below. No matter how much she wanted to chase away thoughts of the fae, the ring, and the dragon, her mind was stuck.

What business did a fae have in Havanya?

"You're awake," Rami mumbled.

Shara smiled. "I haven't kicked you."

"No, but you flinched." He nuzzled the back of her neck. "You're not as light as you think you are."

Shara elbowed him in the chest, and Rami grunted. The pained expression had not yet faded from his face when she kissed him, her brown hair curtaining their faces. "I like you better when you sleep," she teased and earned a beautiful, sleepy smile in return.

Rami trailed featherlight kisses along her jaw. She surrendered to the feeling of his warm lips and the firm grip of his hands on her naked body beneath the sheets. Each touch was a gush of air that blew her thoughts away. Her eyes fluttered shut, and she'd almost surrendered to his attentions when someone pulled the sheets.

Shara gasped as she spun to face the intruder. Brown doe eyes stared back at her, gleaming with entertainment and ringed by tired circles. "At least this time you kept to your own bed."

"Lana, was that necessary?" Shara snatched the blankets and tugged them back over herself and Rami. "What is your problem?" She sucked in a breath as her attention snapped to Solana's untouched bed. "Have you been out all night?"

Solana leered at Rami, an eyebrow raised in a quirk. "I'm sure the Maiden's price for her gifts hasn't turned to laziness overnight."

"I have business to attend to in town." Rami hurried to say. When it was clear Solana had no intention of leaving, he pressed a quick kiss to Shara's lips and got out of bed. A red line spread along his neck as he dressed. "I'll see you tonight."

Solana turned to Shara once they were alone.

"At least one of us had some fun last night, sister." Solana laughed.

The Vrahiid's daughter had been the first to welcome Shara to the Vrah's Keep. She taught Shara the ways of the vrah and their goddess back when Shara knew only dragons and fire. Solana was merely a year her senior, but even as a child, she'd been wiser than her age. Losing family to raiders hadn't stopped her from holding a hand out to a girl broken by grief, even if that girl was fae.

I want to be strong.

I can show you how.

Solana made a hollow girl into something more than a dethroned princess and a Dragon-Blessed. She'd carved Shara into someone worthy of the dragon riders she admired, someone who could be her own hero. Solana didn't have her blood, but she was her sister in all the ways that mattered.

"So, you weren't with Xoro?" Shara asked.

Solana discarded her belt of daggers on the bed and rolled her neck before unbuttoning her leather doublet. "I was tailing a mark."

"You're abusing the Maiden's gifts." Worry coated Shara's voice. The dark rings beneath Solana's eyes, the stiffness of her limbs, and the pallor of her brown skin were all signs that her sister had spent too much time hidden in their goddess's darkness.

"I'm fine." Silent as a cat, Solana padded to the adjacent bathing room.

"Who were you tailing?"

"I'll tell you more tonight. Now I need a bath and you need to meet Icaro at the market."

"Does his wife already have another lover?" Shara settled deeper into the covers. "Do you think the Maiden really needs the blood of another reprobate?"

"Blood is blood. So long as Icaro pays, we don't ask questions."

Shara tracked Solana's movements through sound. Water filled the tub and a bar of soap hit its surface with a splash. Her sister groaned as she descended into its fragrant depth. There would be time to tell Solana about the fae.

If Havanya's heat was unbearable at night, it was even more so now. The midday sun shone proudly in a cloudless sky. Rank sweat mingled with the pungent odor of fish and the far more unpleasant smell of human excrement. Sometimes it was hard to remember the city was close to the sea.

The five daggers strapped to Shara's belt thumped against her legs as she walked amid the colorful stalls in search of her client. In the past year, Icaro had become one of the Maiden's most devout worshippers. The woes of having a young, lustful wife, he said. The truth was, Shara didn't like the man. He made his wealth through usury, and the only reason his young wife married him was to save her brother's life.

This time, she wouldn't argue. Blood was blood, and she'd already crossed the Vrahiid once this week.

"Are you ready for my story?"

Shara stiffened at the voice. Familiar and foreign at once, it was soft and slightly accented. She thumbed one of her daggers and spun to face the silver eyes that haunted her nightmares.

"You can't take a hint, can you?" She looked past the fae to the stalls. The glint of steel was unmistakable. His friends hid in the crowd. One browsed through silks, another held a pearl necklace, and two more engaged in fake conversation.

Their attention fastened on Shara.

"It is a good story. It would be a shame to let it go to waste."

Get out. The words echoed in her mind, making her feel small and terrified. Shara shoved down her mounting panic. "Not interested." She took one step before the fae blocked her path. The bastard was fast. His cronies guarded her back.

"Once upon a time," he began, "humans left their land in search of something extraordinary. They found it. Ilahara."

Shara's knuckles turned white around the hilt of her dagger.

"They drank from the waters of the Ilah and were blessed with strength, long life, and magic. The newly turned fae conquered the land, which was ripe for the taking, but forgetting that it was not truly theirs or uninhabited."

Shara chanced a glance to her side, stomach sinking as everyone cleared away. Vendors, buyers, pickpockets, and children marched with vacant stares. Her gaze lurched back to the silver-haired fae. The same musical cadence had enriched his voice the previous night when he'd held the frightened girl's face. Her skin prickled as realization sunk in.

This was magic.

"Dragons roamed the land and skies long before the fae. They did not appreciate this new race stealing what was theirs. Thousands died bathed in dragonfire. The fae cowered in fear at the looming shadows overhead until one day a boy named Garon—a single boy—spoke a language untaught and unknown. It was Drakasi, the Dragon Tongue. Garon's words stopped the mightiest dragon, the vicious Teirak, who listened to the boy and bowed before him. That boy started a dynasty. The Myrassar. The Dragon-Blessed."

Shara's leg muscles tightened as she readied to sprint. Desperate for an escape, her eyes swept her surroundings. There was nowhere to run, and with the sun so high in the sky, nowhere to hide.

The fae stepped forward, slow and calm. Shara's grip shifted on the dagger. She angled the blade between their bodies to discourage him from coming closer. A curious smile tugged at his lips, but it didn't reach his eyes.

He knows who I am.

Five against one. She'd fought through worse odds against humans, but this fight would not be as easy. She was aware of her body's limits and her adversaries' superiority. They were taller, broader, and the silver-haired fae had magic. The years spent away from Ilahara weakened her gift. A spark persisted, buried deep within, but it was a flicker of what she might have wielded if she had a chance to master her Fire. Though a wild, desperate part of her would summon that spark to carve a way to freedom with blade and flame, she couldn't risk it. Her Fire was a weapon she couldn't control, thus one she couldn't wield.

How did he find me?

Sunlight glinted on the obsidian dragon's ruby eye. Shara took a quick breath. The fae's long, elegant fingers broadened in her mind's eye. Pale skin darkened to an olive tone. Shara remembered a room that felt much too wide, with golden tapestry and sconces fashioned into black dragons on the wall.

"*Can I hold it?*"

"*No, my little rider.*" *Her father's laugh was warm.* "*Only a king can wear this. One day, it will belong to your brother.*"

"Centuries later, another dragon made history. He

gave his life in a desperate attempt to save the last of the Dragon-Blessed. Hundreds of arrows shot down the beast and the girl he so desperately tried to save."

Shara's chest heaved and tears blurred her vision. Even after all these years, she couldn't escape the fires, the screams, the blood. Her family...dead.

Deimok.

Her dragon plummeted, wings no longer able to hold them aloft. Deimok's body ripped through foliage. Branches sliced at them like knives. She screamed, uncaring of her pain, only echoing Deimok's down their soulbond. The dragon hit the ground with a deafening crash. The earth cracked around him and dirt rose to envelop them both. Despite his injuries, he was careful not to crush her beneath his weight.

Shara's hold on her dagger wavered. A sob slipped from her lips for the dragon who sacrificed his life so a girl could live.

The fae no longer smiled. "The girl was believed dead for many years."

"Not you," she cried and scurried to her dragon's face. *So much pain shone in his tear-glazed eyes. Whimpers slipped past his parted maw. Blood trickled from its side, from his open wounds and chest. His heart.*

There is nowhere you could go that I will not follow. The last words he'd said down their bond.

"It really is you," the fae breathed.

The weight of steel sharpened the pain into something lethal. Rage was a wildfire that heated the blood in her veins and sharpened her mind.

She let fly the first dagger. A cry and a heavy thud followed as the blade found its mark—not the fae, but one of his cronies. The silver-haired one's eyes widened, and Shara pressed her advantage. She unsheathed the sword at her back.

The men burst into action.

"No," the silver-haired fae commanded, switching to Ilahein.

Shara threw a second dagger, which struck another fae's eye.

"Stand back." The two remaining accomplices watched the other with furrowed brows, struggling to keep still. Their gazes flicked to their dead companions. Shara focused on the silver-haired fae. He fixed her with a glare. Swords whispered as he pulled them free. "She's mine."

One hundred arrows had kept a god from defending the girl he loved.

Shara angled her sword, knowing how many times her blade would pierce the fae before he died. With a feral cry, Shara lunged. The fae lifted his swords to parry. The impact reverberated up her arm, down her spine, and into her legs. He barely seemed to register it. Shara struck again. Her dagger sliced at his unprotected abdomen, an opening quickly guarded by her enemy.

"Who are you?" she snarled.

"Don't you recognize me?"

For every opening Shara found, she met one of his swords. He dodged the dagger she thrust at his chest, only to have her sword cut his calf. Shara relished in his grunt of pain.

In her peripheral vision, she was aware of his cronies stepping forward yet hesitating to join the fight. The fae lunged, grimacing through the pain, and forced her to assume a defensive stance. His speed and strength were effortless, second nature. Despite her training, he drove her to her body's limits.

The song of steel on steel rang through the empty marketplace. Blades collided in the space between their bodies. The fae leaned into the blow. Shara's muscles shook with the effort of holding him back. Her foot slipped. With a grunt, she fell onto the cobblestones, winded.

Get up. Her limbs turned leaden now that she stopped.

The fae advanced, silver eyes lit with determination. He swung his sword, but a sound like thunder rang in Shara's ears before he could deal the fatal blow.

Swords slid one against the other and metal shrieked. Darkness rippled around Shara. A woman stood between the assassin and her attacker. Lithe, and clad in black. Strands of black hair sprung loose from a long braid. She shoved the fae back, meeting him blow by blow with relentless force.

The Vrahiid's daughter. The Maiden's Chosen.

"Lana," Shara breathed.

To his credit, the fae didn't let stupor break his discipline. The gift to access the Maiden's darkness was common to the vrah, but where the power of most ended with the rising sun, Solana's gifts were different. The wraith burst from the darkness at Shara's feet, not even daylight enough to sever Solana's bond with the goddess.

This time, the fae's cronies didn't hesitate. Solana's appearance shifted the fight's balance. Shara forced her body upright.

The air grew suddenly cold. A brisk chill pinched her skin. Ice fanned out spiderlike for the fae and solidified over their feet with quicksilver speed.

"What's happening?" Solana gasped.

A great column of fire hissed by, barely missing Shara's sister. It crackled over the line traced by the ice and turned blue where the elements touched. The trapped fae desperately tried to escape, but blue flames climbed up their legs like a famished beast and consumed their bodies and screams in a heartbeat.

The fae turned toward the source of the magic. Two figures approached, swords in hand. "Arkael."

Shara didn't miss his hesitation. It lasted a moment,

but it was all she needed.

The sound of the arrows that struck down her beloved dragon echoed in the blood pulsing in her ears. She lunged. This time, the fae wasn't fast enough to parry. A surprised gasp slipped past his parted lips. Shara gritted her teeth as she lodged the blade in his chest, pushing it deeper. Blood spilled over her hands as she twisted the dagger.

He thought I'd fight fair.

The fae's silver eyes closed.

One didn't survive on honor. She'd learned that lesson long ago.

7

"Shara, we need to go."

Blood dripped from Solana's finger where she nicked herself with her blade.

The fae knew who Shara was, and he'd found her.

The fae was dead, and she'd killed him.

Shara was safe.

Wasn't she?

The shadows in the alley stirred as they approached. Solana was here. "How did you find me?"

"I was following them." Solana gestured over her shoulder as she tugged Shara along.

"Princess Asharaya?"

A new wave of apprehension washed over Shara at the stranger's voice, yielding new clarity to her thoughts. She'd almost forgotten the new intruders—two more fae, and both gifted with magic. Two more fae who'd found her.

For years, Shara had stopped fearing this moment would come. Asharaya Myrassar was dead. That's what the fae had known for the past fourteen years. She had a new life now, a purpose, a family. What threat could she pose to the powers of the Magical Lands? Why were they looking for her? How had they even known to look?

Solana extended a hand toward the darkness. Shadows twisted, yawning open.

"The dragons sang the day you were born."

The same words spoken with a different voice surfaced from the well of Shara's memories, belonging to a man with a somber tone and a kind gaze. Maenar Elvik had always been patient with her, even when he struggled to keep her seated and focused. Shara halted, the hairs at the nape of her neck standing on end.

The approaching fae made a striking pair. Clad in matching leathers, they appeared to be around Shara's age and were a vision in contrasts. One's skin was a dark sepia brown and the other's was fair and slightly sun-kissed, bringing out the freckles on the ridge of his nose. The former was dark-haired while the latter was blond.

Silver-blond.

Shara raised her sword with a snarl and acted as a barrier between Solana and the fae. Past and present intertwined. The fae's blood coated her hands and was as warm as her mother's had been. Solana was an able warrior, but a human was no match for a grown fae. As a child, Shara had been powerless to protect those she loved.

Never again.

Solana, however, would have none of it. She stepped beside Shara, sword raised.

"We mean no harm," the blond one said. The similarity to the fae she'd slain was unsettling. He was the first to drop his weapon. His companion eyed him sidelong before following suit.

"Can you talk Ilahein?" the other asked. Unlike his blond friend, his Havanian was more accented and less refined.

The harsher sounds of their consonants suggested they came from a different region of Ilahara. Shara hesitated and then nodded. The fae released a breath. Whether he was relieved or tense Shara couldn't say, but she kept her weapon raised regardless. The familiar weight grounded her, though it was no match for the magic she'd seen the fae wield. "My name is Mykal Todrak. My father is Darrok Todrak, Head of Daganver. Do you remember?"

She did, vaguely. Darrok Todrak had already been Head of Daganver, the northernmost region of Ilahara, home of the Ice wielders, during her days as princess. She remembered that her father laughed when the lord traveled south to Embernest to visit, that he often complained about the heat and that her mother's eyes shined when she said his name.

He'd been a friend to her family. Then again, hadn't Aerella?

Shara swallowed hard. "How did you find me?"

"We tracked you." The blond one advanced slowly, and still Shara flinched, keeping him in range of her blade. He tugged at a golden chain around his neck.

The dagger fell from her fingers like cool water. She remembered the pendant around a beautiful, slim neck. It was simple gold, but the dragon made of small rubies and sapphires perched around it made it extraordinary. The necklace had belonged to Shara's grandmother and her mother before her, and it would have been hers when she came of age.

The blond one extended it in an offering.

Shara stepped forward, transfixed by her mother's necklace. Within her, the kernel of fire stirred in recognition. An heirloom of her family and of Ilahara.

Solana grasped her arm. "If your father rules, then he is no friend of Shara's."

Mykal bristled and stepped back as if slapped. "How

dare you?" he snarled at the same time his friend asked, "You know our language?"

"I do not like being caught unaware." Solana fixed them both with the weight of her gaze.

"I assure you my father's power comes at a high cost." Mykal pointedly ignored Solana and focused his attention on Shara.

That look made Shara's hand slip in Solana's, fingers squeezing once before letting go—a signal to stand down. Mykal's eyes were rife with anger, fear, heartbreak. Every day, Shara glimpsed them in her own reflection, too.

Moved by sudden solidarity, she mustered the courage to take the final step to the necklace. Her heart lurched as the warm gold touched her fingers. A feeling of rightness washed over her only to crash against a wall of guilt. She had no right to hold this necklace, yet she held fast, precious stones digging into her skin. Tears piled behind her closed lids and a shaky breath slipped past her lips. "Why are you here?"

Shara and Solana followed the fae to an inconspicuous inn. The main room was empty save for a few men talking over a glass of wine. The blond, Arkael, spoke to the innkeeper, while Mykal eyed the dank room as if the empty walls posed a threat.

Shara shared the sentiment.

They retired to a small room off the more desolate of the inn's two hallways. The moth-eaten quarters were a far cry from the opulent elegance of the Establishment or the imperial grandeur of the Keep. Stale air rich with Havanya's most unpleasant smells wafted through a broken window. A crack in the wall let the humidity in, spots of it spreading along the old, yellowed wallpaper. The bed, barely big enough for two, seemed ready to fall apart.

"Cozy," Shara commented.

Mykal recounted everything Shara had missed. Ilahara was no longer the place she'd once called home. Aerella banned the Dragon Faith, replacing it with the Pentagod Creed, and made Heads of fae who supported her coup. Only Imiri Vynatis and Darrok Todrak remained of the Heads Shara remembered.

"Imiri was my mother's friend." Another traitor. Not that it mattered. She lifted her gaze to Mykal. "You said your father's power came at a cost."

"After the Coup of Fire, my father led the Uprisings. He lost the use of his legs in battle, my eldest brother died, and my sister was taken by the Argarys." Mykal leaned against the wall, shutting his eyes. "Aerella could've executed him for treason, but she didn't."

"Daganverans are proud and loyal. Even broken, they never would have turned their backs on Darrok Todrak." Arkael turned to his friend with a warm look that may have been admiration.

"Still, the usurper queen disbanded our fleet and impedes our entry into Adara without a formal invitation from the Crown. She decreed that Daganver should pay higher taxes because we're a wider territory. As if cutting our funds could force us to yield." Mykal's smile was bright and full of hope. "But in the North, we remember who the Dragon chose to lead us."

Shara balled her hands into fists. "The dragons are gone."

"You're not."

She laughed without humor. Even before abandoning Asharaya for Shara, she'd never wanted to be a princess, let alone a queen. Ruling had not been her destiny but Elon's. All Shara wanted was to be free, with a sword in her hand and a dragon's warm hide between her thighs. She lost her dragon, but the Vrahiid made her the warrior she always wanted to be.

Mykal's eyes burned holes in her despite the Ice that allegedly flowed in his veins. "You think this is funny?"

"I have not been in Ilahara since I was eight. How can you possibly think I am the answer to your family's problems?"

"This isn't only about my family."

"Asharaya Myrassar is dead. The princess you are looking for is gone."

"That lie can't protect you anymore," Arkael intervened, his gaze apologetic. "Aerella Argarys knows you're alive."

Shara shook her head, wrapping her arms around herself as if that could stop the words from breaching her carefully constructed walls.

Arkael pressed on, solemn. "The fae you slew in the market was her son, Derron Argarys."

Who are you?

Don't you recognize me?

She should have. In fact, she had. His mother's silver-blonde hair and silver eyes had been the specter that plagued most of her life. Yet Shara hadn't wanted to make the connection, even when recognition prodded at her mind. Perhaps she hadn't wanted to reconcile the man she'd fought with the boy who visited the castle often, sparred with her brother, and offered her flowers from the garden.

That boy was gone, and the man he'd become had tried to kill her. Now he was dead by Shara's hand.

"Aerella's seer saw you return to Ilahara." Mykal's voice betrayed a trace of disappointment.

"In Ilahara you believe in prophecies?" Solana scoffed. "Anyone who claims to know the future is a liar."

"Yet Asharaya Myrassar stands before me." Mykal addressed Shara once more. "Even if that future were to change, you've slain the prince. You gave Aerella one more reason to want you dead."

Shara rubbed at her temples.

"That's enough." This time, Solana was the one to stand. A lesser human would have feared a fae, but Solana faced them with her head held high. "How dare you come here and make demands? Shara was a child when she came to my doorstep. Where were your dragons when she needed them? Where were you?"

"I was a boy of eight who watched his family fall apart because of those damned Argarys," Mykal snapped. "I can't even admit to having a Do'strath unless I want us both to lose our heads. My people grind just to live another day. Life hasn't been kind to us either."

Shara took a deep breath. "Listen, I am sorry for what the Argarys have done to your family, but I am not the solution." She held up her hand before Mykal could speak. "I am a stranger to Ilahara in all but name. You think the fae would rally behind a foreigner?" She shook her head. "This is my life now."

Mykal stared, aghast. Arkael gave him an intense look as if trying to calm him with his mere thoughts. Perhaps he was. The Do'strath bond had roots in that of the dragons and their riders. Shara envied those silent conversations, keenly feeling the emptiness her dragon's deep rumble used to fill.

"There must be something we can offer." Mykal made a sound close to a growl, but Arkael ignored him. "Something we might help you with. We have magic and the two of us together," he gestured between himself and Mykal, "we're stronger than most. We've managed to track you all the way here."

Solana's breath hitched and she went unnaturally still. "Could you really find anyone?" she asked.

Arkael nodded, his expression turning somber. "You've lost someone to the fae."

Solana turned to Shara, and in the depth of her dark gaze, Shara saw a trace of hope. Jealousy struck her, hard and unforgiving. Solana had told her about the brother stolen by the raiders. It happened before Shara arrived in Havanya, but she still felt she was competing for Solana's favor. Shara had hoped to fill the void created in Solana at the loss of her brother as Solana had filled the one in Shara's heart, but Shara's brother was dead, and Solana's was not. The hope to see him again was not.

The look in Solana's eyes was like a stab in the back. Solana knew what Shara lost in Ilahara and the nightmares still haunting her. "You can't be considering this," she whispered.

"Shara, perhaps..."

The sudden betrayal stung more than any blow Derron Argarys had dealt her that day. The room was suddenly too small, too crowded.

Solana called her name, but Shara refused to listen. In a single day, everything she'd built in Havanya was falling apart. Aerella Argarys knew she was alive. Derron Argarys tried to kill her. Solana betrayed her.

Air struggled to flow through the thin walls of her lungs. The world spun in and out of focus, but she kept moving. So long as she did, she would be all right.

Shara did what she'd done most of her life.

She ran.

8

They found Princess Asharaya.

Although Mykal had no doubts about what he and Kael could accomplish together, he still couldn't believe they'd succeeded. Asharaya Myrassar was alive. When the last of the Dragon-Blessed finally returned to Ilahara, everyone would know it had been Mykal and Kael, perhaps the last Do'strath alive, who achieved the impossible. He could see it in his mind's eye. The fae of Daganver waiting at the port, children tugging on their mothers' skirts as they pointed toward their approaching ship, young warriors envious of their triumph. His father would lead the welcoming party, eyes shining with hope, reverence, and pride. Mykal could almost feel his embrace and the pat on the shoulder that meant *"you made me proud, son."* The people would rejoice, and between chants of *"Asharaya," "long live the Myrassar,"* and *"long live the Dragon-Blessed,"* they would sing two more names—Arkael and Mykal.

"Mykal."

His Do'strath's voice whisked him from his reverie. Before he could claim the glory earned through years of training and sacrifice, Mykal had to first convince the lost princess to return. If Asharaya could be convinced.

The young Todrak scowled.

"What were you thinking?" Kael asked.

"I'm thinking we shouldn't be sitting here doing nothing." Mykal stood from the bed and pointed to the door. "My father entrusted us with getting the princess home. We found the princess. What are we waiting for?"

"We're waiting for her to want to come with us."

"And we're going to let this Selena do the convincing for us?" A snort tickled the back of Mykal's throat.

"Solana," Kael corrected. "And yes, we are. They're obviously close. If Asharaya is going to listen to anyone, it's her." The woman said as much before leaving a few hours earlier, yet neither she nor Asharaya returned.

Mykal finally unleashed a snort into the world. "How very like you to trust this human. She didn't seem to like us before you convinced her we'd find her brother. We can't trust her."

"And how very like you not to trust her." Kael sighed. "Solana wants her brother, and we're her best chance. She'll do this."

Mykal rolled his eyes, stalking to the window.

On the horizon, the sun began its descent. Evening drew closer, but the stifling heat of the morning was equally so at night. The oh-so-delicious smells of shit and fish were even less enchanting when a breeze carried them right to his nose. Now more than ever, Mykal missed the forests of Daganver. He longed for snow that lasted all year long and the smell of trees and rivers. Even his magic was no more than a muted song as the distance from the Ilah took its toll. Ice struggled to answer his summons, caught in a tug of war between Mykal's will and the invisible hand trying to claw it away.

How had Asharaya survived so long without her Fire?

Mykal's teeth ached from clenching his jaw too tight. *Solana*, he thought with a scoff. Could finding her brother really outweigh her distrust of his kind? Kael seemed to think so, but Mykal had lost family to the enemy. Even if the Argarys promised to return Eileen, he'd never trust them. Why did Kael believe Solana would help? *Because she has pretty doe eyes.* The smell of shit filling his nostrils was almost welcome. At least he'd have a valid excuse when he vomited outside the window.

Mykal hadn't felt so distant from Kael in a long time. For Do'strath there was no being apart. Even when standing in different places, the soulbond kept them together through every minute and breath of their lives. Yet, the more Kael and Solana spoke, the more he'd felt like the odd one out. The only thing missing was his mother's reprimanding whisper telling him to give them privacy. He hated how easy it was for Kael to bond with others and for people to trust him. He hated that no one failed to see Kael was beautiful, kind, and perfect.

"I don't think we should wait for Selena." No one besides Kael was in the room, and they spoke Ilahein, but Mykal whispered anyway. Conspiracies were conspiracies and they demanded conspiratorial tones.

"What are you suggesting? That we whack our future queen behind the head and carry her home?"

Mykal faced his Do'strath with a reckless grin. The amused tilt of Kael's lips turned his Ice into rivulets of fresh water. "Precisely."

Kael's smile faltered. "What?"

Mykal leaned against the wall and crossed his arms. "I know you want to trust the human, but we can't risk failure, nor can we risk losing Asharaya. We need to get her home, and we must do it before anyone else comes looking for her."

Now Kael's smile disappeared completely. "We can't force her to come with us. It's not who we are."

"Not who we are?" Mykal moved away from the wall. "I'll tell you who we aren't. We're not failures and we're not cowards." He knelt before Kael, gripping his Do'strath's knee. "My father is counting on us. If we fail, we'll be remembered as the Do'strath who lost Asharaya. Is that what you want?"

"Of course it's not what I want." Kael covered Mykal's hands with his. "But Myk, if we do it your way, she'll never help us, and we'll never forgive ourselves."

Mykal shook his head. "The moment Asharaya Myrassar crosses the Ilahein border, dragons will return from the Burning Sea and the air will fill with dragonsong. It's in her blood. Once she realizes what a solid favor we did her, Asharaya will thank us. We'll have nothing to worry about." Mykal could hardly keep the excitement from his voice. "We'll become legends."

"I think she's scared of all that. It might not be as simple as you're making it out to be."

Mykal ground his jaw. "Then I'm locking her in ice from the tip of her toes to the traitor's mouth and I'm dragging her ass to Ilahara. I'll hand her to my father and I'll still become a legend." He jumped back to his feet and yanked his hands from Kael's.

You're putting too much pressure on yourself. Kael's warm voice traveled down the bond, and Mykal helplessly closed his eyes as he returned to the window.

In battle, the invisible thread linking their souls was an open channel to their every thought and feeling, but in private moments the line where Mykal ended and Kael began was more defined. Mykal anticipated the moments when Kael would lower his walls and let him in. Mind to mind, heart to heart. It was the most intimate thing he'd ever experienced.

He loosed a breath, air pluming before him. A twinge pinched his chest. Tension settled at the moment he recognized the signs of the Frostbite. Pain would soon follow, and he dreaded his own fear. The first time Mykal had endured the gradual freezing in his chest had been after the Soul Binding. The increase in power provided by Kael's magic caused it, but it was a price Mykal gladly paid for the honor of being his Do'strath.

"This is important to m-me." Mykal stuttered.

The bed shifted as Kael stood. A few moments later, his Do'strath's arms surrounded him. Heat seeped through Mykal's skin and chased away the cold sinking its claws in his heart. "All right." Kael's breath tickled Mykal's ear, sending a new wave of shivers down his body, different from the ones threatening him a moment before.

Mykal released another breath, relieved when it didn't fog. He meant what he said—bringing Asharaya home was important. If they succeeded, he would make his father proud and prove he deserved the title of Head as much as his brother would have. A Myrassar on the throne might put together the broken pieces of his family and see Eileen home.

He also knew how much it meant to Kael that Asharaya made the decision herself. Vaemor Argarys hadn't given his mother a choice. Kael wouldn't be like his father.

Mykal rested his hands on top of Kael's and tilted his head to touch the side of Kael's brow. His Do'strath's smoky wood and citrus scent filled his lungs. "If Selena fails, we're doing things my way."

Kael chuckled. "Solana, Myk. It's Solana."

"Are you sure?" Mykal voice filled with mirth. "I'm pretty sure she said Selena."

"I'm pretty sure you're being petty."

"And why would I do that?" He twisted in Kael's arms

to face him, careful not to break the embrace. Would Kael notice how his breath caught at the nearness or how he couldn't help looking lower to the full curve of his lips?

"Because you don't like her."

Mykal flashed his most charming grin. "I don't like anyone who isn't you."

"That's quite a lot of people not to like."

"We're Do'strath. It's my sacred duty to make sure we have a balance. Everyone loves you, so they mustn't love me."

"That's not true, you idiot. You are loved, and not just by me."

Mykal beamed. "So, you love me?"

"You know I do. We're brothers. Through blood and fire, remember?"

Suddenly, Mykal couldn't bear to be in the circle of Kael's strong, warm arms. Being close enough to see darker flecks of blue in his eyes and light freckles over the ridge of his nose without leaning forward was torture.

Mykal nudged Kael away to put distance between them. Each inch of freedom gained was both a blessing and a curse as he guarded his heart against his Do'strath.

"Through blood and fire," Mykal echoed, turning his back.

If Kael could see him now, he'd know that while for him it meant they were brothers, for Mykal it meant he had chosen to be Kael's completely, without limits.

It meant he loved him, even if it killed him.

9

Shara meandered through Havanya's crowded streets like a ghost among mortals. People chattered and laughed, oblivious to her turmoil. Voices made up the static noise ringing in Shara's ears. Shapes and colors blurred in her unfocused gaze. For the first time, Havanya's liveliness didn't reach her.

Her fists clenched and unclenched around her mother's necklace. In her mind's eye, she saw Solana. Not the beautiful wraith who sprung from the darkness to protect her, but the hopeful woman in the inn's decrepit room. The hitch of her sister's breath rang in her ears and broke her heart.

Befuddled though she was, Shara still gave the market a wide berth. She didn't want to know if someone had taken care of the faes' bodies or if Derron's blood still stained the cobbles.

Derron Argarys.

The Argarys children were the same age as Elon, who

was three years her senior. She had a memory of returning to the castle from an excursion with Deimok, wet and covered in mud. Cassia stared aghast, Elon turned red with shame, but Derron laughed. She'd liked the sound. His kindness was genuine, unlike his sister's.

Today, he tried to kill her and only failed because Shara killed him instead.

She staggered to the nearest wall and retched.

The world spun as she righted herself. Heat burned beneath the surface of her skin, a fire readying to consume her. She was running out of options. Not only was Shara the last Myrassar and a threat to Aerella's usurped power, but she was also Aerella's son's murderer. It was personal now. Shara had nowhere else to run. Wherever she fled, Aerella's wrath would follow.

It's personal for you, too. Shara shut her eyes and reminisced about her mother's gentle hands in her hair and her father's deep laugh. Elon hunched over his journals in the candlelight. The warmth of Deimok's breath against her fingers.

"What should I do?" she whispered, lifting her face to the sky.

Shara returned to the Keep and sought refuge in the familiar. In the training hall, she surrendered to the physicality of sparring with fellow vrah. Hours blurred as she changed opponents, light giving way to the Maiden's darkness. She refused to acknowledge the clamminess of her skin, the sweat beading her brow, the ache of her muscles. Blow for blow, strike, and parry. This was a battle she knew and understood. In it, she channeled her frustrations, desperate to find reprieve from her spiraling thoughts.

Mother. Father. Elon. Deimok. Aerella. Derron.

Solana. Faces and memories chased one another in a relentless cycle. Shara couldn't focus. Whenever she neared a solution, doubts surfaced. She could stay in Havanya and cut through any threat as easily as she did the victims of her murders, but her heart rebelled against the thought. If she let Aerella's war reach Havanian shores, it would only be a matter of time before someone she loved paid the price. Havanya had given her a home and a family when she had neither. She wouldn't repay that gift with death.

Could she return to Ilahara? The thought rattled her bones. She knew nothing of the intricate power plays that ruled politics, nor did she know how to inspire loyalty or how to lead. She was no queen. Why would the Todrak follow her? Why would anyone? No, in Ilahara she'd be alone, and what could she do on her own against the woman who brought down a dynasty?

Shara returned to her room when there was no one left to fight. The hallways had gone silent enough to hear the crackling fire in the sconces and the click of her boots against the marble floors. Face warm and eyes dry, she wanted nothing more than a nice, cool bath.

She'd started to unbutton her leather doublet, weapons already discarded in a trail behind her when her gaze dropped to the bed. Her brows furrowed. She had put her sketchbook back inside the drawer before leaving that morning.

Only when she looked closer did she realize it was one of her older sketchbooks, the pages yellowed at the seams. She flipped through it with care, taking in each drawing with both nostalgia and dread.

Solana's eyes, dark but not depthless.

Two bloodied daggers and a quick scribble of the Maiden's statue in the temple.

Dragons in flight filling every corner of the page.

Her father's hand. She'd even drawn the ruby-eyed

obsidian dragon ring Derron had used to track her.

A woman standing in a hall, silver-blonde hair catching the light of the torches. She wore a long silver dress drenched in blood.

On this page, Shara found a hidden note written in a hasty, messy scrawl she recognized at first glance.

Meet me on the roof.

Shara dropped the sketchbook and raced back into the hallway, footsteps in tune with the violent beat of her heart. Why had he been in her room? Why had he looked through that particular sketchbook? Why hadn't he waited?

She sprinted up the spiraling staircase until she reached the narrow, moonlit stairway leading to the top of the watchtower, one of Shara's favorite spots to draw. Havanya spread out below her, each fire burning in the hearths like flickering stars stretching along the mountain.

Rami had kissed her the first time on this roof on a night much like this one. He was standing in the same spot, a warm breeze ruffling his unruly black curls. Back then, he'd smiled at her and the moon lit up the beautiful green of his eyes. Now, those eyes widened, as if seeing her for the first time.

"Shara."

She swallowed back a lump in her throat. "How long have you been up here?"

"A while." He tucked his hands in his pockets. "I needed to think."

Shara loosed a quavering breath, hugging her middle. "You looked through my journals."

Rami nodded after a beat of silence. "When I was a boy, I remember a man recounting a story he'd heard from a pirate sailing back from the Magical Lands. He said dragons were struck down from the skies with thousands of arrows and that the fae's king and his entire family were murdered. I didn't think much of it. I didn't think..." He shook his head. "It wasn't long after the Vrahiid took you in."

Shara held her breath. Blood rushed to her face, setting her ears aflame. "Rami, I—"

"No." He held up his hands. "You don't have to lie. I saw your sketches. That woman in the silver dress, she's a fae. And the dragons...and that fae in the market..."

Shara gasped. "You were there?"

"For most of it."

"And you didn't think I needed help?" She took a step back. "I almost died. I would be dead if Solana hadn't shown up."

"You think I don't know that?"

"But you did nothing."

"What should I have done?" Rami snapped. "I found out the girl I love is a bloody fae." He pinched the bridge of his nose and smiled, though it didn't reach his eyes. "You're not denying it."

Shara's lip wobbled. "You said not to lie." A warm tear slid down her cheek as she looked away, anger dissolving into despair. Her life was spiraling out of control. First the fae—Derron—then Solana, and now Rami. She'd feared this moment and prayed it would never arrive. "Do you hate me?"

"I want to," he admitted. How much pain could a heart take before it shattered? Rami stepped closer, hesitant. She flinched, but it didn't discourage him. He tucked a long, wavy strand of hair behind her ear, gentle as his gaze lingered on its round curve. Although it had been a clean cut, the illusion held only if one didn't look too closely at the scar tissue. For that reason, Shara preferred keeping her hair down, forsaking the practicality of having it bound during a fight. "But I can't."

A sob cleaved her chest. Shara crashed into Rami and held him tight. Her name was a whisper on his lips as he stroked her hair, her back, her wet cheeks. He dried her tears with his thumbs, green eyes shining with tears only his ridiculous manly pride stopped him from spilling.

Their eyes locked, and all the dread, fear, and anger she'd piled up during the day faded into glee. Rami knew the truth, and he loved her anyway. Shara leaned forward, anticipating the softness of his kiss as his breath caressed her mouth.

"How touching."

Shara froze, her blood turning cold.

It's not possible.

The blood on his leather armor had darkened to brown. A hole tarnished the fabric over his chest where Shara's dagger had been, but the sliver of pale skin beneath was unmarred.

"Hello, Asharaya," Derron said.

"You were dead," Shara breathed, shaking her head in denial. "I killed you."

"You came pretty close." He stroked the punctured leather, her father's ring still around his finger. "A little deeper and you would have ended me."

Shara cursed under her breath. In her haste to reach Rami, she hadn't thought of collecting her belt of daggers. She had no weapons.

"We won't make the same mistake now," Rami threatened, stepping forward to shield Shara. "Draw your weapon."

They had the darkness, the one place Derron couldn't follow. Safety was only a drop of blood away. "The shadows," she murmured, hoping Rami would listen.

"My quarrel is not with you, human," Derron said.

"Then this will be quick."

Rami lunged for Derron. Steel hissed as Derron unsheathed his blue jay swords. Shara held out her hand to stop her lover, a desperate plea on her lips.

In its place, Shara unleashed an agonized scream. Fire, that small, feeble spark within her, surged to the surface. Her veins, her skin, her whole being burned. Pain exploded through every nerve and sinew of her body. Five lashes of crimson flame speared from her outstretched fingers with a thunderous roar. They merged into one, brutal and unforgiving as they consumed everything in their path. Shara's cry was barely audible over the booming echo of fire. She couldn't see past the tears blurring her vision. Her legs wobbled like frail twigs, and they buckled beneath her weight. She barely felt the impact with the hard stone. Fire burned everywhere she looked, ravaging her from the inside, tearing her apart.

Derron was on the ground too, his long hair falling in disarrayed strands around his face. He must have seen her flames and jumped out of their trajectory. His wide eyes reflected the screaming, flailing pillar of flame between him and Shara.

Only minutes before her heart had swelled with unexpected joy. Now, it splintered into thousands of shards of glass that lacerated her chest.

A broken wail clawed up her ravaged throat, salt and ashes coating her tongue.

Rami, the beautiful green-eyed boy who'd kissed her, held her, loved her, was burning.

Shara begged the flames to recede, and though they'd erupted from her body, she had no control over them. Desperation had her turn to Derron. The Argarys were Fire wielders. At that moment, Shara would have done anything if it meant saving Rami. "Help him, please."

Her beloved fell to the ground in a heap of flames.

His screams stopped.

His body stilled.

Shara crawled along the stones. Though every movement created new waves of agony, she didn't falter.

"Rami." Her voice was a broken rasp. The stench of burned flesh was unbearable, but never as much as the stillness of Rami's body. She extended her fingers to his blackened ones. Shara knew every callus on those hands, their strength and gentleness.

As they crumbled into a heap of ashes, she learned their frailty.

The flames burned lower as the body underneath fell apart. Shara screamed, desperately trying to grasp what remained of him.

Rami was dead.

A cruel breeze swept over them and blew his ashes to the wind.

I killed him.

10

Derron Argarys believed he'd learned the meaning of
pain in the long hours of training with Semal Leneris,
where every broken bone marked a new lesson and every
healed cut was a reminder to do better, to push harder.

But no one had ever stabbed him.

His leather vest kept the blade from puncturing his
heart, and still, he felt it pierce his skin and slice through
muscle. Surprise was short-lived. Only agony remained as
he stared into the golden eyes of his slayer. The same eyes
that had belonged to a friend whose family was slaughtered
by his.

Asharaya.

When the tracking spell had led him to that den of
iniquity, a part of him hoped against reason that the young
woman he found wasn't Asharaya. The amber skin and
golden eyes—traits unique to the Myrassar—heralded her
identity, and still, Derron had hoped. Finding her again in
the market had been a blow. In a way, the fighting leathers

and weapons felt truer to the child he remembered than the expensive silks she'd worn the night before.

Asharaya was alive.

Derron's mother had murdered her family, and now he would murder Asharaya.

Instead, Asharaya stabbed him first.

At that moment, Derron hated her. She'd bested him because he'd been too distracted by Arkael and the death of his men to remember she posed a threat. His blood stained her hands, and he would die away from home and away from Cassia. He hated her like his mother wanted him to. Then he remembered Elon. Her brother, his friend. He'd died in a similar way and by the hand of some soldier wearing Argarys colors. The cruel irony wasn't lost on Derron, and he wondered if somehow Elon was watching and if he was happy.

I'm sorry, he wanted to say, *I was only a boy*. To Asharaya or the ghost of her brother, he didn't know. The words never came. There was only blood, and her angry golden eyes as she twisted the blade deeper.

Then there was nothing.

By the time Derron came to, the sky turned a bright orange as the sun dipped below the horizon. A dreadful stench assailed him, and flies buzzed in his ears. Someone had thrown him into a mound of refuse, not even bothering to check his pulse. As much as his current state disgusted him, he had to wait for feeling to return to his legs before he could stand.

Derron was alive, therefore the promise to his mother remained. There was no room for regret or grief for his long-lost friend. The legacy his mother had fought for depended on his success. He still had the Myrassar ring and a job to finish, and though most of his magic had gone into healing his wound, enough remained for one last tracking spell.

Find her, Derron, and end her.

Hand fisted around the ring, he let it guide him to a red building, the only color in a sea of gray. Entering hadn't been difficult. The door was open, and despite the late hour, the place was deserted. On those he met, Derron used his Song—the gift inherited from his father's Meranian heritage—to lure them out of the building. Controlling humans required little effort, their minds lacking that extra barrier magic provided. He followed the thread to the rooftop, where he found Asharaya with a human. A lover.

Derron hadn't meant for him to die.

He barely had time to jump out of the Fire's range. The blast was meant for him, but she had no control over it as was evident by the way she screamed. How there was any magic left in her after so many years spent away from the Ilah was a wonder.

"Help him, please."

Even if Derron were able, he couldn't move. He could only watch in horror as an innocent burned, consumed by flames brighter than any he'd ever seen.

This was his fault. The Fire was hers, but she meant to kill Derron.

This is my fault.

Derron sat in silence as Asharaya's lover burned to ashes. His heart broke at the sound of her crying. He didn't love anyone that way, but if Cassia had been the one burning, he doubted he would survive it. No one should have to feel that sort of pain.

Yet she had once already.

Asharaya was defenseless, spent. He almost felt his mother's hand on his shoulder, urging him to that final act that would wipe the Myrassar from their lives, ending what she'd begun fourteen years earlier. The end of a nightmare started on the day the old crone prophesized the Myrassar's return.

End her.

Derron walked to Asharaya and grasped her arms to make her stand. Though weakened by the onslaught of magic, she tried clawing his face to break free. Derron seized her wrists, applying enough pressure to hold her still. He wasn't worried about a new surge of her fire. The violent outburst of her magic had likely drained what reserve she had, and it would take time to replenish, especially this far from the Ilah.

Asharaya's golden eyes burned with hatred.

"I'll kill you," she vowed and went limp in his arms.

Underneath the acrid smell of cinder and flames, he caught the subtle hints of rose petals, lilacs, and sandalwood. She smelled exactly as he remembered.

Derron set Asharaya down with care and unsheathed his sword. Killing her now would be easy. He could return home to a mother he vowed to serve, to a waiting sister, and to a woman he didn't love.

This is my sister. You would end her while she's defenseless? Have you no dignity, Derron?

Derron's hold on his blade wavered.

Elon had been dead more years than he'd been alive, yet Derron still remembered his friend's soft tone, gentle even when he was angry, and the intelligent gleam of his eyes.

Moonlight shone on Asharaya's amber skin. Her hair tumbled off her shoulder, revealing the side of her face. The boy he remembered and the young woman before him had much in common. Elon's skin had been lighter, but the shape of their eyes and chins was the same. The more Derron looked at Asharaya, the more he remembered her—a princess who could never sit still, a girl always prowling beneath the shadow of her dragon. She'd been beautiful when she was younger, but now that she'd grown into womanhood, she was magnificent.

Something was wrong with her ears. Derron leaned closer, tucking away a strand of hair to have a better look, and paused. They'd been cut, forcibly rounded like a human's. A necessary sacrifice if she wanted to fit in.

She'd only been a girl of eight, and she'd lost everything so he and Cassia could have anything.

Show your power, hide your heart. Those were his mother's words. Her lesson to her children. The secret to strength was the absence of weakness. One couldn't be truly heartless but could learn to hide emotion and turn away from it. To be untouchable, one must be ruthless.

Derron finally looked away, gripping his sword with both hands.

An Argarys blade earned us the throne. An Argarys blade will keep it.

Derron's fist tightened around the hilt.

Asharaya looked like a sleeping beauty. How much death had she seen? How much of it had been his family's fault?

Derron cursed through clenched teeth and stepped back.

What are you doing, brother? His conscience often had Cassia's voice, especially before doing something he'd later regret. *I'm the princess, not her. Leave the past where it belongs.*

Asharaya was his enemy—their enemy. Derron promised he'd take care of it, and he would. Yet for all the times he and his sister walked through the halls of Asharaya's former home, for everything he'd gained and she'd lost, he at least owed her the chance to be conscious when the end came. He could give her the honor of a duel and the chance at revenge.

Derron would kill her, but not like this.

11

Ashari.

He flew over crystalline blue waters that faded into hues of fuming gold and red as far as his eyes could see. An island rose from the burning lava. A volcano occupied one shore, its sides carved by red veins where lava streamed into the sea. An expanse of green occupied the other, where a small stream was the only water source not overcome by fire.

He was not alone. Frantic beats of powerful wings kept his companions aloft, their breaths heavy from more than exertion. They were restless.

Ashari.

A cacophony of growls rose to meet his in a song at once terrible and beautiful. It shook the earth and the oceans and rattled the stars in the night sky. Memories of those they lost enriched their mournful cry. The knowledge of a thousand years rang in every note. Their music was as old as time itself, yet vibrantly new. His was one of joy.

His Dragaelan was not lost. Though distant, he could sense the weight of her soul on the other end of their soulbond, linking their minds by a feeble thread. Her heart was beating in tune with his—weak and distant, but alive.

Ashari.

The word was a soothing whisper in the wind carried by one voice and many, neither human nor fae.

A mountain sprouted in her mind's eye, with villages spiraling around it. That land thrived on lies, theft, and murder. The villages became bigger as she became smaller. Sounds of a restless town replaced the beautiful song. Voices, horses' hooves, cartwheels creaking on cobbled roads. Colors faded into gray—the roads, the buildings, the mist descending from the mountain. Only one emerged from the monotony.

Ashari.

Red like blood.

Ashari.

Red like fire.

In Shara's dreams, woes haunting her in life seemed small and insignificant. Her soul merged so tightly with the dragon that she couldn't say where she ended and he began. Only in dreams could she still chase the wind on Deimok's back and sing with dragons.

Havanya pulled her back each time, reminding her that place wasn't real. Not anymore. Asharaya had lost everything, but not Shara.

The first thing she became aware of was pain. Every breath generated agony. Her lungs and skin burned. Ashes coated her parched tongue. The fragrance of jasmine and lavender surrounded her, along with distant laughter and smothered sounds of pleasure.

This wasn't the Keep.

It took all her willpower to open her sore eyes. Shara squinted to adjust to the dim light. She lay on a lavish bed of golden silk sheets in a room large enough to feel welcoming but small enough to feel intimate. Gossamer red curtains swayed before open balcony doors.

The Lioness's Establishment.

Memories returned in a sickening wave. Rami's note in her sketchbook, wind tousling his unruly curls, his hands around her face, and the promise of a kiss lingering between them.

Do you hate me?

I want to, but I can't.

Shara would have cried and screamed if only her tears hadn't dried and her throat wasn't raw. Despite the numbness of her body, her heart could still shatter.

Fire had burned her lover. Rami was dead and it was her fault.

A shifting shadow captured her attention.

Derron Argarys, the man who'd twice attempted to kill her in the same day, leaned against the balcony's door. A shiver ran through her. She had no weapon and was in no condition to fight, but she couldn't smother the instinct to rise to a sitting position. The flare of pain was a welcome reminder she was alive and could exact her revenge.

The sheets slid over her body. Gooseflesh rose along the naked skin of her arms and chest. Shara gasped, covering herself. Why was she naked? What had he done?

"It was one of the girls." Derron looked over his shoulder as if verifying her state of undress before fully facing her. "You were burning up."

A vision of Rami's flailing body covered in flames flashed before Shara's eyes. She spoke in Ilahein to make sure Derron understood every word. "If you had stayed dead, none of this would have happened."

"You're right, it wouldn't." He lowered his eyes. "He wasn't supposed to die."

"But I was." Shara grimaced. "You are the prince now." The title that belonged to Elon—the prince, the heir, the future of Ilahara. "Elon was your friend. As was I."

"It's in the past."

"Yet your mother wants me dead. Is she so afraid of a Myrassar?"

"The queen fears nothing. This is a precaution."

"What kind of killer gives their opponent time to lick their wounds?"

Derron finally looked away, cheeks flushing. "The stupid kind."

As a vrah, Shara learned early on that blades weren't the only weapons at her disposal. Experience taught her to find weakness and exploit it. Master Crane's had been lust and arrogance. Derron, in sparing her life when she'd been unconscious, had revealed his. Honor.

Skin prickled at the tension building up inside. She was alone in a cage with a lion, but she refused to be prey. Gritting her teeth against a flare of pain shooting up her arm, Shara grasped the porcelain vase on the bedside table.

Derron realized his mistake too late. Once again, he underestimated her will to live. He lunged, but Shara smashed the vase against his head with vigor. The porcelain shattered. Chunks of it clattered to the ground, and hundreds of tiny shards exploded around them. Derron staggered back with a grunt. Blood trickled from his temple. Shara held on tighter to the shard in her hand and let the jagged edges bite into her skin.

Blood slipped between her fingers. She didn't give Derron the time to recover. Shara threw away the sheets to buy herself time, launching them so he'd have one more thing to struggle with.

The shadow of the bedside table shook and stretched as

she toppled off the bed and crashed to the floor.

Her blood touched it, and the darkness sucked her in.

In the dark, the weariness of her limbs disappeared. Colors faded and sounds silenced. Shara's world narrowed into a map of shadows occupying the room: the bed on the right and the bedside table beside it, the shifting mass belonging to the swaying curtain, Derron's elongated shape etched onto the floor.

She couldn't hide for long. Though she couldn't feel it now, exhaustion weighed her down, and soon she'd lack the strength to hold on to the shadows. Reaching the door would require a short sprint and Derron would easily catch her in her current state. The balcony, however, was within her reach.

How high up was the room? Could she make the jump? Perhaps she couldn't, but she'd rather die of a broken neck than be skewered by an Argarys blade.

Like her family.

The thought brought her to a halt.

Myrassar blood stained Argarys hands. Rami died because Aerella wished to add Shara's name to the list of those she slaughtered. Fourteen years ago, Shara had been only a child, too afraid and weak to act. Things were different now. The vrah taught her anger, strength, and vengeance.

Shara tracked Derron's shadow moving closer. She steadied her breath and adjusted her grip on the shard. It wasn't a dagger, but it was sharp enough to hurt.

To kill.

Silent as a ghost, Shara burst from the darkness. She grappled Derron's back, legs locking around his middle while her arm clasped his throat. Derron cursed, trying to wrest her off. She stabbed the side of his neck with the porcelain. Once. Twice. Blood spurted on her face.

Derron snarled. Nails digging in her legs, he thrust her back against the wall. Shara wheezed, the impact pummeling her already battered body. The shard slipped from her fingers and she crashed gracelessly to the floor. She couldn't breathe and couldn't move.

Anger lit Derron's silver eyes. Blood gushed between his fingers as he clutched his neck. *You almost had him.* Shara let the thought comfort her as he grabbed his sword.

The door burst open, and an icy wind blasted through the room.

12

Shara's vision blurred. She strained to see Derron crashing against the wall and the ice daggers that pinned him in place, but his screams resonated throughout the room. When she stabbed him, he'd barely made a sound, which was a testament to the amount of pain he must be in now. The sudden realization cut through the haze of her muddled thoughts. Once, she might have been sorry. Not tonight. Instead, she reveled in the reek of new blood tainting the room.

Someone called out her name. Shara would recognize that voice in a sea of thousands. Solana's face filled her vision. Only hours ago, her sister saved her life in the market. A sense of safety pervaded her as Solana's hands inspected her body for injury. The sting of betrayal took several moments to catch up. "Did he hurt you?"

Shara managed only a shake of her head.

"Maiden be praised," Solana whispered. "I went back to the Keep and you weren't there. Father told me the fae used some form of compulsion to keep him still and quiet. I didn't know where you were." She wrapped the sheets around Shara's naked body and helped her stand.

Shara pieced together the rest on her own. Solana had gone to the Do'strath for help. After all, they'd tracked her from Ilahara with nothing but a necklace.

Ice danced on the tips of Mykal's fingers, sparks of red mingling through the blue. Undeniable hatred burned in his eyes as he advanced on Derron.

Derron breathed out a pained laugh. "Mykal Todrak. I would say I'm surprised, but it appears Lord Darrok has a taste for sacrificing sons for his treason."

Steam surfaced from Derron's skin where ice seared his flesh. The mind compulsion Shara had seen him use in the market wasn't the only magic Derron possessed. As one of the high fae families of Adara, the Argarys were Fire wielders. Derron likely tried to summon that Fire to free himself, but despite his efforts, the daggers wouldn't melt. His gaze shifted from Mykal to Arkael, who stood a few paces behind, his face unreadable.

Derron's expression turned somber. "I see. The blue Fire, Ice resistant to flames—you're Do'strath." His laugh held no humor. "You do know the Soul Binding was outlawed?"

"Really?" Mykal turned to Arkael, voice dripping with sarcasm. "Did you know that?"

"It's not your fault if your father misguided you." Even Shara could see it was a desperate attempt on Derron's part to turn the odds back in his favor. "If you help me bring the Myrassar to justice, all shall be forgiven."

"You talk too much, prince." Mykal stepped forward, Ice crackling as it shaped into a dagger. "Your silver tongue won't get you far." He leaned close to Derron's face and traced the outline of his jaw with the frozen blade. "When I look at you, I think of my people suffering under your mother's yolk. I think of Eileen, my sister, raised in your court of lies to keep my family compliant." He pressed the tip to Derron's throat. "But this far from home, you're not a prince. You're no one's son. You're nothing."

Derron gritted his teeth as Mykal applied the slightest pressure, drawing a bead of blood.

Shara shook in Solana's arms, scrutinizing the scene with rapt attention. *Kill him.* Derron had stolen the life meant for her brother and sailed across the sea to end her. All to please the woman whose hands were stained with her family's blood. He deserved to die. Aerella deserved to know that loss. *Kill him.*

Arkael placed a hand on Mykal's shoulder. "He'd be of better use to us as a hostage." He looked straight into Derron's bewildered eyes. "He's Aerella's heir. Your father could use him to negotiate Eileen's return."

Shara clung to Mykal's reaction. The war waging inside him manifested in his tremulous grip around the dagger. Although the reasoning in Arkael's words was undeniable, Shara understood how it felt to lose to the Argarys. The same rage simmering in Mykal's eyes sparked to life inside her the moment she realized Derron's identity. Mykal probably wanted Derron dead as much as she did. *Use that dagger. Kill him.*

With a groan, Mykal lowered the weapon, and the ones pinning Derron to the wall melted at Mykal's will. Derron slumped to the ground, closing his eyes to steady his breathing through the pain.

"No." Shara tore free from Solana's arms and grabbed a dagger from her sister's belt with the momentum. She lunged, snarling, eyes fixed on Derron. Alive. Unpunished. Free.

Her legs buckled beneath her at the last moment. Arkael caught her before she fell to the ground. "You're burning up," he said.

Shara thrashed against his grip. "Let me go."

"Kael is right," Mykal ground through clenched teeth. "He's worth more to us alive."

"You are a fool," Shara snapped in Ilahein. "I thought you wanted revenge for your family. Will you make prisoners of every Argarys we encounter?"

"We?" The tightness on Mykal's face softened, and Shara's stomach dropped. The hopeful gleam in his eyes made her nauseated. "You'll come with us?"

"Yes." Admitting it aloud left her breathless. Shara was no closer to feeling ready to return to Ilahara than she'd been a few hours ago, but what choice did she have? With Solana determined to find her brother and Rami gone, the human life she desperately wanted to protect had slipped through her fingers like grains of sand. Fighting was all she had left. "But so we are all on the same page, I am not doing it for you. I do not want the throne, only Aerella."

"You don't want the throne?" Mykal blinked.

"Myk," Arkael chided.

"Fine." Mykal ran a hand through his hair, looking up as if in prayer. "I suppose it's a start."

"Good." Finally free of Arkael's hold, Shara channeled every ounce of self-restraint she possessed not to hurl her dagger at Derron. She made a point not to look him in the eyes as she slid her father's ring from his finger, though she felt the weight of his steady silver gaze. The obsidian dragon bit into her skin as she stumbled to retrieve her clothes. Solana stepped forward to help, but this time Shara jerked away from her touch. "It looks like I'll be taking you to Ilahara after all. You got what you wanted."

Solana looked away, but not fast enough to hide the hurt from her face. She wouldn't fight back. Lying was a talent unpossessed by the Vrahiid's daughter.

Shara addressed the Do'strath once she was dressed. "I assume you have a ship?" They nodded. "Then meet me at the docks in one hour. There is something I must do before we leave."

13

Kael had dreaded every mile ushering him closer to human shores. Aerella Argarys had likely made plans to dispose of Asharaya, so he set his expectations somewhere his peace of mind and reality could coexist. He imagined the queen assigned her lapdog, Semal Leneris, to such a delicate mission.

Surely, she wouldn't send her own son.

How foolish Kael had been to think Aerella Argarys would entrust the survival of her dynasty to someone other than her flesh and blood.

Kael's feelings about Derron and his twin, Cassia, were complicated. He hated them once because they were the children of a monster. Then again, so was he. When he grew old enough to discover the truth of his conception, Kael wished he could magic his own blood away and replace it with something cleaner and worthy of his mother's love. How could she look at his pale blond hair and not see Vaemor Argarys, the fae who abused her? The Todrak's deep-rooted hatred made it simple to view all Argarys as monsters, himself included.

Mykal showed him otherwise.

Do you think I would trust you if there were Argarys in you? You're kind, loyal, and good, things an Argarys can never be, so quit whining.

What did that make Derron and Cassia? Kael had only seen them once when he traveled to Adara with Mykal and Lady Alissa for Eileen's sixteenth birthday, the first and last the queen allowed Eileen to spend with family. He spent the journey plotting his father's murder to find upon arrival that Vaemor wasn't there. Derron and Cassia kept their distance, yet he sensed the prince's gaze when he thought Kael wasn't looking. Cassia, on the other hand, hadn't deigned him a glance. Kael often imagined his siblings to be as cruel as their father and as vicious as Aerella, though sometimes he couldn't help the small part that wondered. But not his father. Never his father.

Perhaps curiosity was partially to blame for what he'd done.

After Asharaya left the strange place to which they tracked her, Mykal and Kael searched for the captain of the *Silent Merchant*. Solana agreed to meet them at the established time and left, silent as a cat, without further explanation.

The Argarys prince was a problem. They had nothing to restrain him with and no option but to lug him along. Kael covered Derron with his cloak, lifting the hood to hide the signature silver hair and eyes, while Mykal encouraged cooperation with a dagger pressed to the prince's side.

Mykal was uncharacteristically quiet, even down their bond. Kael tried probing at his mental walls, but his Do'strath kept them resolutely up. Kael knew Mykal didn't like sharing breath with an Argarys, so why hide? It wasn't the first time Mykal isolated himself, and Kael didn't know what to make of it. Once, there had been no secrets between them, but now Mykal often kept his thoughts and emotions locked in an impenetrable fortress, within Kael's reach and yet impossible to grasp.

Kael turned to Derron. "The market was isolated when we arrived. I imagine that was your doing."

For a moment, Derron only stared back before he replied. "Yes."

"Of course, you inherited the Song from your father," Mykal said with an eye roll. "An Argarys and a merman. My, you really are perfect."

A muscle feathered in Derron's jaw. "Do you have the Song?" he asked Kael.

"No," Kael said, and he was glad. No one should have the power to manipulate another's mind and feelings. "So, you expected Asharaya to fight back. How? Mykal and I didn't know she was trained in combat until we saw her."

"Simple. I saw her before you did, in that place where you found us." Tracking them hadn't been difficult. Kael and Derron shared blood, so the spell required no item to channel. "I tracked her there. She was dressed like a cortesan. The man I saw her with was found dead the following morning, so I questioned the woman in charge to find out more. She knew plenty."

"A pleasure house?" Kael's stomach churned. There was no such thing in Ilahara. Humans trained in the art of the bedroom generally served one master. To think he'd believed Havanya a place where humans were free.

"And you obviously booked yourself a room," Mykal scoffed.

"I figured there was no better place for discretion."

"Oh, yes. Discretion."

They reached a back-alley inn near the port. The air smelled of fish, seawater, and other more unappealing things. Mykal hardly held back a noise of disgust. The door wasn't big enough for them to walk through together, so Kael entered first and Mykal shoved Derron in after him. Beneath the hood, the prince most likely glared with the same dislike Mykal showed in the narrowing of his eyes.

The inn was crowded with men and women, mostly sailors. Laughter boomed as ale spilled on wooden tables and the floor. The captain sat at a round table surrounded by other men, some of whom belonged to his crew. A glamour made their ears appear rounded, and they were drunk, judging by their rosy cheeks and bright eyes.

"Gentlemen," Mykal said in greeting.

The captain raised a cup in answer. "Can I offer you gents a drink?"

"Does it look like we want a drink?"

Kael sometimes wished he could gag his friend. "How about one at the counter?"

The captain shifted his long limbs around the mass of men to follow them. One gesture at the barkeep and four tankards of ale slid down the bar. The captain grabbed his. Kael and the others didn't. "What can I do for you?"

"Are you daft?" Mykal hissed. "We must sail back to Ilahara immediately."

"My crew is in no fit condition to sail now."

"And whose fault is that?"

"We don't need to leave at this very moment," Kael cut in, "but as soon as possible. The faster we return to Ilahara, the better."

The man nodded. He was serious with Kael, whereas it seemed he liked to piss off Mykal, who made no mystery of his feelings regarding the captain's former pirate life. "We'll set sail in the morning after we gather provisions."

Kael breathed a sigh of relief. "Thank you."

The captain shot a glance at the robed figure beside them. "Is this who you were sent to retrieve?"

"I'm afraid my stay aboard your ship won't be of the

friendly sort."

Mykal and Kael froze as Derron threw back the hood, revealing silver-blond hair, quicksilver eyes, and the sharp, handsome features of his face.

The captain's eyes widened.

Mykal grabbed Derron's arm in a not-so-gentle fashion. "I told you to keep your mouth shut."

"That is a fucking Argarys," the captain slurred through gritted teeth.

Kael raised his hands. "I can explain."

"I don't want any trouble. I brought you here out of respect to Lord Darrok, but this is taking it too far."

"You owe my father your life," Mykal was quick to remind him. His grip on Derron's arm tightened visibly. Kael had no doubt his Do'strath would dislodge the prince's arm if he uttered another word.

"My debt is paid," the captain said.

"You said you'd bring us back," Kael and Mykal snapped together.

The captain stumbled away from the counter. "Best of luck to you."

"Wait." Kael made to follow the captain, but the man had surprisingly better luck wading through the inn's chaos. By the time Kael shouldered past a pair of arguing men, the captain was gone.

"Good luck finding another ship now," Derron said.

Mykal grabbed his shirt, fist shaking with strain. "You think I won't? I'm finding us a ship, even if I have to carve out one of your pretty eyes and say it's made of real silver to bribe my way onto one."

"Do it," Derron challenged. "Perhaps you'll find some desperate clod willing to sail you back to Ilahara. It won't change the fact it'll be a human crew."

"I wonder, Argarys, how well can you sing without your tongue?"

"Myk," Kael warned.

"My father may want to barter you for Eileen," Mykal continued, "but he doesn't need you whole. Your mother likes the quiet ones, doesn't she?"

"I don't think Eileen would be too happy if you cut out my tongue."

Mykal's nostrils flared and his grip on Derron's shirt tightened. "Speak my sister's name one more time and we'll find out."

Kael tugged Mykal away and grabbed Derron's arm. "Let's go."

"The prince forgot his drink." This time, Kael wasn't fast enough to stop Mykal from smacking a tankard on Derron's head. The prince had only time to grunt before he toppled to the floor, unconscious.

A few curious glances turned their way, but the interest faded quickly, and the humans soon returned to their entertainments.

"Someone had to shut him up," Mykal remarked, slamming the tankard back on the counter. "And since you're so bent on being Argarys's hero, you get to carry him to the docks."

"Myk."

"Don't 'Myk' me." Mykal whirled, poking Kael's chest. "That's the second time today you've stopped me from giving the Argarys what is owed to them. Are you going soft on me?"

"Don't be ridiculous."

"And you don't be a fool." Mykal took a steadying breath before grasping Kael's shoulder. "He's an Argarys. This won't be the last time he'll try to outsmart us. Don't let him get to you with that silver tongue and false puppy eyes."

"Everything I do, I do it for the Todrak. For you. I won't jeopardize our mission."

"Good." Mykal patted Kael's shoulder and started forcing his way through the crowd.

Kael blinked, and then looked between the prince on the floor and his Do'strath's retreating figure. "Are you serious?"

14

Shara kept her head angled to the sky and followed the stars peppered like grains of dust in the dark blue. Havanya was rarely this quiet. The market stalls had been dismantled, though they'd be back by dawn. Would she get the chance to see them again before leaving?

Breath misted before her. The silent, hollow streets felt like a tomb as she shuddered through each stumbled step. Shara craved the warmth of her bed and Rami's embrace. If only she could turn back time and fix every mistake she made. She wouldn't avenge Thalina's child, and she'd make sure the dagger pierced Derron's heart before removing the blade. Better yet, she'd go back even further to a time before the Coup of Fire. Rami, her family, Deimok—they'd all be alive if she drove a blade through Aerella's heart.

The candlelit halls of the Vrah's Keep were exactly as Shara left them. She leaned against the black iron doors to catch her breath and took in her home for perhaps the last time. As the burning incense filled her senses, her ghosts came alive around her. There was a young Solana, extending a hand to a blood-drenched princess. There they were together, not strangers but sisters, rushing down the stairs as they played at being pirates. There was Rami, handsome and wild, sweat glistening on his bare chest as he strolled out the training hall with a heartbreak smile.

Everything was familiar yet different. Shara blinked back the tears blurring her vision and forced one foot in front of the other until she reached the stairs. Air grew colder as she descended. Only a few sconces illuminated the way to accommodate the darkness.

Voices resounded from the depths of the crypt, though Shara never learned their origin. Solana once told her they belonged to the souls the Maiden had judged favorably in their moment of passing, but whether or not that was true remained a mystery. She strained to make out a familiar timbre, dreading and hoping in equal measure to recognize Rami's voice.

At the end of the cavernous space loomed the Maiden. The statue might have seemed real if not for its height, towering at ten feet tall. The sculptor had been meticulous in its rendering. There was movement in the sleek folds of the Maiden's black gown and the cape of starlight billowing behind her. Her face remained hidden beneath the hood, save for the straight point of her nose, the fullness of her red lips, and the ivory coloring of her chin, framed by long curtains of wavy black hair. In one hand she held a dagger, the hilt red with blood. The other she kept extended, palm hovering over the stone font at her feet.

Drip, drip, drip.

Blood fell in large drops from the Maiden's hand. Its scent overpowered even the incense, and the copper tang coated Shara's tongue. The night of her Initiation Ceremony, two years to the day after she'd arrived in Havanya, the Vrahiid offered it to her in a goblet before plunging a dagger in her heart.

A daughter asks to serve you, Maiden, but only you can determine her worth. Guide my hand, and may your will be done.

Shara dipped two fingers in the thick blood and smeared it across her lips. "May your will be done," she whispered, looking up at the Maiden. She felt infinitely small in a way she never had when standing next to the dragons of her childhood. Despite the years devoted to serving the human goddess, she felt like an intruder in this place of worship.

You do not belong here, the Maiden said the night Shara died, in a room made of darkness and stars. *Yet there are things you must learn in the dark.*

And learn she did. Asharaya and Shara had always felt as different as the sun and the moon, but today she'd realized they were only distorted reflections of the same woman. They both craved love and a family to lean on. They both experienced fear and loss. Asharaya had run from it, but in the dark, she learned courage. Today, Shara fought back. The helpless girl that had escaped Ilahara was gone.

"Thank you for giving me the chance to learn. I won't forget it," she said around a lump in her throat.

"So, it's true. You're leaving."

Shara spun at the Vrahiid's voice. Her gaze shifted from him to Solana at his side. She must have traveled through the darkness to reach the Keep before Shara, no doubt to inform her father of their imminent departure and force Shara into another goodbye. Pain lanced through her chest. "Yes."

"And you share my daughter's ridiculous trust in the fae?"

Solana dismissed his words with a shake of her head. Despite the respect passing between father and daughter, something shattered between them when the raiders killed Solana's mother and kidnapped her brother. The Vrahiid never forgave himself for being unable to save them, and neither had Solana.

"I'm a fae," Shara reminded him in a whisper.

"You're my daughter."

"Rami is dead." Shara couldn't bear their pitying glances.

Dougas looked up at the statue of the Maiden. "We mustn't mourn him, Shara. His soul rests with the Maiden now."

Shara shook her head. It was too soon for her to find comfort in religion. "I can't keep losing the people I love. I have to put an end to what Aerella started fourteen years ago. I made my decision. You can't stop me."

"The Magical Lands aren't safe for you," Dougas argued.

"No place is." She took his hands before he could retort. They were larger than hers, dry and calloused. Shara committed their texture to memory, knowing that it might be the last time she held them. "You taught me to be strong, but we must both learn to let go."

Tears spilled when Dougas Spirre hugged her. His affection always came in small gestures, but Shara couldn't remember the last time he held her. "My Shara," he whispered, tears dampening her forehead as he placed a kiss there. "I'm too old to learn new lessons." He cupped her cheeks and gave her a dimpled smile. "I've forged you into a blade men fear. Now be the flame you were always meant to be."

Solana placed a hand on her father's shoulder. "I'll take care of her."

"You'll take care of each other." Dougas took both their hands as Shara's stomach dropped. Solana looked at her expectantly, but Shara couldn't give her the reassurance she needed. She was too numb to think of where she and Solana stood. "May the Maiden protect and guide you in the wars to come."

15

Derron woke leaning against a damp wooden post. He registered the absence of weight on his back where his swords should have been. With consciousness came the awareness of pain. A groan slipped past his lips, ache spreading through his chest, limbs, and head. Vision blurred, he pieced together what happened. The Do'strath, the captain, Todrak hitting him in the head.

He was having a very long day.

"One wrong move and I'll slit your throat."

Arkael stood in front of him, one hand already on the hilt of his sword. Derron never had the chance to see him use it, but he wasn't willing to test his half-brother's abilities without his swords or his full strength.

Given the Todrak's animosity toward his family, it was no surprise Maenar Elvik sent them word of Asharaya's survival, though Derron still hadn't expected Arkael in the market. The brother in the North he'd never gotten to know. His mother didn't want Arkael at court, for he was the living and breathing reminder of the king's transgression, and Lord Darrok overseeing his training complicated matters further.

"Where's Todrak?" Derron asked. His head still ached from the blow to his head, and the slightest movement caused his vision to blur.

"Not your concern."

"We don't have to make this unpleasant, Arkael." Derron had noticed Todrak calling him with an abbreviation, and for a moment, a twinge of regret caught him unaware. This young man shared his blood, yet his enemy was more a brother to him than he was. More than a brother—their souls were bound through a ritual proven to be fatal more times than not.

"You tried to kill the last Dragon-Blessed. Twice."

"Had she been the Todrak's enemy, would you have spared her life?"

"I spared yours."

The words landed like a slap in the face.

Time dragged on in silence. Judging by the sky's blue tinge, Derron hadn't been out for long. The hour Asharaya had given them was likely over, but she was nowhere to be seen. He hoped she'd changed her mind and ran while she still had the chance, though where he didn't know. There was nothing past Havanya and hiding in Ilahara would prove difficult now that his mother knew she lived.

Do you swear you'll always be truthful, Derron, and that you'll fight by my side, through every battle, against any foe? That you'll be my shield and my sword?

I promise, my friend.

Derron swallowed a lump in his throat and suppressed the memory of Elon. His friend and his promises belonged to the past. His duty was to his family, not a ghost. Not to a former friend who was now a stranger. Hesitation already cost him dearly. If Derron didn't find a way out of his current predicament, he'd be taken to Daganver. A hostage and a failure.

Todrak found them some time later, a murderous gleam in his eye as he regarded Derron.

"Had a nice evening stroll?"

Todrak didn't rise to Derron's bait. Instead, his attention trained on Arkael. The two looked at each other as if holding a conversation Derron wasn't privy to. Perhaps they were.

"Ignoring a guest is considered bad form," Derron said.

Todrak whirled on him, fingers coated in frost.

"Your actions in the inn cost us," Arkael said.

"I take it I was right." Derron wasn't surprised. Finding a captain willing to sail to Ilahara was no easy feat. Havanians' distrust of the Ilahein ran deep, and for good reason.

Todrak's lip curled with disdain. "Don't be so smug."

"You should've gagged me if you expected me to follow obediently."

"Now there's a thought."

"Which one is our ship?" a new voice said.

Startled by the sudden appearance of Asharaya and the human woman who'd saved her in the market, they jumped. The young women each carried a small sack, most likely filled with things they'd need during the voyage. Derron hadn't heard them approach. Not their steps or breaths, or even their heartbeats, as if they'd materialized out of nowhere, which he suspected was the case. The human had burst from Asharaya's shadow to save her from his killing blow. He'd never seen such magic.

"Dragon's sake," Todrak gasped.

"So, where's the ship?" the human asked.

Arkael sighed. "There's a minor setback."

Todrak glowered at Derron. "Someone had the brilliant idea to remove his hood. The captain refused to give us passage once he recognized him."

Asharaya raised her brows, sweat beading on her forehead. "We don't have a ship?"

Arkael rubbed his temples. "No, we don't."

The assassins exchanged a glance. Derron often shared the same look with his twin, a silent communication born not out of magic but time and familiarity.

"Wait here," the human said, before walking down the pier.

"Where is she going?" Todrak inquired.

Asharaya shrugged. "To find us a ship."

Derron didn't know how much time passed, only the growing magnitude of his discomfort. He was in the company of the woman he failed to murder, a man who hated him, and a brother who did an excellent job of pretending he wasn't there. Two out of three had come close to killing him today. All had weapons at easy reach. He contemplated using his Song to escape. Surely the captain who had taken him to Havanya still awaited his return, but even Derron had limits. While human minds were as easy to mold as clay, his kind was different. Taking on three fae would require more energy than he had.

Derron's thoughts inexplicably drifted to Eileen. When he used her feelings as a means to rile her brother, a twinge of guilt followed. There had never been anything between them, and there would be nothing until after Eileen's first Bleeding, but Todrak didn't know that and the allusion would haunt him. While Derron wouldn't lose a night's sleep for the northern brute's pride, Eileen deserved better.

I'll escape, he vowed. *I will come back.*

Derron recognized a newly familiar scent of ginger lilies and vanilla. By the way the Do'strath stood a little straighter, they noticed, too.

When the human returned, she wasn't alone.

Beside her was a towering man, his skin golden and his dark, shoulder-length hair tied back in braided knots. The moon's glow cast shadows on the sharp edges of his face, but what drew Derron's attention was the man's veiled eyes. Blindness did nothing to hinder the dangerous aura surrounding him. The size of his muscles beneath his shirt, his large hands, and the confidence with which he swaggered beside Solana served to create an intimidating picture. Watching him, one could have mistaken the cane he carried for a whim of vanity. The perching crow fashioned on the brass handle highlighted the exquisite craftsmanship. Derron also didn't miss the saber at his belt and the long sword on his back.

Asharaya stood from the rock she'd used as a stool and stepped in front of the man. "Thank you for agreeing."

Solana addressed the Do'strath in Ilahein. "Captain Xoro will receive half of his retribution now as a sign of our goodwill." She glanced at the pouch of gold hanging from Arkael's belt.

Arkael hesitated, but he handed the pouch to Solana, who dropped enough coins in the man's hand to fill his large palm.

The man weighed the gold, his square jaw clenched in concentration. Derron wasn't sure if they should trust him. He seemed like the kind of person who could murder a baby for crying.

"We'll also be sleeping in the second cabin," Asharaya added.

"My quartermaster sleeps in the second cabin." Captain Xoro's Havanian was a sharp rasp that made the hairs at the nape of Derron's neck rise.

"Not for the next fortnight, he won't. I'm sure the crew will enjoy his company in the barracks."

The man scowled.

Arkael and Todrak reached for their swords.

The captain smiled and tension drifted. "You're a pain in the ass, Shara."

Asharaya patted his arm. Her smile didn't reach her eyes. "It's always a pleasure doing business with you."

"How are we all supposed to sleep in one cabin?" Todrak whispered to Arkael.

"Shara and Solana will take the bed and we'll hang a hammock for you two," the captain explained in accented Ilahein. "The prisoner goes in the brig."

"The prisoner stays where I can see him." For the first time since she returned, Asharaya acknowledged Derron. "A chair and some chains will suffice."

"And a gag," Todrak added. Derron barely suppressed the instinct to roll his eyes. Asharaya gestured for Derron to walk and he didn't bother protesting. Right now, his best option was to wait. At least neither Do'strath was holding him, which was an improvement for his arm. Then the tip of a dagger grazed his side. "I thought you'd be tired of putting holes in me," he said.

To prove the opposite, Asharaya applied more pressure. Derron kept his mouth firmly shut. He'd had enough wounds for the day.

"I don't like this," Todrak whispered behind them. "I don't trust that man."

"Why am I not surprised?" Arkael teased.

"Don't make fun of me."

"It's not like we have other options."

"What kind of company can an assassin keep?"

Derron, unfortunately, found himself agreeing with Todrak.

The answer came when Captain Xoro waved toward a brigantine moored to the dock. A black flag depicting a skull pierced by a dagger and a crow perched on its hilt whipped in the wind. The words *No One* were painted in white cursive on its flank.

"Told you," Todrak commented.

The *No One* was a pirate ship.

16

The sea glowed in bright shades of salmon pink and crimson red, night fading into dawn as the *No One* departed Havanya's port. Shara might have liked to paint it if she didn't feel so weary. Her head throbbed almost as painfully as her heavy heart and focusing seemed impossible.

The *No One*'s crew hadn't taken interest in them until someone recognized Derron Argarys. The prince. The title flowed in whispers from mouth to mouth. They would recognize the silver-blond hair from their frequent voyages to Ilahara, but if that wasn't enough, Derron also carried himself like a prince. He walked as if the ground beneath his feet had been created for the sole purpose of greeting his passage. An aura of danger surrounded him, along with the awareness that this man differed from the rest. He was powerful and therefore demanded reverence. Shara had been a fool not to see it immediately. If she had, she'd have slit Derron's throat in the Lioness's Establishment.

Perhaps things would have been different, and Rami would be alive.

She wondered if Elon would have developed Derron's same level of confidence had he the time to grow. When she thought of her brother, she remembered his sweet smile, his flushed cheeks when Shara snapped at Cassia, and the gleam in his eyes when he snuck into her room to read a story before bed. Her brother hadn't been as confident as their father or as fearless as their dragons, but he had their mother's gentle heart.

"How is it that you know Ilahein?" Mykal asked Xoro, suspicion coating his voice. "Humans loathe Ilahara."

"There are plenty of things that interest a man like me in your part of the world." Xoro referred to the goods he smuggled and sold to the black markets in Havanya.

"You steal from us, you mean. I shouldn't have expected honor from a pirate."

"I won't have a fae lecture me on honor." Xoro switched to Havanian when he called for Niguel. Shara eyed the longtime quartermaster. At sixty, he was the oldest man on Xoro's crew, with graying hair, round spectacles, and a bloated middle. Shara knew he'd been quartermaster under Xoro's father before a storm took the former captain's life. "Have the boys bring up some chains for our guest of honor and fetch some of that special grog while you're at it."

Niguel flashed a crooked grin. "Aye, captain."

The grog in question turned out to be the foulest concoction Shara ever smelled, but disgust was nothing compared to the satisfaction of watching Derron squirm and struggle against his restraints. Mykal laughed, obviously delighted as Kael held the prince's head firm and Niguel forced the drink down his throat.

"What is that?" Solana asked Xoro as the prince slumped, fear creeping into his eyes at last.

"Something we picked up in the Magical Lands. It'll keep him compliant."

"You're drugging him?" Shara caught the disapproval in Solana's tone.

"He's high fae. We can't risk him channeling his magic," Xoro explained.

Solana's expectant gaze weighed on Shara. Poison was the weapon of cowards and Solana was honorable, but she hadn't seen Derron manipulating an entire marketplace full of humans. She hadn't seen her lover die in flames. If her sister waited for her to speak up, Shara had to disappoint. She had nothing to say.

"You should rest, Shara," Solana said finally.

"No." Shara dried the sweat from her brow as the prince's lids drooped. "We need to plan."

Xoro led them to his cabin. Sheer emerald curtains billowed beside large windows. A desk was neatly organized with ink and quill, a compass, and one of the ship's ledgers, items Xoro could use only with the help of his quartermaster. Maps hung on the walls, trophies from ships looted over the years.

Xoro took a seat behind the desk as the others gathered around it. Niguel spread a map on the mahogany surface and used items in his proximity to keep it flat. Solana stood beside Shara, who moved a fraction to the left to create more space between them and leaned in to study the map. It represented both Havanya and Ilahara, the expanse of sea between them narrowed to a splotch of blue.

Havanya felt small compared to her homeland, but Shara never realized the truth of it until now as she studied the two continents one beside the other on the parchment. Havanya looked like an island at best, while Ilahara was vast and diverse. The northern part of the continent,

Daganver, was dominated by pine forests. Browns and greens mingled with white on the map's surface. West of Daganver were two smaller islands that made up Eathelin, while a large mountain range, Teirak's Maw, spread out on the eastern side and far into its neighboring region of Makkan. The austere geography changed in the southern regions with the forests of Tyrra, the green heart of Ilahara, and the grassy plains of Adara, where Shara came from.

At the heart of the continent was a tree similar to an elm, drawn larger than the rest and rendered in turquoise and golden colors. Webs of rivers branched from the roots and spread throughout the entirety of the continent. The tree was the Ilah, the source of Ilahara's magic.

"This map is inaccurate," Shara said, jabbing her finger to the sea south of Adara. "This is where the Burning Sea should be."

"No one can sail to the Burning Sea. There's no point in putting it on a map," Xoro replied, unaware of the tightening of Shara's jaw. "All right, gentlemen. Where to?"

Mykal's gaze roved over the map. "Daganver," he said, the word filled with longing. "When we sailed to Havanya, we went over Merania to avoid siren waters." He tapped his finger over Eathelin, Merania being its capital.

"Wise." Niguel shuddered. "Those sirens are nasty creatures. Best to stay away from them."

"Believe me, the merfolk are no better," Mykal said.

"We can't sail to Daganver, Myk."

Mykal turned to Kael. The taut muscle of his jaw softened the longer he stared at the other man.

Kael continued, "Aerella will suspect we're searching for Asharaya by now. It will be the first place she'll expect us to return."

"What do you suggest?" Mykal asked.

Kael bit at his lower lip. "There's Tyrra." He pointed to

the western shore. "If we avoid the docks, we could land on the coast and cross the mainland undisturbed. We'll make it to Daganver on foot. Patrols might be a problem, but it's our best option." He looked at Xoro. "Can you do that?"

"It's a fortnight's trip with good winds. We have enough stores for such a trip. I can do that." Xoro's fingers casually brushed the pommel of the saber at his side. "As long as you remember your promise to Miss Spirre."

Mykal rapped his knuckles on the table. "We gave our word," he said, voice clipped. "Get us to Ilahara and we'll find Miss Spirre's brother." Mykal looked each of them in the eye. "Are we all in agreement?"

"We are," Solana said.

Xoro nodded.

Shara's gaze lingered on the map, and she fixated on the castle on the cliff that had been her home. "Yes."

Solana made to grab her hand, but Shara stepped away before their fingers could touch. She could no longer stand to be inside this closed space, surrounded by so many people. Her vision blurred the moment she left the cabin, and she leaned against the wall for support. Fortunately, neither Kael nor Mykal noticed. Any more of their coddling would make her murderous. Shara looked down at her hands as they came in and out of focus. The thought of more flames at the tips of her fingers sent waves of panic crashing against her rib cage, but she found no relief at their absence.

Her Fire had already done the irreparable.

"These aren't mine." The hitch in Solana's voice kept her pinned to the spot. Shara braced the wall and peeked back into the cabin as Solana faced Xoro, golden coins in hand.

"I won't accept payments in gold from my woman," he said, bracing her hips. "Shara will come around, you'll see."

"Shara has every right to feel betrayed. I've never

returned to the house by the sea after they found my mother's body, yet I was ready to ask her to return to the Magical Lands for a boy she's never met. She lost her whole family there, and a dragon that was a part of her soul. It wasn't fair of me to put this burden on her. It isn't fair that she should return there at all or that her past should continue to haunt her. None of this is right."

"But what choice did you have?" He leaned their foreheads together. "You have a chance to find your brother, Spirre. If Shara had that opportunity, she'd take it. Give her time, and she'll see the truth of it."

Shara spun away as their lips met, hot tears in her eyes. She hated Solana because she understood even when she was being selfish. She hated Xoro for assuming she was the one who should understand. She hated them both for being together and in love while she was alone and hollow.

Instead of going into their cabin, Shara stumbled in search of the stairs that would take her to the lower levels of the ship where she could be alone. Her head, her face, her entire body ached, but nothing hurt more than the useless organ beating in her chest.

A draft chilled her to her bones. The hold was dark and stank of molded wood and sailor's grog. Crates and barrels were stacked one on the other, filling the space nearly to capacity if not for the space left to navigate the stores.

Shara lost her footing on the last steps of the narrow stairs, chest cleaving with a sob. Her knees throbbed at the impact, and blood bloomed from the scrapes on her palms. The cut burned, but before Shara could think to look for one of the bottles to use as a disinfectant, a tingling sensation pulled at her skin as the severed halves stitched back together.

The burn softened to a sting before the magic swept even that away.

Fae. Her body was so undeniably fae.

Crushed by the weight of that truth and of Rami's loss, Shara bowed her head and succumbed to her grief. Though her body could heal, there were wounds hidden deep in her soul that no magic could ever repair. Old pain mixed with new sorrows. She felt as if those invisible cuts were bleeding, and she was drowning in that blood. She curled in on herself, cradling her head against her knees, and cried.

17

"May Heradem embrace him in her benevolent arms and may the everlasting Fire of Helrios keep him. Rest and farewell, Ronann Naeraan."

"Rest and farewell."

The congregation bent their heads as the head keeper burned the body of the deceased Lord Ronann upon the white marble altar. Cassia lifted her gaze. What was once flesh, blood and bones would soon be nothing but ashes, the soul caged within already gone. What would remain? A name in a crypt, the faded memory of a face, and the emotion it stirred. Soon even that would disappear.

"Cassia."

She blinked and turned to Eileen at her side. The sickly scent of lilies adorning the benches filled her nose once more. The gathered were leaving the Temple of Helrios, god of Fire and father of truth and justice. A long queue formed in the aisle, but some waited beside the white columns, hands on their hearts as the grieving family passed. Two tear-streaked faces led the mass outside: an elderly woman, sustained by the head keeper, and a man who very much resembled her. Her son, the new Lord Naeraan.

Ascensions were a dreary matter and Cassia never liked them. She wasn't someone who cried over a near stranger's death and playing the part for the local lords' benefit was exhausting. Cassia couldn't remember if she'd exchanged more than five words with the late Lord Ronann. She knew of him, and she'd seen him at functions, but she couldn't quite place his features, his face lost in a sea of many.

Second only to the family of the dearly departed, the Royal family was next to exit the temple. The queen and king first, followed by Cassia, and then Eileen, who was always a step behind at formal events.

The crowd parted for the queen, heads bowed. Even in the temple, they respected her above all else. Her they feared. Queen Aerella looked like a vision. The light from the open doors swallowed the paleness of her hair, and her black gown dragged on the floor like a long shadow.

Lady Caila Naeraan and her son stopped in front of the golden doors of the temple to greet those who had come to pay their respects. Behind them, Adara's sea shimmered with golden light.

"My condolences, Lady Caila," Queen Aerella said.

"Thank you, Your Majesty." Cassia's attention shifted between Lady Caila's wrinkles and her graying hair. A fae's body was slower than a human's to betray the passing of time, and Cassia had only met a handful of fae who truly looked ancient. Lady Caila was one of them.

Maenar Elvik had been another.

Cassia banished the old maenar's memory before it could conjure thoughts of the seer's prophecy and Derron's mission. A month had already passed since her brother left. She hoped he had found Asharaya, and that the deed was done. Despite Derron's reassurances, she knew her brother. He would fulfill his promise for the sake of their family, and later torment himself for killing the last Myrassar. Elon's sister. A girl he'd once considered a friend.

"I spoke to High Keeper Baramun last night. He regrets not being able to officiate the ceremony." Cassia kept her features blank to avoid giving away her mother's lie. The high keeper was the supreme representative of the Pentagod Creed, outranking the five head keepers of Ilahara's five regions who, in turn, outranked the keepers scattered throughout various temples. The only ceremonies he celebrated were those deemed holiest— those concerning the Crown.

Her father, Vaemor, expressed his condolences and brushed a chaste kiss on the woman's knuckles. Growing up, Aerella and Vaemor were often mistaken for siblings, their resemblance as staggering as Cassia's with her own twin, but they were merely cousins. Their marriage was born of their family's desire to strengthen the Argarys line.

The temple sat at the top of one of the coastline's lower cliffs, similar to the Embernest. A staircase had been carved into the cliff to access it, and no more than two people at a time could walk side by side. Cassia followed her parents, Eileen beside her. Her friend kept a hand upon the cliff's wall and her eyes locked ahead. The princess, on the other hand, walked with ease, unafraid of the overhang on the right.

A remembrance feast followed the ceremony in the Naeraan's home. The manor was a few miles from the city, so carriages awaited them at the base of the stairs. Because of the numerous guests attending the gathering, the Crown lent the Naeraan some of the castle's servants for the feast. As guests of honor, the Royal family sat on a built-in dais in the enormous dining hall. Cassia behaved as was expected, smiling and answering with pleasantries when spoken to. However, hiding her discomfort on the chair was proving difficult. Her back hurt and her legs ached. She longed for a walk or a softer chair. The only one to notice was Eileen, seated on her left.

She leaned closer. "Has it started?"

Cassia shook her head, but it was only a matter of time. At twenty-five, Cassia's first Bleeding was imminent.

"I heard the servants talking the other day. One of their daughters started the Bleeding. She's only nine."

"Humans mature faster." And died sooner.

Eileen faced the guests. "You'll break the hearts of many gentlemen once your parents find a worthy match. They can't take their eyes off you."

Tradition decreed the first-born of a high fae family should marry another within the same region. Between the twins, Derron had come into the world first, entitling him to the crown, while Cassia would remain a princess. He should have married an Adarian high fae woman, but their mother preferred matching him with Eileen, a union that guaranteed them a claim to the North. That left Cassia to deal with tradition.

"They could be looking at you," Cassia pointed out to her friend.

"Don't be ridiculous." Eileen's smile remained, but the light dimmed from her brown eyes. "I'm a traitor's daughter."

"Eileen." Cassia squeezed her friend's hand on the table, the action meant as both a comfort to Eileen and a warning to the nobles present. Eileen may have been a Todrak, but she had Cassia's trust.

Her friend returned the gesture in silent thanks, yet her smile remained sad. "You've heard them talking. They almost seem eager to see my family's suffering."

"They're not suffering. Mother is only keeping a close

eye on them, that's all."

Eileen looked over Cassia's shoulder to the queen deep in conversation with one of the guests. "The Yronwood took up residence in Frosthead Hall and my family is under house arrest," she whispered. "They're one mistake away from execution."

"It'll never come to that. We need the Todrak in the North."

The Todrak were a thorn in her family's side. The only reason her mother hadn't executed them was the Daganveran's blind loyalty to the family. Killing the Todrak would lead to a civil war, and after the Coup of Fire and the Uprisings, it was important for her mother's reign that Ilahara know peace. One raven risked jeopardizing years of stability. The queen's spies reported that Mykal Todrak was unaccounted for, and it wasn't hard to imagine the Todrak had moved against the Argarys.

Eileen knew this as much as Cassia. No reassurances would hold, at least not with Cassia, who lacked the ability to find soothing words. She wished Derron were here. He'd know what to say.

"I swear, Lady Vynatis just stood there. You'd think she was watching a couple dancing."

Cassia's attention zeroed in on a nearby table, where a group of ladies sat huddled close in mock privacy, their whispers loud enough to be heard by their neighbors. She stood from her seat, drawn to the conversation and the name they'd mentioned. Eileen followed silently, ever the faithful friend.

"Princess Cassia, what a lovely surprise," one of them squealed, her tone suggesting it was anything but. Cassia was the Princess of Ilahara, and therefore the subject of many of the nobles' gossip. They knew the name Vynatis meant something to her.

Cassia sat with a quick nod of thanks to the human

servant who fetched her a chair, a gesture the ladies noted. Eileen remained standing beside her with a cool expression.

The princess leaned back, wearing one of her best smiles. "What has you all so excited?"

One glance at her friends and the lady who'd been recounting the event preened, eager for the chance to speak to the princess. Lady Maree Louvas was one of the many swooning after Derron, earning Eileen's dislike. "Well, I was recently in Tyrra for a friend's wedding. Imiri Vynatis was there too, and so were two men who were very taken with her." A giggle rippled among the ladies.

Lady Imiri was the Head of Tyrra, and a woman many defined as of loose morals. Her many lovers were no secret, and some found it an amusing topic of conversation. "What about them?"

"They challenged each other to a duel, princess, right in front of everyone. A gruesome affair. They shifted into beasts and tore each other to pieces. I've never witnessed a shifter duel before, and believe me, I wouldn't wish the spectacle upon anyone."

"It's barbaric," another said. "When will the shifters learn to be more civilized? Duels are a thing of the past."

Lady Maree gasped. "Does Makkan still have them? One would think with High Keeper Baramun being Makkani, they would forgo such outdated traditions."

"What happened to the men?" Eileen asked, invested in the conversation in a way Cassia no longer was. Her mind went back five years to one of the rare trips she and Derron made with their father, in which Eileen joined them. They'd gone to Tyrra in honor of the Vernal Festival, the Tyrran celebration of the coming of spring—a season dear to a territory blessed with beautiful and fertile lands. During the celebration, she'd met Johan Vynatis, Imiri's second son. The moment he'd entered the room, Cassia had been unable to look anywhere else. Even now, she remembered the intake of her breath as his eyes found her, and how they'd done so again and again. Cassia would have given anything for him to approach.

He had, and she'd given him everything.

Cassia and Eileen returned to the dais when the servants brought in the third course. Distracted by memories, Cassia didn't notice a servant refilling her chalice until the young man whispered in her ear. "Remember to breathe, princess."

Cassia grabbed the goblet to hide her smile. She didn't draw attention to herself by acknowledging him in any way, but Korban delighted in making her life difficult.

She watched him walk away to serve the other guests. When Eileen nudged her foot under the table, Cassia knew she'd lingered far too long on his backside.

The princess huffed, and she speared the venison with her fork a little too violently. Korban spied her from another table, laughter twinkling in his gray eyes. It reminded her of a feast similar to this one, not an ascension but a birthday—hers and Derron's. She usually didn't notice the human help, yet it had been impossible not to see Korban or the way his attention never strayed from her. Cassia could have had him punished for being too forward. Instead, she'd ordered him to sit with her. He'd been a welcome distraction when her thoughts kept returning to her previous birthday, spent in Tyrra, relishing in Johan's kisses and whispered promises.

The five gods blessed Korban with a winning combination of assets: dark hair curling at the ends, rich brown skin, lean muscle, and remarkable gray eyes. Cassia knew exactly how she wanted the night to end when she fed him from her plate.

One night, she'd promised herself, but one night turned to two, a week into a month, and what began like a game grew into much more. Korban never asked for anything more than a stolen kiss or a chance to see her in the evening. He listened to her complaints, and she'd ask him about his day. She'd kiss him and he'd draw her closer, holding her until nothing but skin separated them, until they were one and there was nothing in their world but each other.

Fool, Derron had said. *You gave your heart to the one man you can never have.* He didn't hate Korban, but their relationship was destined for tragedy. She was a fae princess, and Korban was a human. There was no future for them, but Cassia wasn't ready to let go of him. A year had come and gone and still, she couldn't get enough.

One of the court ladies, Lady Denia Bahys, called attention to herself by standing from her seat at the back of the room. "Your Majesty," she said to the queen, her smile sickly sweet. "How lovely to have you here."

"What may I do for you, Lady Denia?"

Lady Denia bristled as if she both dreaded and anticipated the moment. "We couldn't help but notice the prince's absence. We heard he left for an unexpected voyage."

Whispers ceased, and all eyes turned to the queen. Rumors surrounding the last Myrassar ran rampant throughout the court. It was inevitable. Many nobles witnessed the seer's vision, including Lady Denia. The Bahys thrived under the Myrassar rule and supported Darrok Todrak during the Uprisings. Only Lady Denia remained, the last daughter of a dying house. She had no part in the revolt, but that she still lived was proof of the queen's benevolence. However, mentioning Derron's absence drew attention to Aerella's failure to dispose of every Myrassar and made her appear weak. It was a rotten way to show gratitude.

The queen straightened, her expression giving nothing

away. "What of it?"

"How long until he returns?"

"My son has his orders. He'll return when his work is done and no sooner."

Everyone returned to their meals once the lady sat, but Cassia's appetite vanished. She glowered at those seated at Lady Denia's table, who leaned in to murmur among themselves.

King Vaemor, the only one who'd continued eating, set down his fork and dabbed at his mouth with the napkin on his lap. "Careful, Lady Denia. Eating is a dangerous affair. You could choke on your food."

The lady's throat bobbed as she forced food down. It took her a second too long to laugh, a beat longer for the rest to follow.

Vaemor didn't laugh, and neither did the queen.

Cassia wasn't feeling any better that night. Her back ached, and a dreadful pulsing between her thighs gave her no respite. The inevitability of the Bleeding made it impossible to rest. Soon, her mother would find her a husband, and she would have to stop seeing Korban.

The princess leaned against the window of her room, arms wrapped around her middle. Eileen was her friend, but she was also a woman who would marry the man she loved. Cassia yearned for Derron. He more than anyone understood how dreadful duty could be. Wherever he was, she imagined him looking up at the moon, too, wishing her goodnight. "I miss you, brother."

The sound of tapestry shifting drew her from her thoughts.

Korban flashed a grin as he set the tapestry back into place. Elon Myrassar had shown her and Derron many of the secret passageways hidden throughout the castle, some impossible to find if one didn't pay attention. Cassia had never been brave enough to explore them all, but they likely extended farther than the castle. They'd been designed to bring the Royal family to safety in the event of a siege.

Fortunately, they hadn't served their purpose with the Myrassar.

She sauntered over to Korban. "And here I was thinking you'd forgotten me."

"I can't do the impossible, princess." Korban twined his arms around her waist. Their lips brushed before his tongue slipped into her mouth and warmed her all the way to her core. "I've wanted to do that all night," he whispered against her lips.

"Just the night?" Cassia's finger twisted around a curl at the nape of his neck.

"Perhaps since this afternoon."

"Well, I've been thinking about you since this morning. I win."

Gooseflesh dotted her skin at the feeling of his breath. "The most beautiful girl in Ilahara has been thinking about me since this morning." Korban's lips traveled the length of her neck and grazed the curve of her shoulder. "That means I win."

"Smooth talker."

"What were you brooding about by the window?"

Cassia's smile faltered, and she stepped away. She couldn't tell him about the onset of the Bleeding and what it meant. Not yet. "Derron."

Korban lifted her from behind, and she shrieked, cursing herself a moment later. Although her mother certainly suspected she had a lover, it never hurt to be careful in the Embernest. *Show your power, hide your heart.*

"If you keep worrying so much, your hair will turn

white," Korban teased.

"You'd love me even if my hair were white."

"Well, it would take some getting used to."

Cassia punched him in the stomach, careful not to use too much strength. Even if he looked strong, Korban was only human. "You're the one who should be worrying about graying hair and bloating stomachs."

Korban grabbed her hands, laughing. "My stomach will only bloat if you keep punching me."

Cassia laughed with him, drawing her face closer. "Idiot," she said and kissed him.

18

"I hate ships."

Kael patted his Do'strath's back as Mykal heaved into a bucket. Mykal had been able to resist his seasickness on only the first day. Now, a week into their journey, each day at sea worsened his condition. Kael begged the Dragon to hasten their arrival if only so his Do'strath could feel better. Mykal hardly kept any food down, and his complexion turned a disconcerting shade of gray. "Just a few more days, Myk."

His neck prickled with the feeling of being watched. Looking away from Mykal, Kael found the prince's stare. Sweat beaded his temples, and his expression was somewhat vacant. They gave him essence of renike, an herb growing in proximity of the Ilah. A small dose could addle the mind, so in Ilahara it was administered to dangerous prisoners to hinder the use of magic. How it came into Xoro's possession and what he meant to do with it was beyond Kael, but it was a macabre stroke of luck. Unpleasant as it was, the grog was the only thing protecting the crew from the prince's Song.

A soft knock on the door preceded Solana's entrance into the cabin. Her gaze immediately landed on her sleeping sister. "How is she?" she asked in Ilahein.

"Still warm." Kael walked over to the bed, standing beside Solana as she brought her hand to Asharaya's forehead and then quickly away.

"I have never seen her fall ill with a fever. Not once."

"It's the Burning," Kael explained. "It happens to Fire wielders when their magic spirals out of control. A weaker fae would have burned from the inside out, but her body is strong."

"It won't get any better." Finally strong enough to stand, Mykal stumbled over to the bed. "The closer we are to the Ilah, the stronger her magic will become." He conjured a thin layer of Ice before touching Asharaya's forehead.

That morning Asharaya's legs hadn't been strong enough to hold her upright. She fell the moment she got out of bed, and it was only Mykal's fast reflexes that kept her from crumpling to the floor. Kael fetched Solana while Mykal undressed Asharaya and put her back to bed. By the time Kael and Solana returned, Mykal's hands already hovered inches over Asharaya's skin to cool her with his Ice.

Solana's throat now bobbed as she looked at Mykal. "Thank you."

"This isn't a solution," Mykal said, ignoring Solana's gratitude. "She's a Myrassar. Dragonfire runs in her veins. She needs to learn to control this if she's to survive."

"I do not know how to teach her."

"Clearly not. You only knew how to teach her to be human."

"Myk," Kael scolded and then turned to Solana with an apologetic smile. His stomach knotted at the fearful gleam in her beautiful brown eyes. "We'll figure it out together."

Mykal scoffed. "Where did I leave the bucket?"

Kael clenched his jaw. "Perhaps you need some fresh air, Do'strath."

Mykal gaped at him. "I'm sorry, do you need some privacy?"

"Some respite from your puke would be nice."

Mykal snatched the bucket with more force than necessary, thankfully without spilling its contents. "By all means, have your privacy. If I fall overboard, feel welcome to loathe yourself for the rest of your long life." He glared at Solana as he strode to the door.

Kael closed his eyes, unable to help his flinch as Mykal slammed the door behind him or the warmth in his cheeks at his implication. He couldn't look at Solana as he said, "Forgive him. He likes being dramatic." Now that Mykal was gone, he switched to Havanian for her benefit.

"There's truth to his words." She sat beside Asharaya and took her hand. "I helped her live a lie. If I hadn't…"

"She would have been alone. Yes, Asharaya—Shara—might have lived her life as a human, but at least she knew love. Family. She grew strong, and it was thanks to you. Mykal sometimes forgets the world isn't black and white. It's also gray and every shade in between." He glanced at the prince, whose silver eyes slowly opened to return the look. Derron's orders had been to kill Asharaya, and he almost succeeded, yet they found Asharaya in his room, weak but unharmed.

"I believe your Do'strath and my sister have more in common than they realize." Solana kissed Shara's fingers before standing from the bed. "I don't want to cause trouble for your friend. I'll leave, but if she wakes up, please let me know immediately."

"I will."

Alone with an unconscious princess and a stupefied

prince, Kael studied his half-brother. Questions swirled in his head, but he was better off not knowing how the prince's mind worked and seeing him as the enemy and not a man. The Todrak wanted to remove the Argarys from the throne, and the Argarys would fight to hold on to it. Kael's place in this conflict was by his Do'strath's side, through victory or defeat. Dragon curse him if by the end of it he wouldn't drive his sword through Vaemor Argarys's heart.

"If you're expecting my mother to barter her key to the North for me, you're wasting your time." Derron spoke slowly as if each syllable required immense effort. Kael suppressed the twinge of guilt rising in his chest. "By sending you here, Darrok Todrak demonstrated he cares more for revenge than his daughter. The queen won't accept his terms, not even for me."

"You're her son."

"She always has Cassia."

Could a mother be that heartless? Derron seemed to believe Aerella could be. Were they wasting their time, or was this another of the prince's attempts to distill doubt in them? Kael preferred to believe the latter. "You'd better hope she will. It's the only thing keeping you alive."

Derron leaned his head back against the wall, chuckling. Red gashes marred his wrists where the chains held him. Kael walked over, unfastening the restraints before he could think better of it. He didn't miss Derron's surprised intake of breath.

"You won't be going anywhere in your state." Kael wasn't sure if the explanation was for Derron's benefit or his own. He stayed crouched, eye to eye, blue to silver. Kael's mother said eyes were the mirror of the soul. If he looked into his brother's eyes, would Kael know if he were lying? "You had your chance to kill Asharaya, yet you didn't. Why?"

"I'm a warrior, not an assassin."

"So, it was honor." Kael couldn't say if the answer

relieved him or not. "Tell me, Your Royal Highness, is there honor in power gained with the blood of innocents?"

"You're referring to the Coup of Fire." The prince's eyes narrowed. "I was a child. I did nothing."

"Yes, you did nothing then." Kael stood, staring him down. "And you do nothing now."

Derron looked at a spot on the wall. *No, not the wall.* Kael followed the prince's line of sight to Asharaya. Were it not for the pearls of sweat on her face, one would think she was sleeping. "There is one currency I value more than gold or diamonds." The two men faced each other once more. "Loyalty. True loyalty can't be bought or sold. It can only be earned or given. The Todrak are your family. I respect that, but I won't betray mine."

Kael bit his lip to keep it from trembling, but he could do nothing about his hands. An unexplainable rage took over him. What had he expected? That Derron would see the error of his mother's rule and fight with them because he was the one asking? Foolish. He'd been so foolish to talk to him.

Kael grabbed Derron's wrists.

"Stop this madness, Arkael. If you return to Ilahara without Asharaya, there will be no proof of your treason. You could return home, and all would be forgotten."

"And you wouldn't say a word to your mother?"

"What for?" Derron asked. "My mother may be queen, but she needs soldiers to fight her wars. Without tangible proof, many Adarian lords wouldn't dare cross the Todrak and start a war with Daganver."

Kael clasped the chains around Derron's wrists. "Save your breath. Nothing you could say would change my mind. Mykal and I gave our word."

Derron sighed, his breath tickling the nape of Kael's neck. "It's too bad we have to stand on opposite sides of this conflict. I've always wanted a brother."

Kael's eyes widened, but Derron was already asleep.

He needed air. Kael stood to leave but froze when he found Mykal standing on the threshold. "How long have you been there?"

"I saw Selena walk out." Mykal's gaze flickered to Derron before it returned to Kael, his expression unreadable. "What was that?"

"He was uncomfortable."

"He's a prisoner. He's not supposed to be comfortable." Mykal stepped inside and closed the door behind him slowly, which meant he was trying hard to remain calm. "I told you to be careful around him."

"He's drugged and barely conscious. There's no harm he can do."

Mykal crossed his arms. "Should we let him be free to roam the deck when he laments an ache to his backside?"

"Your father taught us there is honor in mercy, even toward your enemies."

"Not this enemy," Mykal said through gritted teeth. He ran a hand across his face. "For once in your life, can you accept maybe I'm the one who sees things more clearly than you do? Do I have to order you to keep your damned mouth shut around Argarys for you to listen to me?"

Kael sucked in his breath. Mykal never pulled rank, not with him. He reached down their bond to assess the extent of Mykal's anger and soothe his worries the best way Kael knew how—wordlessly, heart to heart, mind to mind—but Mykal's walls were unyielding. Once again, despite his silent plea, his Do'strath wouldn't let him in. "No need. I'll keep my mouth shut from now on, my lord."

Mykal sighed. "I didn't mean it, Kael."

"Forget it, Myk." Kael bumped his Do'strath's shoulder as he passed. "You keep guard. I'll see if Solana wants to talk."

"She already has a lover, in case you haven't noticed."

This time, it was Kael's turn to slam the door.

19

When Derron came to, Arkael was no longer in the cabin and the chains had returned to his wrists. He couldn't remember Arkael binding him again. The fog surrounding his mind was receding, a temporary respite that would allow him little time to plan and not much strength to act. A small kernel of power woke from its slumber, but it wouldn't be enough to seize the men's minds and commandeer his escape. His captors made sure to force the renike down his throat at regular intervals. Soon, they would come with more.

Todrak sat by Asharaya's bedside, his frosted fingers going to her neck and arms every so often. She was asleep, and the occasional flutter of her eyelashes suggested she may be dreaming. It reminded Derron of when he and Cassia were children before he gained a crown while his friend's blood was still warm. The Burning forced Cassia to bed for an entire week, and only the maenar's careful ministrations and Derron's silent prayers to the five gods had seen her back on her feet.

"I know you're awake, Argarys." Todrak didn't look Derron's way when he spoke.

"How perceptive of you."

Todrak turned the full might of his glare on him. For a moment, his eyes flashed blue, but when he blinked again, they were a furious brown. "I won't see Kael hurt. Stop trying to manipulate him."

"I have no idea what you're talking about."

A small cry slipped past Asharaya's lips. Tremors spread down to her hands, and then her arms and legs until her entire body convulsed and she screamed.

"Asharaya?" Todrak's hands flew to her forehead.

At that moment the door opened, and the man named Niguel marched inside with the grog, whistling. He stopped in his tracks at the sight of Todrak trying to keep Asharaya from spasming off the bed. "What in the Maiden's name is going on here?"

"Help me," said Todrak.

Arkael and Solana burst into the cabin, followed by Captain Xoro. "What's happening?" the pirate demanded.

Niguel shook his head. "I don't know, captain. I just got here."

Solana shoved the quartermaster aside and ran to her sister. "Is it the fever?"

Todrak cast a quick glance at Arkael, who hurried to his Do'strath's side. "Kael, hold her legs."

Sweat beaded Derron's brow. The room grew suddenly warmer, and Asharaya's face no longer held its former serenity. Whatever she'd been dreaming about turned into a nightmare, and her tenuous hold on her Fire was slipping.

Solana gasped and jerked away from Asharaya, her hands red.

"Myk, she needs to be cooled down," Arkael said. Todrak

threw his shirt over his shoulders. He sat on the bed and gathered Asharaya against his chest. His arms around her were the only thing keeping the blanket from sliding off her bare body. Smoke lifted where their skins met. Todrak panted, the Fire too hot even for him to endure for long.

The edge of the blanket caught fire, quickly extinguished by a wave of Arkael's hand. The stench of burned fiber filled the room.

Xoro muttered a string of curses. "Put a stop to it before she burns down my ship."

Todrak growled in frustration. "I'm trying."

Derron looked away, a muscle feathering in his jaw. The Fire would consume her before it burned down the ship. No amount of Todrak's Ice or Arkael's Fire wielding magic would save them.

Asharaya whimpered.

Solana slapped her sister's cheek, heedless of the blisters on her palm. "Shara, wake up."

Help her.

Derron shut his eyes as if that could silence the voice in his head that belonged to his friend.

She'll burn, Derron. My sister will burn.

If she did, Derron would fulfill his duty to his family. He'd die in dragonfire, but the Argarys legacy would live on.

Another small cry from Asharaya.

Derron's gaze unwillingly returned to her. She writhed in agony, and her eyes refused to open. If Cassia were here, she'd remind him Asharaya was their enemy now and he should let her burn. Yet with every whimper, it wasn't only Elon's memory becoming more insistent. It was Asharaya's, too. He remembered her as a girl who played with a dragon at least twelve times her size. Grass or mud often stained her gowns, but her hair remained miraculously tidy in wondrous braids. He saw her smile when he said hello or hide behind a wall with a stick to imitate Derron and Elon's fighting stances. When he caught her, she made him swear not to tell Maenar Elvik. It had become their little secret.

Only a small drop of his Song had awoken from the lull of the drug.

Enough to slip past the lowered barriers of her fever-addled mind.

Derron's Song allowed him to do more than simply persuade a person to act as he willed. He could waltz into a mind and summon images of his own creation. He could spy on people's dreams or change them and shape them to his will. *You can make them adore you, my little prince,* his grandmother once said. Catlana Ravyne Argarys was a powerful mermaid, and she insisted on being the one to teach her grandson when she sensed his potential. *You can be a god.*

I don't want to be a god.

You'll be king one day. There's hardly a difference.

Now, Derron used his Song to enter Asharaya's dreams. The rooftop of the Keep looked exactly like that night—the warm breeze, the lights outlining the city sprawled beneath them, the body burning on the ground. Asharaya was on her knees, hands outstretched as if to call back the flames. Tears lined her soot-stained cheeks as she muttered something Derron couldn't make out.

A beautiful woman looked down on Asharaya. Her golden nightgown complemented her amber skin, the front stained with blood. Apart from her green eyes, she strongly resembled the young woman on the floor.

Jaemys Myrassar, Asharaya's mother.

Once, Queen Jaemys's amber skin glowed in the light as if the sun delighted in her presence. Her face was open and kind, and like her daughter, her eyes held a spark of mischief every time she smiled. Derron was happy when she invited him to stay for dinner, but he looked away whenever the former queen hugged her children. His mother never showed such tenderness to him and Cassia, and he wondered if she ever would. This Queen Jaemys, however, wasn't the woman from his memories. A scowl replaced her smile and her skin was ashen.

"It's your fault." The accusation knocked the air from Derron's lungs until he realized the former queen wasn't speaking to him but to her daughter. "They've stolen our home, destroyed our legacy, and what have you done? You hid like a coward, pretending to be human and forsaking the magic flowing in your veins. You've forsaken us, Asharaya."

Somewhere in the distance, the whiz of arrows preceded a cry of agony as they found their mark. Derron searched the skies for the dragon, but he couldn't see it, though his lament echoed with no end.

"I'm sorry," Asharaya cried as she covered her ears. "Please, make it stop..."

"Asharaya," he called, but her mother's accusatory words and the dragon's wails rang louder. She was too far gone in her nightmare, but he had to cut through its haze somehow. Asharaya bent forward, and Derron took a tentative step toward her. Her shoulders shook with the force of her sobs. Instinctively, he reached out a hand to comfort her, but if he touched her it might spook her further. "Shara."

Asharaya's eyes snapped open and settled on him. She choked on a sob, scrambling back. "No, no, no." Crazed, she searched the floor, perhaps for a weapon.

"This is a dream," Derron said. "You need to wake up."

"You're here to kill me."

Asharaya's pants had ripped on the side, revealing a fragment of the black dragon snaking around her leg. Derron had seen it in the Establishment when she stabbed his neck. He'd been too busy trying to stay alive to care that she was undressed, but that detail struck him. "I've never seen such markings before," he said, pointing to it. "What is it?"

"What?" Asharaya sniffled and looked down at her leg. She self-consciously tugged the torn fabric with trembling fingers. "It's a tattoo. Humans make them with needles. The ink stays in your skin like a scar." A small smile touched her lips. "Solana has one behind her shoulder. She says it reminds her of a cat she had when she was a child."

When Derron looked up, Jaemys Myrassar was gone. "Is the scar meant to remind you of your dragon?"

"Deimok," she breathed, brushing the marking on her leg.

Derron looked to the burning remains of her lover. Asharaya had screamed at him to help, and Derron would have done it, but Fire was the weakest of his abilities. He could conjure a small flame, but he couldn't control a Fire of that proportion. There was nothing he could have done.

He could now.

The scene changed, and the night no longer drowned in the wails of a dying dragon. Asharaya rested against a tree trunk. Sunlight filtered through branches and caught in her spectacular golden eyes. Once she registered the change, she stood with a gasp and gaped at the Embernest gardens. The smell of lavender and roses filled the air, and dragonsong echoed around them.

"This is impossible." Suspicion warred with wonder as Asharaya faced him. "Is this truly a dream?"

Derron plucked a rose from a bush, wincing when a thorn pricked his finger. "A better dream than the one that came before." He offered her the rose, a smile tugging his lips at the familiarity.

"It doesn't explain why you're in it."

"I don't know, Asharaya." Derron braved another step toward her with a suggestive grin. "Why am I in your dreams?" Asharaya raised an annoyed brow, and his smile vanished. "You're about to set fire to the ship with everyone on board. Someone had to intervene."

In a few moments, reality slinked within the dream's cracks. When Asharaya realized the gravity of his words, she gasped—a predictable reaction—and then delivered a slap to his cheek. "That's why you're here, then. You can't kill me, so you decided to break my mind instead."

"Break your mind?" Derron rubbed his aching cheek. "I'm trying to save your life."

Asharaya threw her hands in the air. "What were Kael and Mykal thinking in letting you anywhere near me?"

Derron skirted back before she had the mind to hit him again. "Gods, woman, they didn't send me. I sent myself." He held his hands up, one still holding the rose, as a sign of peace. "They're trying to wake you, but so far haven't been successful. I did what I had to do to save us all. To save you."

He extended the rose again with conviction.

Asharaya considered the flower, lips puckered in thought until she narrowed them in a thin line. She snatched the rose and widened her arms. "How is an act of chivalry going to wake me?"

"I'm here to make sure you don't kill us all. When you awake is entirely up to you." As he spoke, their fighting leathers faded. For himself, Derron chose tight-fitting black pants, a white shirt buttoned to the collar, and a blue velvet jacket on top. A red dress laced with golden leaves on the bodice hugged Asharaya's curves. The low cut revealed glowing amber skin reminiscent of her mother, whose locket hung around her neck. Light winked in the dragon's ruby eye. Derron had half a mind to add the dirt he'd been accustomed to seeing, but something about the way she looked in that dress gave him pause.

"So, you're useless." Asharaya looked down at the gown,

and though she made no comment, the lingering moment in which she examined it betrayed her appreciation. She took a deep breath and looked around. "Why did you take me here?"

"It was easier to change the dream into a place familiar to us both."

"Familiar." Asharaya stroked the tree she'd been leaning against before. "I used to be happy here. I had my family. I had Deimok." She turned to look at him, a moment of silence stretching between them. "You were Elon's friend, but I liked to think that we were friends, too."

"I thought of you as my friend," he whispered, averting his gaze.

Asharaya leaned against the tree and looked down at the rose in her hands. "Things were simpler back then. My mother was right. I have forsaken my family. I should have done something. Instead, all I did was run with my tail between my legs. Some dragon I am."

"You were only a girl."

"My mother looked for me that night. The soldiers found her in my room, but I wasn't there because I'd run off to the library to read a biography of Bhaessa Myrassar." She laughed, the sound full of bitter regret. "She was my favorite dragon rider. I wanted to be just like her."

Derron swallowed the lump in his throat. "The Dragon Bride. They say she used to lay with her dragons." Derron doubted that was true, but he believed in the dragons' veneration. If he'd been a creature of Fire, he would have undoubtedly felt drawn to someone as fierce as the beating of his own heart.

"Well, Maenar Elvik made sure the biographies I came in contact with left out that detail." Asharaya laughed. "I was only a child."

"Clever Maenar Elvik." He didn't realize he was smiling until it was gone. "Your mother's death is not your fault."

"But if I'd been with her, I could have protected her." Asharaya inspected her hands. "What good is power if it only brings destruction and death?"

"Your mother was a gifted Fire wielder and she couldn't save herself. Your father was a Dragon-Blessed and he still died. Elon..." Elon trained in the art of combat, but he was a scholar at heart. When he was feeling particularly miserable, Derron often imagined his friend's last moments. He pictured Elon bent over a journal, the soldiers bursting into his room, the sword running him through. "You could have done nothing."

Asharaya stared at him in silence, the weight of her golden eyes unbearable after a few moments. A pit opened in his stomach at her scrutiny. "You're a shit killer, Argarys."

The dream vanished, and Derron returned to his body with a gasp. Asharaya's shaking stopped, and she opened her eyes. A collective sigh of relief followed.

"She's awake," the quartermaster whispered to Xoro.

For a brief moment, Asharaya's golden eyes found Derron's, and then someone yanked his head back and Niguel filled his vision.

"Open up, Argarys." Todrak.

Derron tried clamping his jaw shut, but his mouth was pried open and oblivion returned.

20

Shara savored the opportunity to be back on her feet as much as she did the fresh wind blowing against her face. The setting sun painted the ocean with a shimmer of gold as far as the eye could see. Gone were the traces of Havanya's humidity and the scents she associated with it. The sea's freshness and the taste of salt coating the air predominated the reek of sweat from a week's journey.

As the crew gathered on deck and their chatter filled the silence, she sat by the rail, water spraying her skin. Shara relished every drop clinging to her without turning into vapor. Her temperature had dropped.

For now.

It was only a matter of time before her Fire surged back to the surface. In Havanya, it was a spark, as easy to extinguish as the last flicker on a consumed wick. Now every mile closer to Ilahara strengthened the pull of the Ilah's magic, and her Fire attuned to it. Doubt, regret, and grief added fuel to the flames. How did one snuff out a wildfire?

Shara's clammy fingers fastened around the charcoal as she drew in her sketchbook. Images flashed before her eyes—her mother's disappointed glare, Rami's body in flames, an arrow in her dragon's heart, Solana's hands red with blisters, a red rose plucked from the gardens of her childhood. Art had been her outlet whenever thoughts weighed her down. Giving life to shapes in her head made them real and thus easier to understand.

Once, she trusted the Fire in her veins, loved it even. It made her as strong and fierce as Deimok. With his might flowing through her, she'd felt invincible and in control. The Coup of Fire changed everything.

Shara's breath trembled as she traced the outline of the arrow piercing her dragon's strong chest. Deimok had been made of her same Fire. He would know how to guide her. She closed her eyes against their sudden sting. "Ashari," she whispered to the wind.

For a moment too swift to hold on to, her heart beat strong enough for two. Shara's eyes sprung open, and her heart, now alone, thundered as she searched the horizon. Had it only been her imagination?

"You look like you've seen a ghost."

Shara glanced sidelong at Mykal. His dark complexion turned ashen and he clutched the rail with a white-knuckled grip. "You look like you're about to be sick."

"Do they teach you to be perceptive when you're an assassin?"

"Do they teach you to be a bitch when you're a lord?"

Mykal's lips twisted in a lopsided grin. "Your Ilahein is improving." A moment of comfortable silence stretched between them before he spoke again. "How are you feeling?"

"Better." She turned to face him fully. "I hear I have you to thank for that."

Mykal shrugged as if it were nothing. "I have my own experience with ill-tempered magic." His gaze was lost to the horizon. "Sometimes, not even all the training in the world will control it, but it helps." It was his turn to face her. "Ever since the Soul Binding, I've been suffering the Frostbite."

"Frostbite?"

"It's similar to your fever," Mykal explained. "Magic needs release. If you don't let it out, it strikes within."

Had they been friends, Shara would have reached for his hand. Instead, they were little more than strangers, mere pawns pushed in the same direction by powers they didn't control. Only this common thread of camaraderie linked them, a bright light in a dark tunnel. "How do you control it?"

"I have Kael." The way he said the name made Shara flush like she'd pried in an intimate affair. Thoughts of Rami came unbidden and cut her breath short. The image of his burning flesh warred with that of the warm smile he had reserved for her alone. How unfair that memories of him were now tainted by his death. "Listen, Asharaya, your Fire is a part of you. Unless you want to do the Argarys a favor, you have to learn how to master it."

"You're right."

"And I know you think you want nothing to do with Ilahara, but—" He gawked as if seeing her for the first time. "You...you agree?"

Shara's eyes raked the men as they passed down grog and exchanged bawdy stories to pass the time, huddling in their coats to keep warm. Solana sat with them, leaning into Xoro's side. A knot formed in Shara's throat at the bandages around her sister's hands. *It's my fault.* "I could have killed everyone on this ship today because I've forgotten what it means to be fae." She looked back to Mykal, steel in her gaze. "There is plenty of blood on my hands, but I assure you none of it is innocent. Yes, I must learn to master my Fire, and since no one knows how, the task falls to you and Kael."

Mykal straightened his spine and squared his shoulders. "We won't fail you."

Shara fought against the primitive instinct to run away from the fervor in his eyes. His devotion to the Myrassar name had the shape of hands closing around her throat, ready to choke her. "I'm not asking as a queen," she specified.

Mykal's posture relaxed as he leaned against the rail. "You know, you and I would have been married."

Shara was grateful she was sitting or else she would have dropped dead. "Married?"

Shara hadn't had the time to plan or to envision a future that went beyond midnight encounters and the bloody path of the vrah. Had she remained a princess, her father would have used her as a pawn to fortify this alliance or that friendship. A crown was nothing more than a golden cage.

"Rendal would have married an Ice wielder to honor tradition, but our fathers were like brothers, and we're the same age." Mykal shrugged. "It was a perfect match."

The two stared at one another, and Shara wondered if Mykal tried to envision that future as well. She would have hated the snow and the cold, but Mykal was a good man and he was handsome, too. Perhaps they would have found a way to make it work.

Perhaps they would have both been miserable.

She thought of how his gaze sought Kael in a room and the reverent way in which Mykal said his name. She thought of the red roses in the Embernest gardens, and how young Asharaya's heart raced whenever Derron offered her one.

Mykal looked away first. "Not as a queen, then. We start in the morning. I won't hear you complain about wanting to sleep in, understood?"

Shara smiled and nodded, clutching the sketchbook to her chest as she stood. Niguel's familiar whistling drew her attention. He strode toward their cabin, a tankard of Derron's drug in hand.

"In the morning," she said in farewell to Mykal as she headed in Niguel's direction.

Niguel had a limp to his step, forcing him to a slow amble, which gave Shara enough time to stop him from opening the cabin door.

"Hello, miss," he said with a toothy grin. "It's good to see you back on your feet."

Shara faked a smile. "Is that for the prisoner?"

"Aye."

"I'll take care of it." Shara held on tighter to her sketchbook, lest she rip the grog from the quartermaster's hands. "You should enjoy some rest with your crew."

Niguel pursed his lip. Uncertainty flickered on his face for a moment before it was gone. After all, what reason did he have to doubt her? Derron Argarys was her prisoner, and no one wanted him dead as much as she did. The quartermaster handed her the grog with a shrug. "Be careful, miss. Drugged he may be, but he's got a strong bite, that one." He held up his hand, showing off a red half-moon to prove it.

This time, Shara's smile was sincere. "I'll be careful."

Shara waited for Niguel to join the other men, and then she entered the cabin. The space was too small to contain five bodies that hadn't seen soap for a full week. Despite the small window being open, it wasn't enough to clear the stale air.

Kael lay on a hammock and stared at the ceiling as if it held the solution to his every problem. The Do'strath were insufferable when they got in a fight.

"You should check up on Mykal," Shara said by way of

greeting. "I think he's about to be sick."

Kael sighed, gaze dropping to the grog. "Need help with that?"

"I can manage."

Only when the door closed behind him did she let herself look at Derron Argarys. His silver eyes opened as if he'd been waiting for the exact same thing.

Shara saw his silver-blond hair and imagined his mother's gown drenched in her family's blood.

She saw his silver eyes and remembered his stare when she woke from her dream. Had it been relief or guilt she'd seen there?

He helped me.

Gooseflesh dotted her skin. Not even in her drawings had she been able to face that moment. The picture of Derron's deep-set silver eyes framed by long lashes and the sheen of sweat on his brow burned in her mind. If drawing made it real, wasn't it easier to let the memory fade?

"Will you put up a fight?" Shara asked, dangling the tankard.

"I don't like the taste." When he'd stepped into her nightmare, Derron's voice held the familiar velvet musicality that she'd learned of in the Lioness's Establishment. The deep rasp the renike had reduced it to startled her and sent an unwelcome pang in her stomach.

Shara looked down at the grog to suppress the feeling. It smelled as bad as dry piss, but for a moment she flirted with the idea of chancing a sip. Her skin tingled as she fastened her hold around the tankard. Would the renike help her escape her thoughts and magic?

"You should have let me burn." The words surged before Shara could stop them. "It's what your mother would want."

"If you burned, we burned with you."

"You lied in the dream, then. You weren't there for me,

but for yourself." In a way, it was a relief.

"Why else? I'm an Argarys."

She clenched her fist. "Did you always hate us? When you played with Elon...when you gave me flowers. Was any of it real?"

Derron avoided her question long enough that she thought he wouldn't answer. "It was real for me."

Shara walked over to the small bedside table, empty if not for a pitcher of water and a basin to wash their faces. She set down the grog and braced the wood, exhaling through her nose to calm her nerves. The Derron Argarys in her dream reminded her of the boy she knew, but the calm demeanor, his charm, and the reassurances had been nothing but a carefully constructed lie to warrant his survival. There was no trace of her friend in the man he'd become. Perhaps he'd loved them once and hadn't wanted to be a prince any more than she wanted to be an assassin, but he'd molded himself into his mask.

They both had.

Shara poured some of the grog into a cup and then watered it down. The rest she hid beneath her bed, hoping the stale air would mask the stench. Mykal's words echoed in her ears. *We won't fail you.*

How foolish to place so much hope in a woman he didn't know.

Shara grabbed the glass and strode over to Derron. "Open up, Argarys." He drew back his head. "It'll still taste like piss and you won't have your Song, but at least you'll be awake." Or at least that's what Kael had pleaded to Mykal a few days earlier.

Derron sneered. "No."

Shara grabbed his jaw. Prying his mouth open proved more difficult than she anticipated, yet she managed to pour most of the grog into his mouth and to keep his head back long enough to force him to swallow. Anger flashed in his eyes, but by that time Shara already decided he was no longer worthy of her attention.

She dropped onto the bed, limbs thankful for the reprieve, and flipped through the pages of her sketchbook with leisure until she found the drawing she was looking for.

A hasty map of Ilahara she created after seeing the one in Xoro's cabin.

"Why this small mercy?" Derron asked after a while.

Shara traced a path on the map, from Tyrra to Adara, and circled a castle on a cliff. The Embernest.

"Because I'm a Myrassar," she said.

And she wouldn't be going to Daganver.

21

Clink, clink, clink.

High Keeper Baramun thrummed his ringed fingers on the visitor's side of the oak desk. Cassia's gaze followed his hand to a wine goblet, and her lips pursed at the sound of his drinking. A drop slipped past his lip and dribbled onto his chest. To his luck, it hadn't caught on the white fabric of his tunic but on the medallion around his neck. It represented the five elements of the gods: Fire, Water, Wind, Earth, Ice.

Helrios, Oceana, Anemon, Heradem, Borethes.

The Head of the Pentagod Creed had a warrior's build, tall and broad-shouldered. Most of the faithful believed the gods' greatness echoing through him made him appear larger than most men, intimidating with his black eyes and golden mane. Others said he'd been a fierce Avian Shifter from Makkan before the gods' calling. Cassia believed the latter.

The warrior-priest sat across from her mother while

the queen finished signing her correspondence. A goblet of wine remained untouched on her left. From where she sat on the divan in the queen's sitting room, Cassia had a good vantage point of Ilahara's two most powerful fae. The queen's invitation to assist in the meeting was another opportunity to learn how to navigate the politics of their kingdom, an opportunity Cassia didn't take lightly. She observed in careful silence, restraining her tongue even when the high keeper's obvious attempts to irritate her mother grated on her nerves.

The queen signed off the last letter with a scrape of the quill against parchment. Dramatic, but Aerella liked it that way.

Cassia smiled.

"I apologize for keeping you waiting, Your Holiness," Aerella said. "Had I known I'd be occupied, I would have postponed our meeting."

Baramun's smile was as sharp as a blade, yet he didn't seem offended, only amused. "Still no maenar, I see."

The queen sighed. "Lur is taking its sweet time."

"The Maenari are certainly doing their best to find someone worthy of the position."

Aerella gave him a tight-lipped nod. "What may I assist you with, Your Holiness? Or are you here for the mere pleasure of our company?" The queen addressed Cassia's presence for the first time. The high keeper's visits weren't uncommon. The queen often invited him as their guest, even more so in the past months.

"I heard troubling reports from Heartstar." Cassia fidgeted in her seat. Heartstar was the seat of power in Tyrra, home of the Vynatis. "A Soul Binding gone sour."

Cassia's attention flickered from the high keeper to her mother and back. The Soul Binding was the ritual that created Do'strath. Two warriors who bound their souls through the most painful magic fae had ever known. A secret gathering of Dragon worshippers was no novelty, but with the seer's vision of Asharaya's return to Ilahara and the rumors the Crown desperately tried to contain, this seemed to be a message.

Ilahara had not forgotten the ways of the Dragon.

"The fools got what they deserved." Aerella wrapped her satin shawl around her shoulders with the calm of someone who had everything under control. "No matter. I already knew of the issue. Imiri Vynatis assured me she would deal with the transgressors. As you can see, you have no reason to doubt the Crown's friendship."

The high keeper leaned back in his chair with a grin. "I never doubted."

The conversation turned idle and Cassia found it harder to follow their quick banter as her thoughts returned to the dead Do'strath. She wasn't as learned in the Old Faith as she was of the New and wasn't as curious as her brother to know more, but if so few survived it had to be brutal.

So much pain, all to be closer to the dragons they worshipped.

Derron liked dragons. He found every excuse to travel to Lur, the city in which scholars studied to become maenari, in order to read about them. The Library of Lur was the one place their mother hadn't been able to remove every trace of the creatures. Rulers changed, new religions emerged, but history remained untouchable. Cassia often joined Derron, although she bored quickly of the library and its dusty tomes. The queen punished her son once she learned of his treks and made Cassia watch because she covered for him. Even after years, the memory made her queasy. She knew that books were Derron's way of being closer to Elon and that it was the reason why he kept returning to Lur even after his punishment.

Cassia never did.

"Have you heard of Lady Denia?"

The high keeper's voice dragged Cassia's attention back to the room. "What about her?"

Baramun turned to her, eyes raking her figure. "She's been found dead in her home. Grapes were found by the body. It would appear she choked."

The list of people dying in Adara was growing at an alarming speed in the past weeks. Cassia recalled her father's words to Lady Denia only yesterday. She doubted anyone who had been present at the banquet had forgotten them. The courtiers would have one more event to gossip about.

The queen stared at Cassia as if waiting for her daughter's reaction.

"She should have been more careful with her food," said Cassia.

Aerella's smile was subtle, but it grazed the corner of her lips. Warmth swelled in Cassia's chest.

"We'll have a beautiful ascension ceremony in her honor," High Keeper Baramun said as he stood. The queen did the same. He courteously kissed her knuckles and then his attention moved to Cassia. "Princess."

"Your Holiness." She held out a hand for him to kiss. His lips lingered on her knuckles a moment too long, and as he leaned back, his dark eyes locked to hers, their depth unreadable. Cassia fought the urge to shrink away. "You grow more beautiful by the day."

The princess kept a smile on her lips until a servant girl escorted him from the queen's quarters. Where Derron's room was a mess of art and music, their mother's rooms were pristine and tidy with not a fleck out of place. No art adorned the white walls apart from the silver flame sigil hanging behind the desk. The drapes and carpets were the customary Argarys blue as were the cushions on the divan and armchairs. The door leading to her bedroom remained resolutely shut as always.

"You look pale, Cassia," the queen observed.

Cassia sat in the seat the high keeper occupied only moments before. "And here I thought I was growing more beautiful by the day."

"Have you bled yet?" At Cassia's shake of her head, the queen sighed. "It's only a matter of time, you'll see."

Her mother spoke of the Bleeding as a grand occasion, but Cassia didn't share the sentiment. The sooner she bled, the sooner she'd have to marry. Last night, her legs tangled with Korban's, she'd entertained the reckless idea of keeping him as her lover, but would he agree?

"Any news of Derron?" Cassia asked.

"No, and we won't have any until he returns to Ilahara. It won't be long now."

There would be at least two more weeks of waiting, and Cassia prayed it wouldn't be longer. "You sent your heir to dispose of a slimy little worm who's been hiding for fourteen years. If anything, I think Asharaya is clever, perhaps protected by people who could be dangerous. Wouldn't it have been safer to send Semal?"

"It has to be an Argarys," the queen said, with a tone that brokered no argument.

Cassia allowed herself a moment to slouch against the backrest. She heard those words before.

Aerella came around the desk to touch her daughter's arm in a rare moment of motherly reassurance. "Derron is strong and capable."

Cassia took a deep breath, wringing her hands. "There's something I wanted to ask."

A knock on the door interrupted her.

"Ah, Semal." Aerella gestured the man inside.

Semal Leneris bowed for his queen and walked to the desk, stealing a smile from Cassia with a wink. Aerella pretended not to notice, but Cassia caught the ghost of a smile on her mother's lips. He carried several letters, which he placed in front of the queen. Letters that he'd written in her calligraphy and that she would have to sign.

Semal spoke to the queen, not with words but gestures. Cassia made sure not to miss any movement of his slender hands or expression on his pale, once-handsome face. Semal and Aerella had grown up and trained together. The training and battle were evident on his body, the muscles of his arms and biceps ghosted by a loose gray shirt and tight-fitting pants.

From where Cassia sat, the scar marring the left side of his face, the missing ear, the irisless green eye were on full display. Semal kept his white hair short and trimmed to the head as if inviting others to look at the scar. The day Aerella won her throne, Semal had been too close to the earth-shattering roar of the beast he fought. It was a wonder he survived, but he'd been deaf ever since.

Cassia remembered a day her father had counseled his wife to find someone more suitable to be her advisor and general, but Aerella's reply had been cold and simple.

I don't need his ears. I need his loyalty.

Vaemor never brought up the subject again.

The ships are in place as you ordered, Semal said.

"And the Nahar?"

An ache between her thighs made Cassia squirm in her seat. She excused herself from the room with barely a nod of acknowledgment from her mother. Pain spiraled up her lower back. She needed to lie down.

Cassia returned to her living room to find Eileen sitting on the couch, her green dress standing out in the princess's white and silver quarters. Eileen sprang to her feet the moment Cassia closed the door. "Did you ask her?" When Cassia hesitated, she added, "About my family. Did you ask her what she plans to do with them?"

"Eileen..."

Her friend's face crumpled. "You promised."

"The high keeper was there, and then Semal interrupted us. I was going to, Eileen, but there was no time."

"The truth is you think they're traitors and you don't care."

"That's not true."

"Darrok Todrak is my father, Cassia, or have you forgotten? You can't ask me to idle by in this stupid court and pretend everything is okay. Everything is not okay." Eileen's voice rose, in tune with her anger. "Your mother promised they'd be safe if I behaved."

"My mother promised no harm would come to you if they behaved, but they didn't," Cassia corrected, punctuating each word. She was quickly losing patience with Eileen's tantrum. All she wanted was to lie down. "Yet here you are, unharmed. You seem to have mistaken who the villain is."

Eileen let out a wordless scream, her balled fists turning blue with Ice. She flung her hands, and icicles flew toward Cassia.

Cassia lifted her palm. The Ice melted without so much as a flicker of flame. Anger turned her legs clammy with sweat. "Instead of whining about your undeserving family, pray your brother's path hasn't crossed Derron's, because if that were the case, for whom would you worry? A brother you barely remember, or the man you claim to love?"

Ice vanished from Eileen's hands. Eyes wide, her friend's lips trembled with the force of unshed tears. Northerners rarely cried, and though she grew up in Adara, Eileen wasn't any different. "Cassia."

"What?"

Eileen pointed and the princess looked down. A gasp tore from her lips. It hadn't been sweat on her legs.

"You're bleeding."

22

"This is painful to watch."

Shara squeezed her eyes tighter but couldn't stop the irritated twitch of a muscle in her temple at Mykal's remark. She tried to shut out his voice and the expectant weight of Kael's and Solana's gazes.

Focus on the shape of the Fire.

It was no longer one spark but many, splitting off from a larger flame in her core.

Now give it a new shape.

Kael, by far the more patient of her fae instructors, explained magic was no different from a limb. As the mind created the impulse to move a finger or bend a knee, so too could it change the shape of its element and externalize it. Shara needed only to train her mind to recognize that impulse as something natural.

Easier said than done.

Shara spent her first day of training understanding how to make that happen. She reached a place where her mind was so lost to the Fire she could morph it under invisible hands, no longer a spiraling bonfire but a perfect orb of brilliant red and shimmering gold.

Now try to release it onto your palm but be careful. Using too much at once will drain your strength.

The first time, panic seized her. Rami's scorched flesh was too vivid a memory. No sooner had she raced into the cabin than Shara retched the meager dinner of dried meat onto the floor under Derron Argarys's observant silver gaze.

Three days into her training, Shara still hadn't succeeded. No matter how much she convinced herself she could control her Fire, her resolve shattered at the first tingle of heat against her palm. If she couldn't control the flames' intensity, if she lost control...

"Give her time," Solana snapped at Mykal. "Her training has just begun."

"It's only an orb. How hard can it be for a Dragon-Blessed?" Mykal retorted.

Shara snarled in frustration. The orb of Fire spiraled up and set her eyes aflame. Its heat warmed her face, and magic tingled below her skin's surface. "You do it if it's so easy."

Mykal's eyes sparkled in amusement. Embarrassment colored her cheeks as he extended his hand. His eyes lightened from brown to frosty blue. In moments, his Ice shaped into a beautiful rose.

Shara bit her lip to suppress a frustrated scream.

"If you continue to doubt yourself, you'll never control your Fire," Mykal said, and then extended the rose to Kael with a dashing grin.

Kael flushed, cheeks almost as red as Shara's Fire. He eyed Mykal, then the rose, and finally cleared his throat and turned to Solana. "Perhaps something in your vrah training could help us. Your shadow power is a form of magic she's familiar with."

Mykal's grin vanished and he crushed the rose in his palm. "Yes, Selena, enlighten us. Can you fashion flowers from shadows?"

Shara suppressed a smile while Solana ignored his jab and shook her head, which only seemed to irritate Mykal more. "The Maiden's gifts are an exchange. Blood is the key to access the darkness, and we can only hide inside it and navigate through it. We cannot create something new like your magic."

"So, your presence here is useless." Mykal crossed his arms.

Solana's boot tapping against the barrel she sat on revealed her irritation. "Apparently, so is yours."

"Let's take a break," Kael proposed.

Shara didn't want a break. She had only four more days before they made it to Ilahein shores. Four days before she no longer had Mykal and Kael's assistance.

She took a sip of fresh water and cleared sweat from her brow with the sleeve of her blouse. Drinking didn't wash away the tightness in her throat as she looked to the horizon. Soon, Ilahara's silhouette would replace the flat line of the sea. According to her escorts, mossy shores awaited them in Tyrra, with breathtaking cliffs and enchanting waterfalls framed by wild, thick forests. Shara couldn't remember if she'd ever seen Tyrra. When she thought of her homeland, she saw flashes of the Embernest—the library with the large armchair, the golden castle on the cliff and the waterfall below it, dragons singing, and Shara joining them from her window.

Four days and Asharaya Myrassar would be going home.

Though mastering her magic wasn't going as well as she'd hoped, Shara's tenuous plan wasn't a complete disaster. She'd been able to steal an empty bottle from the hold and she filled it with Derron's leftover grog whenever she was the one to administer it. There wasn't much, but every drop would prove useful once they reached the shore. The reduced doses of renike made Derron more vigil, a necessary evil that was hard to digest. Not that she had much choice in the matter if she wanted her plan to succeed.

Perhaps moved by an instinct of self-preservation, the prince played his part. He pretended to sleep when they weren't alone and kept quiet when they were. Shara presumed he'd try playing his advantage on land, but she wouldn't give him the time. Xoro predicted they'd arrive in Tyrra at night, and when they did, she'd drag Derron into the darkness and make her escape. She wouldn't be able to move far with another traveling with her, but she needed only to get far enough.

Mykal and Kael would be furious. Perhaps Solana would be sick with worry. Someday they'd thank her. Without Shara or the Argarys prince, the Do'strath wouldn't commit treason, and they'd be free to help Solana find her brother. Her sister sailed to Ilahara for him, after all.

Shara instead would travel to Adara with the prince. The renike would keep him from using his Song, but Derron had to be able to carry his weight to guide her to Adara. She had to hope he'd agree to it if only to lead a lamb to its slaughter, that is if they didn't encounter the patrols Kael mentioned or Argarys sympathizers in the meantime. The chances of reaching the castle undetected were slim, but perhaps she'd be able to slip into the darkness and remain unseen by the guards. Then Shara would find the queen, and she'd make her watch as she slit Derron's throat before killing her, too.

Maybe Aerella would kill Shara instead.

Either way, there would be an epilogue to the story that had started fourteen years ago with the Coup of Fire.

Shara pawed at her mother's necklace around her neck, the dragon's shape a balm to the anxiety gnawing at the pit of her stomach. She searched the horizon and imagined the position of the Burning Sea. They were too far to see its fumes, but she hoped against reason to catch a shimmer of red on shadowed wings. Her fingers found the obsidian ring she'd slid onto the chain. *Dragons are the Ilah made flesh*, Maenar Elvik said during one of the few lessons she paid attention to. *The legends say their soul returns to the Ilah when they die, and they are reborn from the Burning Sea.*

"Ashari," she whispered, fingers closed around the ring.

Shapes flickered on the horizon. Shara squinted, hardly able to make out their color, but she realized what they were a moment before the lookout in the nest shouted, and the hairs at the nape of her neck stood on end.

"Sails!"

Solana rushed to the forecastle deck first, where Xoro gripped the rail with his quartermaster, who looked through the spyglass to analyze the ships and be his captain's eyes. Xoro's tension manifested through taut muscles as he faced the direction of the possible threat. Solana brought her hand to his.

"Six ships. Galleons by the look of them. Line formation. Blue flags with a silver flame," Niguel reported.

"Argarys," Kael said.

Mykal and Shara cursed under their breaths, exchanging an awkward look before focusing once more on the discussion.

"Your queen is setting up a welcome party," Xoro said. "Niguel, have the men ready the cannons."

Solana grasped his arm. "One ship is hardly a match for six. Don't be a fool, my love."

"The *No One* is swift," Xoro said, trying to reassure her. "We can take them."

Solana's hands slid down into his, and she brought their joined hands to her chest. "There's honor in choosing your battles and knowing when to step back."

"Aerella must have set up a perimeter in case the prince failed and we returned with Asharaya. There will be more ships closer to the coast."

At Kael's words, a shiver raced up Shara's spine. She fixed a glare on the ships. Aerella had considered the possibility of her son's failure and developed a tactic to seize her either way.

Shara would be damned if she let Aerella take her without a fight.

Licks of flame rose below her skin's surface. Dragonfire flowed in her veins, the most powerful fire of all. Hers was the power that could change the game and level the playing field, if only she could summon the flames and control them.

"There could be as many as two hundred fae on each of those ships." Niguel swallowed hard. "Captain, I don't think the men are ready to face those odds. If we're boarded, it's over."

"What other choice do we have?" Mykal cut in. "If Aerella is expecting us in Tyrra, she will expect us wherever we go. I say we combat now."

"There is another way." Shara turned at the urgency in Solana's voice. "You said you wouldn't sail through siren waters. Would Aerella?"

Mykal harrumphed. "She is the queen, and the Nahar are in her jacket." Shara assumed he'd meant pocket. "Of course she would."

"Siren waters don't belong to the Nahar. Those are hunting grounds, outside even the queen's jurisdiction." A spark lit Kael's eyes. "If we can get through, we may be able to reach Daganver shores."

"Where Aerella will likely have another patrol waiting

for us on land," Mykal protested in Ilahein.

"It's too dangerous, captain." Niguel's voice shook.

"The ship can't sprout wings," Xoro snapped through gritted teeth. He massaged his jaw and took a resigned breath. "We have enough provisions for a week at best, but not enough to circle back."

"It will be enough," Kael said.

Mykal shook his head. "I don't like this."

Shara didn't either. The voyage from Daganver to Adara would take months on foot. Not only did she doubt she'd have enough grog to keep Derron compliant, but the longer she traveled, the harder it would be to hide from Aerella's allies.

"Human minds are easy prey to sirens. Without the crew, we'll never be able to maneuver the ship," she said.

Solana curled her lip in thought. "I can get us past the sirens."

Shara's blood chilled.

"I need only some darkness to cross through on the other side." Solana squeezed Xoro's fingers tight. "I can make the jump."

"No." Shara stepped forward, her heart giving a panicked jolt. "You can't travel with an entire ship. That's madness."

"I'm the Maiden's Chosen."

"You're human." Shara hoped the words would land like a blow, but her sister remained as immovable as the statue of the Maiden in the Keep's crypt. "You're not invincible."

A hopeful smile formed on Solana's lips. "Trust in me, sister."

"Then it's settled," Xoro said, weary. "We sail for siren waters."

"Captain—"

"Do not question my orders," Xoro hissed through his teeth. "The decision is made."

Shara bit her lip, turning back to open water as the nerves in her stomach knotted to the point of pain.

Things were not going according to plan.

23

For the third day in a row, Derron was alone in the cabin. The sudden leniency confused him at first until he heard the muffled swears and the repeated crackle of summoned Fire.

Asharaya was training.

That she was learning to control her magic was a benefit while he remained a captive. Dragonfire slumbered beneath her skin, and she was the sole barrier between it and everyone aboard the ship, including himself. However, mastery of Fire would make her even harder to defeat and a greater threat to his family than she already was. Derron's single ally at this point was time. The renike made it impossible to keep track of days, but they couldn't be far from Ilahara. The Ilah's pull grew stronger. Asharaya couldn't learn everything in a handful of days.

Derron could only guess at her plan. She'd reduced his ration of renike, and while he remained unable to summon power, he was vigil and capable of thinking of more than combinations of musical notes. Was she taking pity on him because he'd saved her from the dream? Unlikely, but that left only one other option. She needed Derron strong.

Whatever Asharaya was planning, he had to be ready.

Footsteps echoed outside the door. Three sets, all hurried. Derron bent his head and pretended to sleep.

"Is it wise to speak here?" Todrak whispered, cautious and conspiratorial at once.

"Argarys wouldn't wake if you screamed in his ear, not with the renike I gave him." Derron's eyes almost snapped open at Asharaya's lie. Asharaya waited for the door to click shut before she spoke again, and he listened in on the conversation with renewed curiosity. Whatever they were discussing, Asharaya wanted him to hear it. "We need a new strategy. No matter what Solana says, she can't drag an entire ship through the darkness. The Maiden's toll for such an effort would be too great."

"True, although she seemed confident she could." Arkael, and by the loud sigh that followed, he'd cut Todrak off before he could speak.

"Wouldn't you be if you thought you could save innocent lives from certain death?" asked Asharaya. "You saw Niguel. He's terrified of the sirens."

Sirens? Only the foolish and desperate would sail through siren waters.

"The sirens will make him waltz to his own death. He'd be an idiot not to be afraid," Todrak said with Asharaya's same matter-of-fact tone. "But since Selena decided fighting two hundred Argarys soldiers was folly, and you agreed with her, we have no choice but to keep agreeing with her. We don't have other options."

"It's two hundred soldiers per ship, Myk, and there were six," said Arkael.

Mother. Derron suppressed a gasp. Had Semal's captain sent word that the stranger he'd sailed to Havanya hadn't returned? Impossible. Derron couldn't be sure when or if the man had set sail again, but they certainly had the advantage. He'd never reach Ilahara before the *No One*, and no raven could deliver messages across a fortnight's worth of sea. The queen had taken precautions in case it wasn't Derron who returned with Asharaya. While Derron recognized it as a good strategy, he winced as if he'd received a blow. Had she never believed he'd succeed? Given his current state, perhaps she was right.

"So, we'll have better odds with the sirens," Todrak countered. "While Selena does...well, whatever it is she does, we can buy her time. That is if the sirens show up at all."

"When have the sirens ever passed on the opportunity for a meal?" Arkael asked him.

"Are you listening to me?" Asharaya snapped. "The Maiden's price for her gift is blood. To bring a ship and this many people through the darkness would take more from Solana than she has to give. Do you think I'm going to let you gamble with my sister's life?"

"Shara—"

"Shara? Not Asharaya Myrassar? Tell me, Mykal, do you only remember my birthright when it suits you?"

Todrak gasped. "Are you pulling rank?"

"No, she's trying to get past that thick skull of yours." Derron couldn't remember Arkael's tone ever sounding so clipped when talking to his Do'strath.

"We don't have an alternative."

"Yes, we do," Asharaya said.

Tension charged the following silence. It rolled over Derron in waves, and he couldn't shake the feeling of being watched.

Todrak laughed. "Absolutely not."

"He's strong enough," Asharaya retorted. "I've seen him use it before."

"You want to give Argarys control over an entire ship? Are you insane?"

"If I stayed with him in the cabin, I could make sure he doesn't use the men against us," Asharaya said. "I still don't have enough control of my Fire to help you against the sirens, and you'll have a better time fighting if you're not preoccupied with my safety."

Derron held his breath. Asharaya wanted him to listen to their plan because he was part of it. Despite the animosity between them, fear for her sister's safety made her desperate enough to seek his help. *Show your power, hide your heart.* His mother's words echoed through his thoughts as he set aside empathy and considered his options.

Todrak scoffed. "And I'm supposed to believe you'll sit idly by while your sister is on deck?"

"I'm doing this to save her life," Asharaya said through gritted teeth.

"Your pretty little knife isn't going to help us if Argarys decides to screw us over."

Arkael spoke through Asharaya's cursing. "If Derron had control of the men's minds, the sirens' Song would be useless. They'd be easier to fight if we weren't worrying about the men."

His brother was putting more faith in him than he deserved. To have him use his Song, they'd have to stop giving him renike. Derron would have his magic back and with it a ship's worth of men to help him seize Asharaya and the Do'strath. *You're not considering this?* His conscience spoke with Elon's voice, and shoving it aside was more difficult than he cared to admit.

"If we let Argarys seize power, he'll use it to kill us," Todrak insisted.

"I'll slit his throat before he gets the chance," Asharaya said.

"His grandmother is merfolk, a descendant of the sirens that are waiting for us to become their dinner. He's one of them."

"His grandfather was Adarian. To the sirens, the prince's blood is impure. For all we know, he's in as much danger as the rest of us. It's in his interest to help us," Kael argued.

"He's still the prince."

"Sirens don't follow fae laws. His title means nothing."

Todrak growled in frustration. "I won't agree to this. I'll never agree to this."

"Could you set aside your hatred for one moment and at least try to listen to what we're telling you?" Asharaya snarled.

"I have listened, and I'm disagreeing," Todrak barked back. "If you try to order me to do it, Dragon help me, there's no family loyalty that will hold. You'll have one more enemy, Princess Asharaya."

The sound of heavy footsteps filled the silence, and then the door slammed shut.

Pretending to sleep proved difficult. Too much was at stake for Derron to sit still. His enemies presented him with the opportunity to tip the scale in his favor. Derron could finish what he started and prove the queen's trust hadn't been misplaced. He'd take care of Asharaya, and he would do it alone, without an entire fleet at his back.

Arkael sighed. "Forgive him. He doesn't mean half the things he says when he's angry."

"If Argarys controlled the ship and you and Mykal kept the sirens at bay with magic, we'd be able to cross without putting Solana's safety in jeopardy. The moment we're out of siren waters, I'll shove the renike down Argarys's throat myself. It's a solid plan." A pause before Asharaya added, "Talk to Mykal. You can still change his mind."

"Not on this, but I agree with you. We can't let Solana

risk herself when there's another way, especially when we have no guarantee her plan will actually work."

"Then what do we do?" Asharaya asked.

The silence that followed was unbearable. Derron almost opened his eyes to gauge their expressions. "We'll stop giving Derron renike without the others knowing. I'll keep a close eye on him until we reach siren waters to be sure he doesn't try to take advantage." Arkael's voice shook, and Derron wondered what his brother dreaded more—the betrayal he was enacting against Todrak or the fact he'd have to trust Derron.

"Mykal is going to see right through us if I'm not on deck," Asharaya said.

"Not if I convince him that you staying in the cabin is the best way to keep you safe and us focused."

"You heard him earlier. He knows I would never stay behind while Solana is on deck."

"That's why when we tell you to stay in the cabin, you have to be convincing." Practicality crept into Arkael's voice. "Fight Mykal for a while, and then I'll propose a compromise. You'll stay on deck until the sirens arrive, and then you'll return to the cabin. I trust you'll know how to keep Derron cooperative."

"And you're sure Mykal won't suspect what we're doing?" Asharaya asked.

"He won't expect me to go behind his back." A pained note laced Arkael's words. "This will be our secret, Shara. Let's hope for the best."

"Argarys will do what he thinks is best to keep himself alive." Derron felt Asharaya's stare on him. "We'll do the same."

24

Not a single light flickered in the room. *Frigid air flowed over Cassia's skin even with Fire simmering in her veins. Her breath plumed as she paced. Cavernous walls closed in on her and the taste of earth parched her tongue. The faint trickle of a river echoed from a nearby tunnel—no, from above. If she could find the source, then perhaps she could escape.*

She couldn't.

Every time she needed release, she was forced into this darkness. Forced to hide when all she wanted was to fly, to soar over mountains, roar to the skies, shake the earth's foundations. I am here, *she wanted to scream.*

She did, and the sound was neither human nor fae.

Cassia woke with a start, heart pounding and throat raw as if the sound in her dream had been hers.

Ever since she was a child, the room recurred in her

dreams. At first, she sought Derron for comfort, slipping into his bed because if anyone could keep the darkness away, it was her brother. Derron invented a game to help her fall asleep where they counted his heartbeats until hers slowed and she finally slept. The room was only a nightmare, he said, and it would go away.

It didn't.

There was no way to predict when the next dream would come. For a time, Cassia thought they were linked to her moods and that her mind conjured the dark space whenever she was angry or sad, but then she saw it again even on the most wonderful of days.

She'd seen the room the night Korban kissed her for the first time.

Now, Korban slept deeply beside her. Cassia brushed away a lock of hair falling across his face, and then got out of bed, cradling her lower abdomen. This was her fourth day of the Bleeding, and while the pain receded, a constant ache remained. Korban teased about her fussing, especially when she refused his advances. *Human girls start dealing with it when they're far younger*, he'd said.

Too bad he was a human boy and didn't know anything about it.

Cassia sat at her vanity. Silver roses were carved into the white frame. She stared at the perfect oval of her face and wished for the mirror to show a more angular version of it, with thicker eyebrows and a better jaw line. She missed Derron. If everything had gone according to plan, it wouldn't be long until he made port in Tyrra.

Thoughts of Tyrra led her gaze to the vanity's third drawer. Casting a quick glance at Korban through the mirror, she slid the drawer open, careful not to make a sound. A stack of letters bound together with ribbon was stored inside. Her fingers tickled as she pulled it out and carefully undid the knot. On the first letter, her name written in Johan's familiar script caused tightness in her chest. She imagined him bent over the parchment in the candlelight as he jotted down tender words meant for her alone, a mirror to the gentleness he so rarely let others see.

"If you need some color on those delicious lips, I'd be happy to oblige."

Cassia peeked at the corner of the mirror. Korban, now awake, lounged naked on her bed with barely a slip of silk covering his unmentionables. She smiled and hid the letters before he could notice them. "When I need them to look thoroughly kissed, I'll know who to ask."

"Was I not thorough enough last night?"

"I'm to meet my mother and High Keeper Baramun over tea. It wouldn't be appropriate to keep them waiting. You should leave before the maids help me dress."

Korban's face darkened. "Are you dismissing me?"

Instead of answering Korban's question, she grabbed the bottle of her vanilla and white rose perfume and sprayed some on her wrist. The smell had become a part of her as much as her silver hair and eyes.

"You've been acting strangely, princess."

"Just go." It was only a matter of time before he'd be gone from her life forever. Cassia kept her back to Korban as he dressed, closing her eyes when she heard the brush of the tapestry. He'd left without saying goodbye.

It's better this way.

The queen and the high keeper waited in the drawing room, one of Cassia's favorites for its large windows facing the sea. The Myrassar royals used to celebrate their private festivities there. That a royal family could gather to enjoy each other's company away from the court's leering attention was a notion foreign to Cassia. Her mother taught her to see every act or occasion as an opportunity to show power. Only then would their enemies fear them.

Baramun eyed her the moment Cassia stepped into the room.

Cassia curtsied for their guest. "I hope I'm not late." The two sat around the small table, tea ready to be served. A human girl stood in the corner, head bent and eyes cast low.

Aerella smiled. "Not at all, my sweet." Behind her, the large windows offered a breathtaking view of the sea.

The Embernest perched atop a high cliff. The castle's front towered over the city, while its back faced the ocean. Water streamed heavily down the cliff's surface and washed into the sea, leaving this side of the castle under the endless whisper of waterfalls. As a young girl, Cassia often fell asleep by the window where the sound was loudest and, somehow, relaxing. Beyond the horizon, she made out the faint red glow of the Burning Sea.

The queen patted the spot beside her on the divan. "Come."

Cassia obeyed, even if she didn't like how close she was to the high keeper, who sat on the nearby armchair. This seemed to be the silent signal for the servant to act. She approached without a word, eyes never meeting theirs as she poured tea into their cups. Baramun took Cassia's before she could and offered it to her.

"There is a particular glow about you today, princess," he said.

Cassia accepted the compliment with a smile.

The princess managed a sip before the high keeper took the cup again and set it back on the table. "I'm told you've bled." He held her newly freed hand as if handling a flower. His were smooth in the same way a retired warrior's could be if given the opportunity to lay down his arms. "A woman such as yourself deserves an equally impressive man."

"Are you so keen to celebrate my matrimony, Your

Holiness?"

"Indeed," the queen intervened. "We're here to talk about your future."

Cassia wriggled free of the high keeper's tender hold, bracing herself for her mother's decision. That she had consulted the high keeper on the matter made sense since he would oversee the ceremony, but it stung that he had a part in choosing her future husband when Cassia didn't have any say in the matter.

"You will wed into House Farwynd," the queen declared.

Cassia frowned in confusion. "But the Farwynd are the current Heads of Makkan. I thought they swore a vow of celibacy upon appointment as the Heads." Unlike other territories, Makkan didn't have a ruling family. Instead, the two ruling Heads were chosen through a competition among pairs of siblings within the high fae families of the territory. Those who proved their strength over all others triumphed and won the Seat of Volaria. Their rule lasted so long as either sibling endured. At their deaths, a new competition was held, and two new Heads were chosen.

"They have," Baramun agreed. "I haven't."

Cassia's head snapped to her mother, unpleasant shivers wracking her body. She hoped she misheard. "Him?" It didn't make any sense. The Crown had no reason to secure his allegiance through marriage. The New Faith thrived because of the Argarys. Baramun was powerful because of the Argarys.

"Arrangements were made so that you could become princess, my sweet. The Farwynd supported the Coup of Fire in exchange for your hand in marriage to their brother, High Keeper Baramun."

"I'm supposed to marry a high fae of Adara. It's tradition."

"A tradition that belongs to the past."

Cassia was too numb to wrest from Baramun when the

high keeper touched her arm or to feel the cold kiss of his rings against her skin. She only stared, drowning in the pitch black of his eyes. "I wish to claim you as mine."

"It's a great match," the queen said. "The might of the Farwynd and the power of the Argarys. Makkan and Adara bound by blood."

Cassia's hands squeezed into fists. The room grew warmer the harder she fought to leash her emotions. "So, am I to be a mere pawn in Makkan's hands?"

The queen remained unperturbed by Cassia's words. "Not in Makkan's, my sweet. Mine."

Cassia jumped to her feet, shoulders stiff. The servant in the corner shrieked as fire flared in the sconces on the wall. Marrying a lord from Adara was one thing, but playing doll for a man who seemed to delight in making her squirm was another. The high keeper didn't seem surprised by her reaction. If anything, he looked amused, as if any fight Cassia put up would only make the prize that much sweeter. The princess suppressed a shiver. "I deny your request, Your Holiness," she spat out the words.

The divan scraped against the polished floor as the queen stood and gripped her daughter's chin. Her sharp nails dug into Cassia's flesh. Unlike the high keeper, she wasn't amused. "There's no version of your future where you won't marry High Keeper Baramun."

Her mother released her, and Cassia stumbled back. Vision swimming with tears, she rushed to the door before her mother could see her cry. No sooner had it shut behind her than a warm drop traced a path down her cheek. The fire in the sconces flickered with no rest, attuned to her discomfort.

"Cassia."

She hadn't noticed Vaemor until he called her name. Heat flooded her face. Her father was the last person she wanted to see her in this state. "Have you fallen so low from Mother's good graces that you must eavesdrop?"

Vaemor took a step toward her, reaching for her cheek as if to wipe away her tears. Cassia bared her teeth in warning. She stopped wanting any affection from her father a long time ago, and that wouldn't be changing now.

The king's hand dropped, heavy at his side. "Don't antagonize her. She'll make you regret it."

"The last person I need advice from is you."

Cassia stormed from the hall without deigning to glance at him or daring to look back at the room that had sealed her fate.

The high keeper's laughter seemed to follow her like a phantom she couldn't outrun.

25

In only two days, the climate shifted from temperate to brisk as the *No One* sailed close to the Daganveran and Tyrran borders. It would only be getting colder the nearer they sailed to Daganver. Shara looked to the west, where etched against the red and golden sky was Ilahara's faint silhouette shrouded by distance and clouds.

Hopefully, they'd live long enough to see it.

Despite the Ilahein terrain in the west, the crew looked to the east. The Siren Coves loomed ever closer, and tension was palpable.

Shara's knowledge of sirens came from stories of mesmerizing creatures with the upper body of a woman and the tail of a fish. Their beauty and colorful fins made them legends, but their Song's lethal power made them feared across the seas. In Havanya's taverns, Shara learned to tell the true stories from the false. Liars boasted about epic battles and long nights of sex that Shara had a hard time imagining, but she'd never forgotten the haggard looks of those who met the sirens and lived to tell the tale. *They make you think you'd do anything for them,* one man had said, hands trembling as he placed them around his tankard. *They don't let go of your mind until the last moment, and then there's only screams and death and you know you're fucked.*

Granite caves loomed like shadows in the dusk light. Come nightfall, their color would bleed into the sky and make them difficult to see. Mist enveloped the Siren Coves' entrance, but a blue glow pierced through it, pulsing in and out of view in tune with the panicked beat in her chest.

Shara rubbed the ruby dragon of her mother's necklace and the obsidian one of her father's ring. She found herself doing so whenever she needed to focus. It wasn't quite as steeling as the touch of a blade, but there was something equally comforting about their warmth against her skin.

Waves slapped against the *No One*'s flanks, impervious to the silence that had taken over the once lively ship. Gone were the nights in which the men gathered on deck to sing their raunchy songs. They were phantoms kept in motion by Xoro's barked commands, spirits lost to the darkened sea and the horrors protected by its depths. Wood groaned as the men shuffled about the deck. Some passed cotton around to clog their ears and limit the Song's effects. Others knelt, hands clasped, and whispered prayers to the Maiden. Shara's blood curdled at the sight. The Maiden was a goddess of death, not mercy. The deity they called upon for protection was as likely to look favorably on the bloodshed about to be unleashed.

Not all the men would survive the night, even if Shara's plan to use Derron succeeded, but she promised herself to save as many as she could without sacrificing Solana. She wouldn't accept any version of this night where her sister bled to death.

Kael stood beside her, knuckles white as he clenched

the rail and looked toward the Coves. "There are over fifty men on this ship and they're all going to die if our plan fails."

"A little optimism wouldn't kill you," Shara whispered. "And stop fidgeting. If Mykal finds out we're lying to him, we'll have to worry about more than just the sirens." It hadn't taken long for Kael to convince Mykal that having Shara stay behind was the best course of action. Soon, she would have to return to the cabin to enact their plan with Derron. Shara gave Kael a playful nudge to diffuse the tension. "Don't let my glorious performance go to waste."

"He won't find out." Kael chanced a glance over his shoulder, where Mykal scrutinized them on the opposite side of the ship. "I shut him out. He won't see anything through the bond."

"It's not the bond I'm worried about." Shara turned to look at him. "Have you ever stolen cookies from the cookie jar?"

"No."

"I could tell." Shara sighed. "Maybe he would be less on edge if you gave him a kiss."

Kael turned crimson. "Don't be ridiculous."

"Does Mykal offer Ice roses to all his friends?" She smiled as she gave Kael's hand a reassuring squeeze. "Mykal won't find out." She looked at Solana, seated on the stairs of the poop deck. Eyes closed, her sister's lips moved in prayer against her dagger. "We'll all be fine."

Kael followed her gaze and returned her squeeze.

A pang struck Shara's chest. Betrayal lay at the end of her road with the Do'strath. The best course of action would be to keep her distance to avoid unnecessary complications, yet she held on to Kael's reassurance. "We shouldn't leave Argarys alone too long. I'll go check on him."

Kael pursed his lips and nodded, looking back at the sea.

The pang in Shara's chest intensified into a painful clutch. She clenched her jaw as she entered the cabin. If only better were also easy. Shara couldn't fool herself and the Do'strath into believing she could play the role of a revolutionary princess. She was a Dragon-Blessed in nothing but name, a stranger to the people they wanted her to inspire, and a foreigner to the land they wanted her to rule. Better to disappoint them now while she still had some dignity left.

Shara leaned against the door and held out her hand, nerves tight. She breathed in, her Fire flickering in answer as she dove inward. When she breathed out, tiny licks of flame danced on her palm. Her heart hammered, but she focused on her breathing, pushing away all thoughts of Rami's burning body. The flames spun closer to one another, tangling as they touched. Shara's hand shook, yet the Fire held.

Two days of restless training with the image of Solana lying in a puddle of her own blood had gotten her this far. Shara had every intention of staying true to her promise to Kael, but life had barreled into her plans too many times for her not to be wary. If she had to fight, she needed to be ready. She prayed to the Maiden and the Dragon that what little magic she'd mastered would be enough.

Shara closed her hand in a fist, smoke lifting from the cracks between her fingers. When she looked up, she met Derron's stare. "I figured pretending to sleep was pointless," he said.

"You're exhausting."

Derron watched her as she paced toward the bed. "Exhausting is sitting on a chair for weeks with the only reprieve being one of the Dragon-Blessed's bodyguards taking me out for a potty break."

"I don't have bodyguards," Shara snapped. "And if you don't like potty breaks, feel free to shit where you are. You can't possibly stink worse than you already do."

"You don't exactly smell of roses yourself."

Shara's memory jumped back to the rose Derron plucked for her in the dream, and then even further back to warm summers of her childhood when she blushed over flowers Derron gifted her from the garden. She crossed her legs on the bed, leaning on her knees. "Why did you give me flowers?"

He didn't try hiding his wide-eyed surprise. "You were the princess and my best friend's little sister. It seemed courteous."

The explanation would have broken her heart as a child. She never thought more of it back then, but the gesture had been enough to set the butterflies in her stomach aflutter.

Since when are you a blushing, flower-loving maid? Shara could almost hear Rami's voice teasing her, and it was enough to inflict a new stab to her heart. It was exactly the sort of thing Rami would have said, and he would have been right. Perhaps she'd stopped appreciating flowers after the Coup of Fire because they reminded her of Derron.

Even as a young boy, Derron was handsome. In her eyes, he was the most handsome of Elon's friends, even more so because he wasn't afraid of Deimok's presence by her side.

He'd grown spectacularly into his features. Derron's face was made up of perfect angles, with the right combination of smoldering gaze, straight nose, and soft lips that probably made many in Adara—and possibly the entire continent—swoon. His was the kind of beauty made for portraits and profiles on silver coins. Though he hadn't been born a prince, he looked the part.

Shara blinked, catching herself as she stared. "I liked the flowers," she said with a small shrug. "And I actually liked you before you tried to kill me."

Even though he bit his lip, it didn't hide his smile.

"That's fair."

"As I'm sure whatever sympathy you may have felt for me vanished the moment I tried to kill you."

His smile dropped.

"Listen, Argarys, I know you must have thought about murdering everyone on this ship at least once a day, and I wouldn't blame you. No one wants to be a prisoner." She paused, bitterness on her tongue. In her mind's eye, Solana prayed to the Maiden and Kael looked haunted as they stood on the deck. "Kael and I are both counting on you to make the right choice."

"Is it really a choice if you'll be holding a knife to my throat?" Derron asked.

"I said I'd slit your throat. I never made mention of where I'd be holding my knife." The thinning of Derron's lips almost made Shara smile. "I know you don't care about me, but don't betray Kael. In a few days, we'll reach land and whatever must unfold between us can do so then."

Shara didn't wait for Derron to give her any assurances. Even if he gave her his word, she was more inclined to trust in the power of persuasion held in a sharp blade. All Shara could do now was hope Kael was right about the sirens, and that Derron's will to survive would overpower his desire to escape.

Shara stood, and for a moment she jumped out of her body.

She was flying, the world small and insignificant beneath her. Crystalline water reflected the muted red and gold of the sky. Wind roared in her ears. A growl echoed at the base of her throat—not in anger, but something akin to nervous excitement. Distantly, a blue star flickered in and out of existence.

Ashari.

Shara returned to her body with a gasp. Derron looked at her with a confused frown, but she barely put it into focus before she rushed from the cabin. Her heart beat in frantic rhythm—strong enough for two. She bolted onto the deck, eyes darting between the blue glow of the Siren Coves and the sky. Her belly fluttered with wild hope at every glimpse of wings etched against the dark canvas overhead only to drop when the shadows remained too small to match the mighty boom pulsing in her chest.

"Shara, what's wrong?" Solana asked.

"It's him."

"Who?"

Before Shara could answer, a voice drowned out Shara's budding hope. At first it was one, carried on the waves as if born from the water itself. It was the most melodious sound she'd ever heard, and soon another voice joined, and then another until Shara could no longer count the many different tones that made up the Song.

Her blood chilled as she looked over the rail.

The sirens were here.

26

In the silence descending outside, men called to foreign gods. The recited prayers were a far cry from the evening chanteys, gatherings Derron heard through the closed door of his cabin-prison. Every breath clouded as the air grew colder, numbing the tips of his fingers and feet. Slithers of mist crept below the door and spread toward him. Someone whimpered, a sharp contrast to the lilting voices rising from the abyss.

The Song held one voice and many, soft and enchanting. Female voices, young and beautiful, carried on the waves, the mist, and the magic surrounding the ship. Derron was immune to its allure, but the music prodded at him, trying to seize his heart and mind.

Come find us, it said. *Come look at us.*

Asharaya leaped out of a shadow and barged into the room. Derron flinched, closing his eyes and muttering a curse under his breath. "Did you have to do that?"

Asharaya ignored his question. She looked crazed as

she hurried to his side. "The sirens are here. I don't know how long the cotton is going to stop them from claiming the men."

"It won't."

"Then you have to get to them before we lose them all."

"You could at least untie me."

Asharaya's dagger seemed to materialize in her hand, and the tip pressed against his throat. "If those men die, we'll all turn into siren dinner," she said through gritted teeth. "Start singing, Argarys."

Derron grinned. "So, you were aiming for my throat after all."

"I have more than one dagger," she hissed. "Don't make me use them."

Not daring to push her further, Derron steadied his breathing as his power speared through the door and infiltrated the men's minds. He hummed to give his Song a steadier grip, wading through the thick wall of the men's fear, a web growing wider the farther it spread. With the final dregs of renike still in his system, Derron needed to press any advantage he had.

Brother, the voices sang, only for him. *Join us.*

Derron wiped away the men's dread once their minds were his and replaced it with purpose and determination. Now that he had them under his control and the sirens surrounded him, Derron cursed his pride and stubbornness. The desire to prove himself to his mother had kept him from claiming the ship and meeting the queen's fleet. Doing so would have been the most sensible course of action, but they were too deep into siren waters to do so now. He told himself he wouldn't have been strong enough. The renike was taking its sweet time leaving his system, but this was only an excuse. The truth was Derron needed the chance to validate his mother's initial trust. That was what he wanted.

Wasn't it?

A storm is coming, he made the crew think. *We need to be ready.* Some of the men still whimpered, but most stopped their praying. Those he'd taken searched for the incoming storm.

The cold press of Asharaya's blade disappeared. "Is it working?" she asked, her voice small and edged with worry.

"For now," Derron answered. "But I don't know how long I can hold them. The effects of the renike aren't completely gone."

Asharaya knelt by his side, her eyes fixed on the door. "Hold on to them for however long you can."

One man's call resonated like a knell in the crew's silence and over the sirens' Song. "I am here," he exclaimed, as he raced to the ship's rail. Despite his captain's bellowed order to stand his ground, the man kept running, captive to the siren who held him in her thrall.

You must stop him, Derron urged the man nearest to the sailor, but his command was too slow. The sailor climbed over the rail and jumped into the water with a loud splash. His adoring words turned to cries of agony as the sirens dragged him beneath the waves. On deck, someone cursed.

"Selena." Todrak's voice held a command and a plea at once.

"She's trying," Arkael snapped.

Asharaya jumped to her feet. "What's happening out there?"

Derron's shackled hands balled into fists. "I'm neither strong enough nor fast enough to control them all."

"Yes, you are." Asharaya crouched in front of him. Even as a child, Derron remembered she could never keep still when she was nervous or excited, and it seemed that hadn't changed. "I've seen you control an entire marketplace.

You...." She bit her lip. "You saved me from my dream in spite of the renike. You can do this."

Derron wanted to argue that he'd been at his full strength in Havanya, but the desperate hope in her voice held his tongue. He knew she was telling him those things only because she needed him to succeed to protect her sister, but for a moment Derron entertained the foolish idea that she truly believed in him. He imagined the fervent light in her eyes was born not out of necessity but of trust. Of friendship.

"You can do this," Asharaya repeated in a low, urgent voice.

Derron's hum refined into a whispered tune that urged his Song to move faster. The gift didn't necessarily require the use of his voice, but sound gave texture to his command and strength to his magic.

As if sensing his intentions, the sirens grappled at minds still ripe for the taking. The ship rocked as their agitation grew. Waves crashed against the *No One.* Derron firmly planted his feet to the ground, keeping the chair from toppling over. His chains made it impossible to do more.

He found Captain Xoro and wrestled with his iron will. *Lead your men, captain. The storm is here.*

He followed a thread of loyalty to the quartermaster. *Follow your captain's lead.*

The one linked to the captain's heart led to Asharaya's human sister. The sirens' Song seemed to recoil from the darkness surrounding her consciousness. Derron tried wading through it to protect her from an attack should the sirens grow bolder, but his attempts were futile. Solana's mind remained impenetrable.

"All men, at your positions," the captain ordered, and the quartermaster echoed the command a moment later. Shouts rose as the men called to each other, the sirens forgotten.

Derron had to concentrate on the humans, but his Song searched for the halo of dragonfire surrounding Asharaya. Magic acted as a natural shield between her mind and the Song. Breaking through it would require more than the sirens were willing to give.

For now.

The ship lurched, and Derron's chair toppled to the floor. Asharaya moved to stop his fall, but he crashed onto the wooden planks. His breath wooshed out of him and his already tenuous hold on the Song began to slip. Outside, shouts of fear mingled with the addled appreciations of men who raced to their deaths.

"Don't let go of them," Asharaya pleaded as she struggled to right his chair while he remained tied to it.

Stand your ground, Derron ordered, but his command wavered. Threads of his Song thinned and snapped loose from his control, and the sirens were quick to attack the minds of the unclaimed men.

"Argarys..."

"I'm losing them," Derron said, panting through exertion. Asharaya shook her head, but there was no point in lying. Derron knew he was reaching the limit of what he could give. "I won't be able to hold onto them much longer."

Asharaya cursed under her breath. She pressed a dagger to her lips as she paced to the door and back.

"They need you out there," Derron said. The words stilled Asharaya, who turned to face him with a skeptical frown. "I'll do what I can from here."

"I promised Kael I'd stay here with you."

Derron laughed bitterly. "To what end? I can't go anywhere, and even if you fear the sirens want to help me, they never will now that I've interfered with their hunt." He held her gaze, giving Asharaya time to see the truth of his words. "If we lose this fight, we're all dead."

More splashes, one following another in quick succession, came from without, and Asharaya's grip on her dagger tightened. Her eyes flicked once to the door before she turned back to Derron and gave him a tight nod. "Don't make me regret this."

27

Come find us. Come see.
Voices grated against the walls of Shara's mind as she rushed back onto the deck, weapons drawn. A man ran past her, heading for the rail. Shara chased after him. She grasped his shirt before he could take the plunge. The man struggled against her hold, but she yanked him back and struck him behind the head with the hilt of her dagger. The man slumped to the deck, unconscious. *Better unconscious than dead.*

Shara's skin crawled at the sirens' attempts to invade her thoughts. Heart racing, she peeked over the rail. The creatures were flashes of color beneath the waves. Long hair billowed about them, and the multitude of colors from their scales shimmered as they circled the ship and skirted the blue and red flashes of the Do'strath's magic. They were too quick to strike—phantoms with eyes like beacons of glowing light that chilled the blood in Shara's veins.

We have waited so long to find you.

Shara fought against her own body and kept a careful distance from the rail. She couldn't afford to lean too far out lest the creatures try to make her lose her balance.

She chanced a glance to the poop deck, where Niguel controlled the helm and Xoro stood like a pillar of strength between him and Solana. The captain's hand grasped her sister's shoulder, gaze directed at a horizon he couldn't see.

The steady drip of Solana's blood on the wood was a ticking clock in Shara's ears. Dusk enveloped them like a shroud, yet the darkness all but rippled at her sister's call. Shara knew Solana would remain steadfast in her determination to deliver the *No One* and its passengers to safety, but she hoped the Maiden would refuse to heed her Chosen's prayer.

Over fifty men.

To carry even one passenger drained a vrah's strength. If Solana found the words to change the Maiden's heart, Shara dreaded the price of such a request.

It wouldn't come to that.

Shara's focus flitted about the men on deck. Some who had been running stopped in their tracks and some clarity returned to their otherwise vacant expressions. Shara loosed a breath of relief. It seemed Derron had been able to regain some control. At least for now.

Kael noticed her approach first. A worried look broke through the mask of his concentration, but Shara could only give a subtle shake of her head to alert him of the obstacles to their plan.

Mykal quickly glanced her way and let out a frustrated groan. "You were supposed to stay in the cabin."

"We're losing the men," Shara said, by way of explanation.

"Thank you for your acute observation." Blue danced on Mykal's fingertips as he looked over the edge at the sirens. "There are too many of them."

As if in answer, a violent wave crashed into the *No One*. The ship tilted, and Shara lost her footing, flying toward the edge. Shara grasped the rail, her chest pounding, to stop her fall into the fathoms below. Water barreled into her and drenched her clothes, but her Fire kept her warm against the cold trying to seep into her bones.

Green glowed beneath the waves and illuminated a heart-shaped face, translucent as a pearl. Gray-green scales peppered its side, forming a pattern from the siren's hairline to her cheekbones. Shara glimpsed gills like gaping wounds on her ribcage, the long tail, and the weightless flow of veiled fins.

Beautiful, and deadly.

The siren's lovely features turned monstrous. She bared her fangs and lashed at Shara with a clawed hand.

The *No One* shifted sharply upright, and instinct made Shara release the rail. Her backside slammed into the deck, and her heart threatened to spill from her mouth. A moment longer and she would have toppled into the water.

Kael helped her to her feet. "Are you all right?"

Shara nodded, not trusting her voice to remain steady.

Mykal's eyes gleamed blue as he turned back to the sea. "I've had enough of this."

"No." Shara grasped his arm before he could release his Ice. "If you freeze the water, we'll be stuck here."

The ship creaked.

"Aimed attacks," Kael reminded them, exchanging a look first with his Do'strath and then with Shara.

"Keep her steady," Xoro called from the poop deck.

The Do'strath stood on either end of the deck. On one side, Mykal held out his palm. Ice lined with red speared from his skin with impressive speed and pierced the water's surface. Steam formed where it fell, wails lifting from its depths as blood surfaced like clouds. A siren emerged with a pained rasp, her hand pressed to her shoulder where blistered skin circled the spear's entry wound. Mykal's Ice had burned her.

On the other end of the deck, Kael didn't miss a beat. Blue Fire spurted in quick succession from his palms to trace a scalding perimeter around the *No One*. The creatures jerked back from the steam, but in moments, veins of Ice spread like vines where scorch marks marred their smooth skin. Shara watched in wonder as the sirens sank, no more than statues lost to the abyss. Flames that could freeze and Ice that burned—the Do'strath's magic merged into one weapon.

Sinister sounds echoed below. The ship rocked, caught between waves as the sirens stirred. Kael's Fire kept them at bay, but its warmth wasn't enough, not with the heart of Ice living within it. His was not the magic that would save them.

Shara steeled her breath and reached for her Fire.

You are scared.

The intruder spoke in a voice female and foreign, soft as a lullaby. Invisible claws sank in her skull and pain lanced through her. Shara was deaf to her own cries. The siren pried through memories of Fire spiraling from her outstretched palm and Rami's dying scream as it consumed him.

Dragon-Blessed, the siren sighed, a jolt of excitement woven through the syllables. *You are not in control.*

Shara whimpered, eyes squeezed shut. Mykal's and Kael's voices were distant, wrapped in a haze. She couldn't make out the words. Tears formed behind her lashes. Lead weighed down her arms as she clutched her temples, wrestling against the siren's hold and against Rami's screams.

There is a way to stop the fear.

Heat grazed Shara's face. Fire simmered below the surface of her palms, ready to burst free and consume her.

Shara gritted her teeth. She begged her body to heed her voice and not the siren's, but the creature's hold was cast iron. Now that she knew Shara's gift and the threat it posed to her and her sisters, she refused to yield.

The dragons are gone, the creature hissed. *It is time you joined them.*

Shara screamed, but no sounds emerged from her lips. The cold touch of Mykal's hands circled her wrists as he tried to help.

"Fight back," he bellowed.

I can't, Shara wanted to cry but couldn't. Her efforts had been for nothing. Fire would consume her, and she'd die in agony and flames like her family and Rami before her.

A dragon does not fear the flames.

A new voice pierced her mind that was ancient and new, raw and infinitely warm. It rumbled through her body and into her blood, and it silenced the siren in her thoughts.

Shara's heart hammered in her ears, strong enough for two.

The siren's hold wavered. Shara immersed herself in the new, steeling presence and drew from its strength to claim back her mind. With a howl rivaling those of the creatures surrounding them, she thrust her hands toward the water. Brilliant red flames roared to life. As Fire scorched the sea, towers of smoke rose everywhere the jet of her magic struck.

The sea—the siren's domain and their greatest ally— turned into their boiling prison.

Shara stumbled back as she released her hold on her magic. Air rushed back into her lungs and carried the blood-laced odor of the sea. Mykal laughed while Kael smiled, eyes alight with silent pride.

The sirens were retreating.

Shara's plan had worked.

She only had time to release a breathless chuckle before hands grabbed her and crushed her against a wiry body. The smell of ginger lilies and vanilla faded beneath ten days of voyage and the copper tang of blood. "You scared the shit out of me."

It worked. Only as her arms lifted to circle Solana did Shara let herself believe it. Many of the men were still alive. Derron had worked with them and Solana was safe in her arms.

They'd survived.

"Lana."

The *No One* jolted beneath them. Shara pushed away from Solana, cold shivers landing like whip lashes as she fought to keep her footing. Xoro gave new orders and the men scurried to secure the riggings.

Thunder echoed in the distance as a drizzle poured down on them. Waves grew, stirred, and churned. A storm was coming.

The *No One* veered despite Niguel's strain to keep her steady. The bowsprit pointed toward the Siren Coves' eerie blue glow.

The crack of thunder silenced Shara's curse. A wave shot up and jostled the ship, a tower of destruction hovering over them. Shara's eyes widened. She grasped for Solana as if it made a difference.

Water rained down upon them, and so did the sirens.

28

"Took you long enough." Derron groaned as a pirate removed his manacles. Over a week of enduring chains had chafed his skin, and bloody blisters circled his wrists. He made to massage one of them and hissed at the needling pain. It would take a while for his skin to recover.

The man blanched. "Apologies, sir. I-I had to look for them keys in the captain's quarters, sir, and the lass is in a mood tonight. A storm's raging outside."

Derron expected neither an answer nor an apology, but his Song made this human want to please him, and the man feared failure. The realization stuck like a layer of grime on Derron's skin. He would never grow comfortable with this side of his power. "No, forgive me. You've done well. Now you must go. Your comrades need you."

The man deflated and took his leave with a curt nod.

Derron stumbled into the nearest wall, holding himself against it to recover his balance. The *No One*'s dangerous bobbing made it difficult to stand upright on his unsteady legs. Devoted to the men's focus and his own freedom, Derron lost track of the fight unfolding outside.

Freedom.

With the men in his thrall and the sirens out for blood, it would take a minor effort to overcome those who opposed him. He'd have to remove Asharaya's sister from the equation. The inability to control her made her a dangerous liability. Solana was unaware of his manipulation of the men. Trained assassin or not, she wouldn't see an attack coming until it was too late, especially if the attack came from her lover. The Do'strath needed to go as well. They were strong, but the humans had the numbers. It would take one push and the sirens would do the rest.

Then it would be only him and Asharaya.

Kael and I are both counting on you to make the right choice.

Derron balled his fists until his wrists barked in protest. Pain gave him focus. This wasn't the time for what-ifs and regrets. Arkael may be loyal and good, and a better brother than Derron likely deserved, but he was also a stranger—a boy from the other side of Ilahara who Derron was getting to know, a soldier in Darrok Todrak's army, and a threat to his family and the life he knew. And Asharaya...

If only things could be different.

Todrak screaming Arkael's name banished all thoughts of Asharaya. Derron lumbered to the door. The pirate hadn't closed it properly on his way out, so he shouldered it open further. Blood drained from his face. The sirens clawed their way across the sodden deck toward unaware sailors, some of whom died without realizing it, their minds still ensnared by Derron.

Fight. Defend yourself. The men burst into action at Derron's silent command. He couldn't find Todrak but caught a familiar flash of silver-blond hair. Arkael was on his back, struggling against the siren clawing at his face.

Derron didn't think and spun back into the room. He grabbed the chair and smashed it against the wall, once, twice, until the legs gave way and he held two makeshift weapons.

He ran.

Gone was the quiver in his limbs and the weariness of captivity. Derron sped through the melee. Rain plastered his hair to his face and the clothes to his skin. Sounds were drowned out by the panicked tempo of his heart. Wide arcs of the wooden pegs cleared a path between him and the siren attacking Arkael. Derron avoided as many men as he could and shouldered past the rest when there was no alternative.

Alerted by his steps, the siren whirled in his direction. Betrayal flashed across her deformed features. *You are in their minds, traitor*, she hissed in his mind. Claws swept at Derron's chest, but he swiveled to the side and countered in the next breath. Derron drove a wooden peg into the siren's heart, gritting his teeth as he forced the splintered edge through her skin. The creature's shrieks filled his ears, and her blood sprayed both his face and Arkael's. Derron forced her off Arkael's body, removing the makeshift weapon only when the siren stilled.

Arkael took Derron's outstretched hand with a wide-eyed stupor. Derron doubted his expression differed from his brother's. His head spun in a whirlwind, but he forced himself to focus. If he lost concentration, the crew would be easy prey to the sirens once more.

"You're sweating," Arkael pointed out.

"I'm fine."

Arkael gasped, his hand shooting forward. "Myk, no."

Derron spun in time to avoid Todrak's sword. "What in the Dragon's name and all five fucking gods are you doing?"

"What am I doing? What are you doing out of your

bonds and on your feet?" Todrak pinned Arkael down with a furious stare. "You went behind my back."

Arkael swallowed hard. "I'm sorry. There was no other way to protect the men."

Asharaya and her sister approached them, blood-splattered and frantic. The sirens who managed to breach the deck were either dead or back in the water. Derron didn't let himself count the bodies of the men lying dead. "Gentlemen now is not the time to fight among ourselves." Asharaya pointed ahead, rain-soaked hair shooting sprays as she whirled to face the eerie blue glow of the Coves. The skeleton of a past shipwreck greeted them at the entrance. "Unless you want to become siren snacks, I suggest holding on to something."

Inside, the waters turned into rapids. The *No One* veered toward the walls and rocks. Sirens shot out of the water, beautiful faces twisted into terrible features of razor-sharp teeth and murderous eyes. Their clawed fingers sank into the ship's flanks. Wood splintered with every blow.

Derron sagged against the rail. Blood dripped from his nose and his breath wheezed out in heavy gasps. Men dropped their weapons and abandoned their posts, calling for the sirens as they rushed to the edge.

His control was fraying.

Solana sprinted for the helm. With one hand, she stopped the wheel from spinning and righted the ship before it crashed against the cavernous walls. With the other, she grasped Xoro's shirt and stopped him from following the quartermaster to the rail. She called back the quartermaster, but the young woman's call met deaf ears. Solana looked away as Niguel jumped overboard, a stupefied smile on his lips. Derron couldn't say he held any sympathy for a man who whistled while he drugged him, but even his stomach churned at the sounds of the quartermaster's screams.

Solana bent her head, tears streaking her blood-smeared face.

Asharaya held on to a rope and grabbed Derron. His face was reflected in her eyes, glossed with tears she didn't shed. "Don't give up, Argarys."

Derron's gaze drowned in hers, golden and incandescent. The eyes of a dynasty thought lost forever. The eyes of a friend he couldn't forget. Life turned them into enemies, yet here they were, a prince and an assassin working together toward a common goal.

He took a deep breath, but his body shook. Asharaya braced him as he burrowed within his well of magic and grasped what remained of his strength. His temples pulsed along with the beating of his thundering heart, but he forced himself to imagine strings tied to the men. "Stop." Derron yanked on those strings, invisible hands fisted around them. *Don't jump. Survive.*

Captain Xoro stood straighter, holding on to the helm.

"Look, ahead," Todrak shouted. "There's light."

Arkael laughed. "We're going to make it!"

Derron seized Asharaya's rope and sagged against her. "Don't faint now," she muttered under her breath.

Their enthusiasm was short-lived. Rocks blocked the other end of the Coves, making it impossible for their vessel to pass through. Broken carcasses of ships loomed before them and smothered any hope of survival. They would crash. Their bodies would break upon those rocks, and the sirens would have what remained. "Hold on," Solana warned from her post at the helm.

Arkael grabbed Todrak's middle as if he'd shield his Do'strath's body with his own.

Asharaya made to dash for her sister, but the rope tangled around her ankle. Derron's weight impeded her attempts to free herself. "Solana, take the ropes."

Solana let go of the helm with one hand and pulled a

dagger from her belt. "I can fix this."

Asharaya pushed hard against Derron's chest. "Solana, get the fucking ropes."

Solana plunged a dagger deep into her arm instead. Her scream silenced the sirens and pierced Derron's concentration, waking the men. Blood poured from the gash in her forearm, but she breathed through the pain, lifting her bloodied hands in the air. The sound she made was one of pure, undiluted fury. The helm screeched as it spun.

Shadows trembled along the walls, and the darkness tore apart at her will.

29

The weightlessness familiar to Shara in the Maiden's domain ripped away. Every spot where the sirens had clawed her ached. Cold seeped into her bones from her sodden clothes. Derron's weight crushed her as he leaned on her for support, and the copper tang of the blood dripping copiously from his nose tainted her tongue.

Solana had done it. The *No One* sailed through an ocean of shadows, lost in time. Shara's breath hitched, unable to comprehend the enormity of what her sister had done. She saved their lives and risked her own in the process.

Don't take her from me, please, Shara prayed. So much blood had spilled on this night. Wasn't it enough to sate the Maiden's hunger? *Don't take more than she can give.*

Sudden light burned Shara's eyes after seconds spent in total dark, blinding in its brilliance. Sound exploded in a deafening cacophony—men screaming, thunder rumbling, wind howling as it tore at the sails. The *No One* soared, suspended in midair as it barreled back into the world. For a moment, the light of the stars looked like thousands of comets.

Solana's arms slackened, and before her name fully left Shara's lips, her sister's body slumped heavily to the ground. Blood poured from the many cuts her sister inflicted upon her human body. She'd gambled everything in hope that her goddess's favor would be enough.

The *No One* crashed into the sea. The impact reverberated through Shara's body as water hammered over them without mercy. A wave struck her from behind, punching the air out of her before another, more violent wave slammed into her front. Water filled her nose and mouth and blinded her to her surroundings.

Shara's feet slipped. She could no longer feel the deck beneath her. Flailing her arms, she tried to claw at the rope, desperate for purchase. It stroked against her fingers with a rough touch.

Gravity dragged her down.

Shara screamed as the rope slipped from her grasp and her body soared over the railing. Wind whipped at her until a hand closed around her wrist. Her body slammed against the *No One*'s flank, and Shara grunted. It hurt to breathe or to lift her head, but she did it anyway, fingers gripping her savior's blistered wrist.

"Derron." The name was a breathless whisper. The white around his bewildered silver eyes mirrored Shara's shock. He'd saved her again, and this time Shara could find no rational explanation for it.

"Pull her up," Mykal called. Shara's gaze flitted to Kael and Mykal rushing across the deck to help.

In a fraction of a second, Shara witnessed the war painted on Derron's face, and his hesitation fed the spark of fear in her core. He was considering whether to let her fall into a watery grave and thus preserve the Argarys legacy from the Myrassar threat. Her eyes stung, but even now as terror seized her, she refused to beg.

Derron's hold around her hand tightened. "Help me," he yelled over his shoulder.

Relief settled over Shara like a warm blanket.

Shara heard a loud splash of water, and then a hiss of rage.

Clawed fingers sank into her ankle in quick succession.

Pain was a distant echo compared to the dread following Derron's refusal to let her go, even as his body was too weak to battle the weight of the sirens dragging her down. Kael stretched out his arm, but Shara could see he wouldn't be able to reach them in time.

Shara held Derron's hand as they fell, the knowledge that these would be her last moments crashing mercilessly upon her. Solana carried them past the Siren Coves, but no farther than that. They were still in siren waters, and the creatures had a score to settle with the Dragon-Blessed who used Fire against them.

Shara crashed into the water, gasping at the bite of cold. The storm stirred the sea. Waves crashed into her, pulled her down, and tore Derron's hand from hers. She barely had time to lift her head above water and draw breath before the sirens were upon her.

Ten, fifteen, maybe more. Shara couldn't count the tails circling her. The sirens attacked in synchronized formation. It was all she could do to writhe and protect her throat. Her mind snagged on colors to escape the agony of her body. Crimson blood tainted the water. A black sea burned into her wounds as it tried to claim her life. Silver claws tore apart her skin. White flashes of fangs birthed new pain. In her peripheral vision, Derron wrestled the sirens in an attempt to yank them away from her body.

The daggers at her belt weighed her down. Shara couldn't reach for them, not caught as she was between the sirens' murderous embrace. Bloodlust contorted their beauty. It was her blood on their fangs. Her blood on their faces.

Teeth sank into her shoulder, and Shara managed a weak wheeze. Her eyes rolled back. The thundering of her pulse turned sluggish.

This is how my story ends.

A story written in blood, fire, and sacrifice. She was the girl who'd seen a dynasty fall and survived. The human morphed into a blade by the vrah and the fae blessed by the dragons with their Fire. All her life she'd fought to stay alive.

So long as she had breath, she would keep fighting.

Shara closed her eyes, numb to the pain, and searched inward with the last of her strength.

Her heart was weak, but there was another, stronger beat tethering her to this world. A heart of Fire begging her to hold on.

A dragon does not fear the flames.

Shara's lips formed the words without a sound, and her Fire heeded her summons for one last time. It ruptured from her body, and the sirens screamed, withdrawing from scorching flesh. Fiery columns rose along her arms and burned through the shredded remains of her shirt. Every inch that wasn't below water became flame. For the first time in a long while, Shara's gift didn't terrify her. It incinerated her fears and wrapped around her heart. Fire was her weapon, not her enemy, and so long as she burned, the sirens couldn't touch her.

Kael's voice rang out, though it sounded distant, as if from a dream. How far had the waves carried her? Shara searched for Derron and found him not too far away. There were cuts on his arms where the sirens had fought against his grip. When she made to reach for him, Derron jerked away. She must have looked terrifying, given the look of unabashed horror on his face.

Shara's vision distorted and dimmed, swimming in and out of focus. An icy chill swept over her as exhaustion weighed her down. It was all she could do to stay afloat and search her surroundings for a pocket of darkness to summon. The nearest shadow was too far, and her strength nearly spent.

Shara edged closer to Derron. The sirens were vultures with greedy eyes, drinking in the sight of the dying embers on her skin.

"Save yourself," Shara whispered, voice breaking on the last syllable. "It's me they want."

Derron considered her for a drawn-out moment, and then his attention returned to the sirens. Body tense, he angled himself to shield her as the sirens regrouped, an act of chivalry that was short-lived. Shara had not lived her life as a damsel, and she refused to die like one. She treaded to his side and rallied what strength she had left.

The sirens lunged with a battle cry.

Shara snarled.

The dragon roared with her.

A jolt of adrenaline shot through her body. Shara's heart stilled, and then raced at an impossible speed in her chest.

As fast as a dragon challenging the storm to reach his soulbound.

Leathery wings boomed like a cannon blast. Shara heard it so often in her dreams it should have been familiar. Instead, the sound rattled her core, filling a void of fourteen long years and breathing new life into her soul.

Shara lifted her eyes to the sky, blinking through the tears hampering her vision. The shadow was as familiar as her own face. He'd been alive in her memories, her dreams, her heart. Black as the obsidian ring around her neck. Red as brilliant as the ruby on her mother's necklace where the light touched his scales. His eyes burning pits scorching the darkness.

A tether snapped into place between her soul and the dragon's. *Ashari*, she breathed down the bond. *I am here.*

Ashari. Deimok's voice belonged to neither human nor fae, meant for her alone. The deep sound rumbled through her blood and soul. Even when she thought she'd been able to leave her old life and magic in the past, Deimok's memory had anchored her to it. He was the thread linking Shara and Asharaya, and he'd returned to her.

He'd kept his promise.

The sirens scattered and shrieked as they sought refuge from the unforeseen threat. Deimok didn't falter. Dragonfire cackled, erupting from his parted maw. Shara's memory didn't do it justice. The Fire shot out in a vortex of red and gold, powerful enough to raise waves of its own as it met water. Steam and smoke exploded through the air. Screams echoed through the night and the reek of boiled blood and charred flesh filled Shara's nostrils.

This was the might of the Ilah made flesh. This force had blessed her dynasty when Garon Myrassar spoke to Teirak. This power—his power—flowed in her veins.

Deimok let out a battle cry, a sound both young and old, filled with longing, rage, and pain.

"A dragon." Shara had nearly forgotten Derron, now ashen-faced at her side. "Your dragon."

Deimok soared over them and chased off the sirens. Shara couldn't tell where the dragon's emotions ended and hers began. She discerned only his bloodlust enflaming her own. The dragon roared again as he flew lower, his wings blowing torrents of air against Shara's face.

A strangled sound slipped from her lips. She extended her hand, longing for the contact with his scales. A shrill sound rippled from the depth of Deimok's throat. Even in the dark, a sheen of tears was visible as he offered his hind paw. It was large enough to envelop her whole body, with only a sliver of space to hang her legs between each sharp talon. They could rip Shara apart with no effort, but his massive size wasn't a threat—not to her. Never to his soulbound.

Scales burned hot as coals against Shara's skin, rough to the touch, though Deimok was heedful of her wounds. Shara buried her face in his warmth and held on tight as if the very air could rip him from her again.

Real, he's real.

You are safe now, Dragaelan.

Shara sagged and closed her eyes. She shivered at the onslaught of wind from Deimok's liftoff despite the protective cocoon of his talons.

"Wait," she muttered, the words barely a breath. Strength rushed away now that adrenaline was gone and Deimok's heat gave her a sense of safety long since foreign. *Solana.*

Deimok's confusion reverberated down the bond. The name meant nothing to him.

The ship's shrinking shape was the last thing Shara saw before her world went black.

30

A dragon had returned.

No one had seen the creatures since the Coup of Fire. Some thought them dead, either by Argarys arrows or grief, but Mykal never stopped believing the dragons would someday return to those who clung to the Dragon Faith. As children, he and Kael would sit by the window of his room in hopes of catching a glimpse of leathery wings against the starry sky.

Dreaming and living were two entirely different matters.

Once he understood the magnificent creature was real, joy filled his heart and set his pulse into a frenzy. With a delighted laugh, he grasped his Do'strath's shoulder and drew him close, his anger set aside in the thrill of the moment. They'd fought for it and believed in it with every beat of their hearts and every fragment of their bound souls. Mykal and Kael had sailed to Havanya to find the brightest piece of the Dragon's burning heart and bring her home.

A dragon has returned.

Kael pressed his forehead to Mykal's. "You did it, Myk."

Mykal melted from the way his Do'strath's body leaned into his. His mind unraveled at the undiluted joy illuminating Kael's face.

"We did it."

Now, despite stupor clinging to his thoughts, practicality forced him to action. Finding Asharaya was imperative. Mykal trusted the beast to have taken her to a secure location, but his presence by her side would be a beacon, and every cell in Mykal's body was wary of the Meranians.

Then there was the matter of Derron Argarys. Mykal stood to the side as Kael and two men hauled Derron back onto the ship, sodden and pale as if he might faint without a moment's notice. A dark part of Mykal wished he would— the same part that refused to believe the usurper prince had helped them, which rebuked the notion he'd raced from the cabin to save Kael and not kill him. He watched Kael hold Argarys upright and stare at his enemy with a mix of worry, surprise, and hope, and it felt like a snake hissed and snapped in his core.

When Mykal wanted to, he caught no similarity between Argarys and Kael, but with the snake lashing out in dismay, he couldn't miss the silver-blond hair, the same straight nose, or that they looked painfully like brothers.

They were brothers, and for that reason, Kael had betrayed him.

Mykal couldn't deal with it. Not yet. He sought any excuse not to be near his Do'strath and solidified his mental walls until not even the sound of a breath passed through the other side. There were more important things than his rage and his broken heart, and he could deal with them later.

The *No One* suffered significant losses—eighteen men, including the quartermaster—but enough hands remained to maneuver the ship. Sometime after the dragon's arrival, the captain found his way to Asharaya's sister and now cradled her to his chest. In some ways, he reminded Mykal of his father—unflinching and rough but fierce in his loyalties and commanding despite his disability. Grief hollowed the captain's sharp features, a harsh reminder of his humanity. Mykal swallowed, hesitantly regarding Selena...Solana.

"How is she?" he asked in Havanian.

"She's alive." The captain's arm tightened around his lover. "I didn't think...I almost lost her."

Mykal nearly grasped the man's shoulder in solidarity. He, too, underestimated the cost of Solana's magic, but Asharaya hadn't. Asharaya tried to make him understand, and Mykal had been unwilling to listen. He dug his nails into his palms, and the spike of pain replaced shame with focus. When Asharaya returned, he'd make sure she'd find her human sister alive. It was the least he could do.

"Those..." Mykal bit the inside of his lip. What was the Havanian word for wound? "Those cuts need to be cleaned."

They carried Solana to Xoro's cabin. As Mykal washed the wounds with a lucky bottle of alcohol that had survived the attack, the captain ordered his men to make an inventory and quantify the ship's damages.

The boatswain-turned-quartermaster returned with his report after a short time. They had broken a mast and the flanks underwent damage, but they would stay afloat until they made port. Kael followed the man inside the cabin, and Mykal's heart bled. When his Do'strath looked to him, Mykal turned away. Kael nudged down the bond, but Mykal made sure his walls held fast. He turned instead to the captain as the door shut. "I must borrow your map."

The first light of dawn filtered through the window by the time the three men had thoroughly considered Eathelin's territory and pinpointed the archipelagos as where the dragon could have taken refuge with Asharaya. She was wounded and weak so he wouldn't have taken her far. They would begin the search after the men had a chance to get a few hours of rest. Hopefully using Asharaya's journal to track her would save them some time.

Mykal left the cabin with squared shoulders and didn't linger so his Do'strath could follow.

"Myk."

Mykal's agitation grew with each stride to their cabin. There weren't many steps, but there were many reasons for his aggravation, and the biggest one waited inside. Derron Argarys lay unrestrained and unconscious on the bed, replenishing his strength to better destroy them in the morning.

The door closed behind Kael. "You saw what happened. Without Derron's Song, more men would have died. We made a difficult choice, but it paid out."

"We would all be dead if Solana's goddess hadn't come through." Mykal clenched his fists. "I told you there was no other way and to trust her, and still you and Asharaya went behind my back. You put us at risk for nothing."

"There would have been no one to save if we hadn't."

"Do you want me to thank you?" Mykal's voice rose an octave, and the Ice in his core trembled.

"No, I want you to look at me."

Mykal shut his eyes and inhaled deeply. *I'm calm*, he whispered to his Ice, but magic knew the truth and his heart's turmoil. He felt like a fly caught in his magic's web, and like a spider taking the first steps toward its prey, the Frostbite began to spread toward his heart. "You betrayed me," Mykal said in a shaky breath. "I never thought I'd live to see the day."

Kael's voice cracked. "I didn't mean to."

Cold snaked into the muscles of Mykal's abdomen, and

he winced. "But you did it anyway." He brought his arms around his middle, afraid his heart might spill from the tear in his chest. "What is happening to you, Kael? I thought you believed in my family's cause. I thought we were enough for you, that—" The words caught in his throat. *I thought I was enough.*

"I do," Kael said. "You are. This isn't about me choosing. I've made my choice long ago when I asked you to be my Do'strath. You think I'm trying to replace you, but I can't. I won't. You mean everything to me. Please, Myk, just let me in and you'd know."

"I can't," Mykal said, voice breaking. *I'm okay. I'm in control.*

"Stop shutting me out." Kael grabbed Mykal's arm and forced him to turn. His eyes were wide. "You're freezing."

"I won't share you with him," Mykal snapped, grabbing Kael's arm in return. "I'll have all of you, Kael, or I won't have you at all."

Heat rose up the column of Kael's neck. Mykal's breath caught as he followed the line of red to the sharp cut of Kael's jaw. His lush lips parted in surprise, the bottom one fuller than the other. Beneath the Ice, Mykal's blood boiled and a wave of desire, primal, demanding, and filled with longing and fear, washed over him. It was true Mykal wouldn't share Kael with Argarys or with anyone else, but he'd sooner die than live in a world without him.

Mykal leaned forward and pressed his lips to Kael's. The impossibility of the moment kept him from asking for more than that simple touch. Now that the sudden burst of courage was gone, Mykal was stunned into inaction. For years, he'd been too afraid to blur the fine line between them. Hearts were such fragile, breakable things, and the last thing Mykal wanted was to cause Kael pain. He'd been content with being Kael's friend, and then his Do'strath.

Until now.

Kael's body stiffened against his.

Mykal stepped back. His stomach sank into nothingness and a flush rushed to his cheeks. *What was I thinking?* The timing was wrong. Everything was wrong. "I shouldn't have done that."

"Stop talking." Kael grabbed Mykal's shirt and yanked him close. His mouth crashed on Mykal's like a river barging through a dam. Their bodies pressed close, and Kael's heat spread through Mykal. Ice receded in favor of his Do'strath's warmth. Kael kissed him the way Mykal dreamt of kissing him, without fear or hesitation.

Mykal surrendered to it and stumbled as he backed Kael up against the wall. They parted long enough to draw breath, and then their mouths collided once more. The sinful stroke of Kael's tongue made Mykal shiver and emboldened him to trace his Do'strath's hips. Mykal attuned to every hitch in Kael's breath, every demanding touch of his body. Lost in bliss, Mykal couldn't remember why he'd waited so long to kiss Kael or a valid reason to stop. A crevice broke through his mental walls and Kael's mind snatched moments—Mykal lost in the blue of Kael's eyes, Mykal counting the freckles on the ridge of Kael's nose, Mykal cradled in Kael's arms after the Frostbite, pretending it was a lover's embrace.

Let me in, Kael's voice whispered down the bond. His arms wound around Mykal's neck and his hands tangled in his hair. Mykal moaned into his mouth, hands dipping lower to Kael's backside.

The door opened, and they jerked apart. Mykal suppressed a growl and whirled to the intruder. "What?" he snapped, the word slipping in Ilahein, though the sailor understood him nonetheless. His eyes flicked between Kael and Mykal. Their swollen lips and crumpled clothes likely revealed what had transpired between them.

"We've got company."

31

Kael burned in every place Mykal's body had touched his. He followed his Do'strath and the human on deck. Derron hadn't stirred once, a testament to the prince's exhaustion. Kael couldn't believe he'd kissed Mykal with his half-brother in the same room.

He'd kissed Mykal.

He could still taste the winterberries and pines that saturated Mykal's skin. The scent of Daganver's forests. The smell of home. When they'd kissed, his heart thundered the same way it did whenever they rode through the snowy paths, but more so. It felt reckless and safe, familiar yet new.

Kael blinked away the memory of his Do'strath's lips on his and the flurry of emotions that came with it. There would be time to face what had transpired in the cabin— the fight, the kiss, where they stood—but now was not that time.

The *No One* creaked and moaned beneath them as they

approached Captain Xoro on the port side of the vessel, where his new quartermaster described the scene in hushed conversation. Something moved in the water. The shape could have been mistaken for a large animal, but a closer inspection revealed a dozen smaller silhouettes—bodies bearing an abysmal resemblance to the sirens.

Mykal bit back a curse. "Just our luck."

"The sirens aren't gonna stop until they make a bloody meal of us all," one of the men cried.

"It's not the sirens," Xoro said, and Mykal and Kael nodded in agreement. "We'd already be dead if it were."

Indeed, the creatures rising from the water not five strokes from the *No One* weren't sirens.

They were merfolk.

Beautiful bodies shimmered with droplets above the surface, while long, colorful tails hid below. Unlike the sirens, merfolk had no scales over the length of their skin, nor did they have gills to breathe. Everything down to their pointed ears was fae. Nature had interwoven the loveliest aspects of both species after the love affair between the fae Vembren Nahar and the siren Sahariel put an end to the Siren Wars and over a century of bloodshed.

The merman at the head of the group was broad and muscular, with dark hair falling over his golden shoulders and blue eyes the color of the Ilahein sea. Kael recognized him. Raxan Nahar, favorite cousin of the Head of Eathelin, was hard to forget. Breathtaking like the rest of his kind, except for a slight crook to his nose from a broken bone that had never healed quite right.

People loved Raxan Nahar.

Kael hated him.

The merman's lips stretched in a sensual smile. "Mykal Todrak. It's been a while."

"Nahar." Mykal brimmed with irritation. "I see you're still sporting Kael's parting gift," he said with a clever smirk of his own, scratching at his nose where Raxan's was broken.

Kael couldn't help his smug smile. He considered himself a sensible man at most times, but Raxan brought out the worst in him. The merfolk of Merania were once on amicable terms with Mykal's family, which had given the Do'strath many opportunities to visit Eathelin's capital and make the acquaintance of Merania's favorite bachelor.

Raxan's smile didn't falter as his attention shifted from Mykal to Kael. "I didn't see you there, half-breed."

"Said the one who's literally half fish," Mykal countered before Kael could.

"You always have a quick response," Raxan said, smiling. "Let us board so we can talk like civilized people."

Xoro's hand shot to the saber at his belt. "No one is boarding my ship."

"I'm afraid I must insist." The unmistakable texture of magic woven into Raxan's words made the humans instantly pliable to the merman's terms.

Kael and Mykal could do nothing to prevent Raxan and his people from boarding the *No One*. Tails morphed into legs the moment the merfolk's bodies left the sea. Even if the Do'strath had a small reservoir of magic left, they couldn't risk the sailors, especially when the merfolk could manipulate them to their advantage. By using his Song, Raxan reminded them who had the upper hand, because he knew they wouldn't risk innocent lives if they could avoid it.

With a nod from Raxan, the merfolk set to search the ship, seawater dripping from their naked bodies. Mykal and Kael exchanged a glance. It didn't take a genius to know they were looking for Asharaya. Perhaps it was a stroke of luck that the dragon had taken her far from the Nahar's reach—and possibly the queen's.

But they stowed away another royal.

"What brings you to these waters, gentlemen? Honeymoon?" Raxan inquired. "I don't recall being invited to the wedding."

Kael silenced the urge to break the merman's nose again.

Mykal crossed his arms. "You think you're clever?"

The merman mirrored the movement. "I think you're about to sink."

"Get to the point."

Raxan grinned. "You've never been much of a talker."

Kael's teeth would have splintered if he clenched his jaw any harder. Though the words were harmless, the clear allusion hit a raw nerve after the kiss. He was one breath away from throttling the merman.

Raxan's grin faded, but Kael's murderous instincts didn't. The merman looked to the sky, cautious as if it would drop on his head at any moment. "We heard the unmistakable roar of a dragon not too long ago. Witnesses claim to have seen it fly in this direction." His attention returned to the Do'strath, and he waited for a confession they wouldn't give.

"Witnesses, or your sirens?"

Kael and Mykal spun in the direction of the cabin from which Derron emerged. Despite his tattered clothes and the hair still damp from rain and seawater, he stood tall and elegant, every bit the prince he wasn't supposed to be.

"Your Highness." Clever Raxan wasn't fast enough to hide the surprise from his voice.

"Let's not pretend the dragon doesn't exist. It does. We've seen it," Derron said. "I think you're old enough to remember the size of a dragon, General Nahar, so I hope you realize it's evident you won't find it on this ship."

Raxan's eyebrow twitched. "Clearly."

"Then why are your soldiers searching my ship? Or better yet, why did your sirens feel entitled to attack the crown prince?"

"Siren waters are hunting grounds, Your Highness. You know as well as I that my cousin holds no power over our sisters' hunger."

"Is that what you'll tell the queen when you try to explain why her heir almost died in your territory?"

In the beat of uncomfortable silence that followed, Kael glanced sidelong at Derron. He didn't look like someone who had woken up moments before. How long had he pretended to sleep? Kael's cheeks flushed as he considered that he and Mykal might have had an audience.

Raxan pinched his lips. "I must confess, Your Highness, I find it odd you're traveling with the son of Darrok Todrak, especially in times as sensitive as these."

Be ready, Mykal whispered down the soulbond.

What about the men?

We won't have a choice if Raxan becomes a problem.

Kael didn't even swallow the lump in his throat lest Nahar caught his nervousness. He reached for the small seed of Fire remaining after the confrontation with the sirens and felt Mykal do the same with his Ice, his Do'strath's magic an extension of his own.

"The merchant vessel upon which Lord Mykal and his companion traveled had an unfortunate encounter with pirates," Derron said. "I did what any sensible man would have done and offered them passage home."

Kael's surprised intake of breath drew Raxan's attention. Beside him, Mykal stared at Derron with furrowed brows. He lied for them, denying their treason.

Why?

"I find myself in an awkward position." Raxan looked from Derron to Mykal, gaze softening with a silent apology. "I'm under orders to escort Lord Mykal and his friend back to Merania, where they'll be questioned by the Head of Eathelin, Andren Nahar."

Mykal squared his shoulders.

"On what charges?" Derron demanded.

"Treason," Raxan replied. "We're not searching for a dragon, Your Highness. We're searching for Asharaya Myrassar. But, of course, you know that."

"Asharaya Myrassar never boarded this ship, General." The conviction in Derron's voice was unwavering. Another lie. He stole a glance at Kael, there and then gone.

"Yet after fourteen years, a dragon has returned to Ilahara." Raxan clicked his tongue, and the ship lurched forward, nearly toppling them. Merfolk rose from below the ship's keel with lengthy ropes in hand.

Mykal looked over the side of the ship and then turned a death glare on Raxan. "Did you just harpoon our ship?"

"You're in no condition to navigate, and in good conscience, I cannot let you continue on this way." Raxan stood straighter. "Given the circumstances, the Head of Eathelin officially invites His Highness as his guest. In the meantime, you'll be allowed to clear your names, and then we can put this nasty business behind us."

Raxan gestured to his people to lug the ship forward. Kael wasn't sure how many were swimming underneath the water's surface, but they couldn't be more than ten. That they could haul the ship at all was a testament to their strength.

Kael started toward Derron, but the prince didn't give him a chance to talk. Derron followed Raxan and engaged the merman in an amicable conversation at odds with his earlier tone. Kael could only stare and try to make sense of what the prince had in mind.

Mykal sidled closer. "How are we going to find Asharaya if we're sailing to Merania?"

"For now, let's settle for sailing out of here with our heads on our necks."

And hope the Meranians didn't find Asharaya first.

32

With nature's gentle melody playing around her, Shara slowly returned to consciousness. The sea sighed, stretching toward the rocks like lovers coming together. Birds chanted soft, low verses and a crisp wind whispered as it ruffled her unbound hair, still damp and rough from seawater. *You're safe*, it seemed to say, and Shara released a soft breath as that truth settled into her bones.

Warmth heated her side, and a heady, earthy scent enveloped her as her head filled with a steady thump mirrored in her chest. Shara refused to open her eyes, afraid it might break the enchantment and rip away this sense of belonging and completion.

She leaned into the sturdy presence beside her, and her body barked in protest. Rocks pricked her legs. Every joint ached from staying in the same position for too long, muscles sore from the previous night's battle. Awareness returned in broken fragments like insidious flies clinging to her skin no matter how many times she swatted them away. Each movement caused shivers of discomfort—an aggravating predicament, given the weight in her bladder she could no longer ignore.

Worst of all was the tightness of her skin and the crawling sensation spreading along her upper body. Shara jerked and scratched the crook where the shoulder met neck.

Stop that. The reprimanding rumble rattled her senses.

Shara stilled. Her finger prodded at the raised ridge where the siren's teeth sunk deepest. Before her body had burst into flames. Before...

She opened her eyes and saw herself reflected in twin pools of smoldering red.

"Deimok," she whispered around the lump in her throat.

They'd met on the eve of Elon's tenth birthday. The dragon was meant to be her father's gift despite her mother's protests. *The dragons are our strength, and he's my heir,* King Gailen said, with a tone that brooked no argument. Elon hadn't looked thrilled, but her brother preferred a quill to a sword and the flap of a turned page to the beat of a dragon's wings. But young Asharaya's blood tingled with excitement. She knew every dragon in the royal pens, but the one meant for her brother had been captured the previous morning in a glade on the southwest coast of Adara, a mere day's ride from the Embernest.

He was magnificent.

Though the dragon was a young male, he was large for his age. When they released him from his pen, he snapped at the stable boys and roared in outrage as he stormed into the courtyard. The ground shook each time his wings' talons struck the ground, lifting puffs of dust that clouded around them. Despite his fearsome appearance, however, Asharaya had sensed his true emotions as if they'd been her own. He'd been ambushed, drugged, caged. Anger was the only defense he knew against fear. Asharaya sensed a thread connecting her soul to that of the dragon. If she could be brave enough to follow that thread and navigate the fierceness of his emotions, she could placate his fury. She could earn the dragon's trust.

Elon shut his eyes, teeth clattering. Asharaya stepped forward, hand extended.

Asharaya, her father scolded, but whatever reprimand had been on the tip of his tongue faded when the dragon stilled and his roars quieted. His smoldering red eyes locked on the seven-year-old girl before him.

Don't be afraid, she said in Drakasi. *Trust me.*

After a moment of stillness, the dragon neared his face to her hand and touched his snout to her palm.

The dragon and the princess had been inseparable ever since. They'd had only one year together before spending the next fourteen years apart. Much like their goodbye, fear, blood, and a desperate need to survive tainted their reunion. Deimok's death had been Shara's nightmare, but his return was a flare of light in a dark oblivion following the siren's onslaught. It had felt like a dream.

Now she was awake. The sun shone on a new day, warm and full of promise. The sirens were gone.

And her dragon was here.

If you tear your skin apart, it shall never heal properly.

Shara's vision blurred with fresh tears, and a smile tugged the corner of her lips. "I'd rather have a scar than live with this insufferable itch," she said, her bravado ruined by the emotional quake in her voice.

Deimok puffed out a breath, the invisible thread that bound them warming. *You have not changed, Asharaya.*

Shara would have laughed, but a sob came out instead. She threw her arms around her dragon's snout, fitting her face in the space between his nostrils. A screech echoed in his throat, and his warm breath caressed her bare torso.

The last time they'd been this close, Deimok's lifeblood spilled onto her hands, searing in its warmth. It poured from his nostrils, his powerful maw, the gashes from the hundreds of arrows that pierced the softer skin of his belly and his heart. Shara flinched at the memory and held him tighter. Her fingers grazed along his dry scales to trace the ridges and spikes framing his face. "This is a miracle," she murmured before she pressed a salty kiss to his skin.

The sound he made sounded like a harrumph. *This is only magic.*

Shara leaned back, but kept her hand to his face, unwilling to break their contact. "So, the stories are true. The Ilah brought you back."

After a time. It has been only several weeks since I emerged from the Burning Sea. When I returned I...I could not feel you. I thought I failed, that you faded along with the rest.

"A lot has changed," Shara said with a sad smile. "I have much to tell you."

Invisible hands held Shara's heart in a vise, and guilt took residence in the pit of her stomach. Distance from the Ilah had weakened her magic, but the anguish in Deimok's voice forced her to face the truth. Shara had allowed it. Every time she refused to acknowledge her magic she'd helped it go dormant. By being afraid, she'd nearly extinguished the bond between her and her dragon. Had Aerella's seer not had her vision, and had Asharaya's magic not erupted at the threat to her life, she wouldn't be here with Deimok.

Aerella's seer. Despite Shara surviving the Coup of Fire, the crone had only foreseen her return some weeks before as Deimok emerged from the Burning Sea. Had her dragon's rebirth triggered the vision?

She turned to the sea, imagining that island surrounded by lava as she scanned the horizon. *The dragons sang the day you were born*, Maenar Elvik had said. Did the dragons sing for her still?

They will not come, Asharaya. Shara's stomach dropped. *To many of my kin, this new life is not a gift. To live without their Dragaelani has hollowed them to naught but their grief. They have become husks of their former selves.*

Shara squeezed her eyes shut, steeling herself before facing Deimok. For the first time, she let herself look at his flank—or the little left exposed by his wing. Words failed her. The grip on her heart tightened. Derron told her hundreds of arrows had struck Deimok, and the truth of those words stood before her. Raised ridges peppered Deimok's side, splotches of white scars interrupting the black of his scales.

"My sweet boy," she breathed as she traced one. The heat of his body was replaced by that of his blood—scorching, a brilliant red. Nature's melody darkened, morphing into the shouts of dying men, the clamor of swords, the roar of Fire. The aches of her body became the pierce of every arrow that struck Deimok's skin.

I feel no more pain. His voice was soothing.

"I want to see them," she said, her tone carefully controlled.

After a moment's hesitation, the dragon drew back his wing. The scars lined his skin in different sizes and angles, not only on his flanks but beneath his belly like a map laid out for her to follow. Shara traced them with trembling fingers and tried to count them, though the numbers soon drowned in the ocean of her thoughts.

She couldn't help but think of Aerella Argarys, the pale phantom whose choices had determined the course of Shara's life. As a child, the Coup of Fire had meant the death of her family and the loss of her dragon. The memory had been too painful for her to stop and analyze it further.

Tracing the scars testifying her dragon's death and rebirth, Shara now waded through memories, teeth clenched against the shaking of her body and the thundering of her heart.

Aerella had been a member of her father's council. Had her father admired her tactical mind and ambition? Her position must have served her to learn how best to dispose of the Myrassar's greatest strength, which is why she attacked at night when the dragons were locked in their pens. She must have coveted alliances beforehand to secure her reign's longevity, and right under King Gailen's nose. Shara remembered catching a glimpse of Aerella's silver hair in the melee as Deimok carried her away. Aerella Argarys had fought for her throne. If the price hadn't been her family, Shara might have respected her.

But the price had been her family.

Shara placed her hand on Deimok's chest where the most gruesome scar resided. She envisioned the visceral red of his blood as it dripped along her amber skin. *Aerella will pay for what she's done,* Shara vowed down the bond. Heart to heart, mind to mind, the words an oath meant for him alone. She gave Deimok images of his shadow blocking out the sun over the Embernest and of their Fire devouring the place they'd once called home. Aerella's empire would burn to the ground until only ashes remained.

Deimok splayed his wings, nostrils flared and pupils dilated. They both wanted revenge and needed the closure that might come with it. Aerella Argarys had stolen their world, and now that they were together—dragon and rider, the last Myrassar—they would take it back.

Shara held out her hand, and Deimok touched his snout to her palm.

The agitated twitter of birds made the dragon's head snap up. Shara followed his gaze to a flock storming in their direction, the feathers of their wings fanning about them in pastel shades like long trails of silk.

Lie low, Asharaya, Deimok said.

Shara obeyed, her senses attuned to the possible danger. She creeped to the edge of the cliff they had taken refuge on and instantly regretted that she had yet to relieve herself when her belly pressed into the ground. Deimok crouched low beside her. Patches of moss bloomed along his back, a glamour to camouflage them among the island's mossy boulders and rocky cliffs.

At first, Shara recognized only the outline of a ship, but Deimok's tension fueled her wariness so she looked harder, squinting. Slowly, as the ship neared and her sight sharpened, she noticed more details. The mast was broken and lacerations marred the ship's side. The black flag depicted a skull pierced by a dagger and a crow perched on its hilt.

Recognition almost made her jump to her feet. "Those are my friends."

Asharaya, stay down.

Ropes harpooned the *No One*'s keel. Shara followed their braided pattern below the water's surface, where waves rippled and parted. She couldn't see the shapes, but the memory of the sirens made each wound on her body prickle. Solana was on that ship, perhaps still unconscious. Shara couldn't bring herself to think of the more terrifying alternative without feeling sick.

It made no sense. If those were sirens, her friends should already be dead.

Merfolk, Deimok said. *They swim toward Merania.*

A shiver slithered down Shara's spine, bringing with it the echo of Mykal's voice. He'd often expressed his doubts on the Nahar, whom he said were faithful to Aerella. Shara's absence, perhaps, had been a small advantage. Without her, the Nahar had no proof to incriminate the Do'strath for their association with her. It had been her plan all along—to clear their name by abandoning them and pursuing revenge on her own.

But in her plans, Solana was healthy and ready to find her brother with the Do'strath's help.

In her plans, Derron Argarys was with her, not on the very ship the merfolk had intercepted. One peep from his mouth would damn the Do'strath. Why shouldn't he talk? He'd been a prisoner on their ship, drugged and bound. If he didn't take advantage of such a monumental stroke of luck, he'd be a fool. What would become of Shara's sister without the Do'strath's protection? What would Aerella do to the men responsible for Asharaya Myrassar's return?

Flashes of memory burned her vision. Mykal on the *No One*'s deck, gifting her a moment of camaraderie when the world seemed bleakest. Kael's gentleness and his proud smile. They'd gambled everything to find her, a princess long lost, and when they found an assassin in her stead, they still offered her friendship. If Shara abandoned them now, their blood would be on her hands.

Shara's gaze narrowed onto the ship.

"Then we must go there also."

A small rock skittered down the cliff's face as Deimok flicked his tail. *Asharaya, the merfolk cannot be trusted. Should you be captured, their leader may surrender you to the usurper. If not, he will try to keep you as a prize. They are vain creatures, drawn to beauty and power, and you possess both in great quantity.*

Shara's lips curled in a smile. "Then we mustn't be captured."

Asharaya.

Shara's mind churned. She needed to act quickly. The longer the Do'strath remained in Merania, the harder it would be to help them. On the horizon, the sun slowly climbed toward its apex.

As a fae, it would be near impossible to save them,

especially with her magic nearly spent after her outburst against the sirens. But as a vrah...

Shara turned to Deimok. "We act at nightfall."

33

Cassia breathed in the fresh air of another beautiful Adarian morning. Crisp winds pinched her cheeks, made cooler by the first hint of the southern winter. The sky was dark when she rode out of the Embernest, but now it turned into a delightful shade of blue as the rising sun bathed it in morning light. The heavy thud of her horse's hooves drowned out every thought, and the cold wind awakened her numbed senses. She held tightly to the reins, spurring her horse faster. The speed was liberating, and for a moment it felt like flying.

Like freedom.

Cassia stopped atop a hill. Everything, from the grassy plains around her and the country fields she couldn't see to the sprawling city in the distance, belonged to the Argarys. It was another day in Adara—another day where its citizens would work, laugh, dream, and love under the shadow of the golden castle.

If only Cassia could say the same about herself.

Her horse grazed on the grass, panting after the long gallop. She absentmindedly stroked its neck while her gaze stopped west, to Tyrra, where she'd left her heart eighteen months earlier. When the queen told Derron he'd marry Eileen, Cassia believed she would be destined to an Adarian lord, and she walked away from the one man she'd ever truly loved.

You need to concentrate on your future, Johan, and that of your territory. I'll only be a distraction.

I love you, Cassia.

I know.

The princess bit down on her trembling lip as a tear escaped her lashes. She brushed it away and grabbed the reins. "Time to go back."

The city bustled with activity by the time she returned. The sweet smell of bread and sticky buns wafted from the nearby bakery. Children ran through the cobblestoned streets, packs bouncing on their backs as they headed to school. Carriages jammed the narrower streets and angry shouts filled the morning. Merchants and customers negotiated prices. When they noticed the silver-haired woman walking among them, their shouts turned to murmured praises and their heads bent in deference. Wide eyes followed Cassia's retreating form.

The soldiers at the gates hardly blinked at her approach. "Your Highness," they said, bowing their heads in unison with their fists to their hearts as the gates groaned open to let the princess through.

Someone had readied a dress on her bed while she was gone. The dark blue fabric was stark against the white sheets and had silver circlets around the wrists. Diamond dust caused the gown to glitter when the light touched it. A beautiful cage.

Cassia turned to the tall mirror. She hated the person reflected on its surface. Even in the long blue vest she wore over her breeches she didn't see Cassia Argarys, Princess of Ilahara, daughter of Aerella, but Cassia Farwynd, wife of Baramun. Her future self, unhappy and unloved. The dark circles under her eyes dulled the silver in them. Two days had passed since she learned of the betrothal, and every miserable second slowly poisoned her.

Cassia loved her life, but at that moment she desired to be someone else.

Derron would damn the consequences and fight his mother if he were here because his love for Cassia made him stupidly brave. A similar sentiment saw him return to Lur even after they'd endured Aerella's wrath. She wished she were that brave and strong.

Derron was being forced into a marriage, too, but he'd marry Eileen—kind, smart, beautiful Eileen. He might not love her now, but he could learn to. Gods knew he already cared for her. That would never happen with Baramun, who'd only ever acknowledged Cassia's beauty and title. He never asked for her opinion or showed any interest beyond her cleavage.

Derron had it easy. He would marry Eileen. He would be king.

What would it be like to walk in her brother's shoes?

Cassia stared at her reflection and imagined her shoulders broadening and her hair shortening ever so slightly. She pictured a jaw that would be more angular and clean-shaven. Her eyes would hide a trace of regret only those who knew her well could see, and her heart would beat to the rhythm of duty, honor, and love.

For a moment, she imagined to be Derron.

A gasp came from her bedroom door. Cassia turned to face Eileen, whose brown eyes brimmed with tears. She clamped a hand to her chest as if to keep her heart from jumping out. "Derron?"

Cassia smiled. Eileen blushed and then frowned a

moment later.

"Cassia."

Cassia couldn't help a triumphant giggle. She turned back to the mirror out of habit but saw only her reflection.

"Drop the glamour."

Cassia sighed and let go of the illusion she'd crafted. Glamours were complicated magic and required the sort of concentration and patience not many possessed. Those who used them generally altered only small details to avoid dispensing too much energy. "What gave it away?"

"The smile." Eileen considered Cassia's clothes. "Going somewhere?"

"Is this a truce?" Ever since Cassia's first day of the Bleeding, Eileen had kept her at arm's length and ignored Cassia when she spoke. She averted her gaze when the princess tried to make eye contact and found any excuse not to see her.

Cassia was on her sixth day of the Bleeding.

Eileen closed the door with a gentle click, eyes downcast when she took a seat on Cassia's bed. Her fingers grazed the shimmering gown, but she remained silent.

"Did you come here to apologize?"

Eileen's brows shot up. "Apologize?" She looked like she was going to strangle Cassia. "I have nothing to apologize for."

Cassia slumped next to her friend. "I don't want to fight."

Eileen seemed to soften and she patted her friend's hand. "What's wrong?" she asked. "Is it the Bleeding? Does it still hurt?"

"Not so much anymore. It'll be over soon."

"Then what is it?"

Cassia glanced at the dress, dreading the thought of wearing it but having no other choice.

A beautiful cage.

White orchids and lavenders decorated the great hall. Both plants were common in Adara, especially the lavender, whose color turned fields into oceans of purple. They symbolized love and devotion, and every long table was embellished with the cursed things. Cassia loathed the look and smell of them. She loathed the already-speculating nobles sitting at the tables, the sounds of silverware as plates were served and drinks were poured, the bustle of servants as they masterfully spun around the tables. She spotted Lady Maree Louvas holding one of the flowers with her fingers, aware of their meaning as much as Cassia. Her eyes were bright as she chattered with her friends.

Cassia preferred roses.

She and Eileen made their way to the table on the dais. Vaemor and Semal sat on either side of the queen. Cassia's father inclined his head to them, a goblet of wine already in hand. Semal reserved a warm smile for them. Cassia's eyes settled on her mother, whose gaze directed her to her seat.

Beside High Keeper Baramun.

A servant appeared as if summoned and showed Eileen to a seat at the opposite side of the table beside the king. Her friend turned to Cassia in confusion as the princess begrudgingly sat by the high keeper's side. She fixed her attention on the hall.

"You're exquisite today, my beloved."

"I'm not your wife yet."

Baramun chuckled. He plucked an orchid from the centerpiece in front of them and offered it to her. "Soon."

Cassia considered burning the flower instead.

"Princess." Korban stood in the space between her and Baramun as he served her. "We were worried the food would go cold before you arrived."

Beside her, Semal watched with an expression of admonishment and the high keeper curled his nose. "You dare speak to the princess, human?"

Cassia called upon every bit of self-control to refrain from slamming her fist on the table. "I don't need coddling, Your Holiness. The boy merely made an observation." She turned to Korban, whose smile was warm with mirth. Gods knew what possessed him to be this reckless. "You may leave us."

He nodded, but his smile wavered.

It's better this way.

Cassia was all too aware of the knowing look in Semal's good eye. She implored him to let it go with a sidelong glance. There was no need for the queen to know about her human lover now that it wouldn't matter. She was going to end it with Korban as she'd done with Johan.

The queen stood, chalice in hand. All eyes turned, drawn to the powerful woman in the beautiful silver gown. "Friends," she intoned. "The five gods smile on us today."

At her table, Lady Maree Louvas exchanged an excited look with her friends.

"We celebrate a blessed union between two great Houses of Ilahara."

A collective gasp rippled through the crowd.

The queen turned to the princess and the high keeper. Baramun stood, but even though her mother's glare burned into her, Cassia maintained a rare moment of rebellion and remained seated.

Baramun commanded the attention of the crowd now. The high keeper in front of his flock. "I have formally asked for Princess Cassia's hand in marriage." He took her hand, a gesture that awed the crowd, but they couldn't feel the grip of his fingers as he forced her to stand. Cassia plastered on a venomous smile, but it didn't hinder her betrothed's malicious grin as he gazed down at her. "And she has accepted."

Clapping and cheering drowned out the sound of silverware clattering to the floor at the end of the hall. Cassia searched for the source of that noise, but Baramun forced her eyes to his.

She jerked away from his touch.

"There must be something we can say to appeal to the queen." Eileen sat on Cassia's bed while the princess paced. Both still wore the gowns from the feast. Her friend ushered her away the moment the banquet was over and before anyone could congratulate her on the unwanted engagement.

"All my mother cares about is power and allies. She was clear on her thoughts regarding Baramun. The marriage will happen, whether I want it or not." Cassia sat at her vanity and refused to look in the mirror lest she see her tear-glazed silver eyes. "I've been intended for a foreign lord all along. I just wish..." A sob threatened to overwhelm her, so she refused to speak until she was in control again.

"That Tyrra forged this alliance and not Makkan?" Eileen finished.

Damn her emotions. Cassia couldn't stop the tears from falling down her cheeks. What would Johan think once he heard of this arrangement with the Farwynd? She'd left him out of duty to her family, unaware her mother had disregarded tradition long ago.

Show your power, hide your heart. Ironically, Cassia clung to her mother's words in order to find her center. Crying wouldn't fix things.

"Talk to her, Cassia." Before she could protest, Eileen held up a finger to silence her. "Perhaps one could argue the wisdom of this choice. Have you seen the nobles when the announcement was made?"

"I heard a lot of cheering."

"Yet some of the lords didn't seem too happy about the arrangement," Eileen observed. "One of them was supposed to be your husband."

"She can't risk losing Makkan."

"She can't risk angering the Adarian nobility, either."

They spent the rest of the day hidden behind the safety of Cassia's walls. Eileen left to grab a book from her room, a scandalous romance a proper lady shouldn't read. Her friend had a thoughtful word for everyone, even the servants, and they returned her kindness by providing the foulest reading material from the city. The story distracted them both, but when exhaustion claimed Eileen, Cassia was alone with her thoughts once more. They had several hours before sunset, but Eileen already slept like the dead.

Speaking to her mother was a lost cause, yet Cassia decided to follow her friend's advice. She tiptoed out of the room, determined not to wake Eileen, and headed for the queen's chambers. The hallways were devoid of the usual bustle of courtiers and servants, which meant the queen either rested or held an important audience. It didn't stop Cassia. Once she was in front of her mother's door, she raised her fist to knock when her attention was drawn by an unfamiliar voice from inside.

"The sirens never lie, Your Majesty."

Cassia chanced to open the door a sliver. The queen sat at her armchair with Semal beside her, and Vaemor leaned over a basin out of which came the voice she'd heard. The voice didn't belong to a stranger, but to the Head of Eathelin, Andren Nahar. This form of communication was exclusive to those with the Song. Their voices carried through Ilahein water as long as another with the same ability was there to listen. Derron should have let them know of his return in the same way.

Her mother gripped the armrests of her chair. Semal

spoke beside her. *If a dragon was seen, it means she's here.*

"And that Derron failed," the queen said, her low voice grating against Cassia's ears.

Cassia drew back, heart pounding and ears ringing. *A dragon in Ilahara. Derron failed.* If Asharaya was alive, it could only mean...

Vaemor made a frustrated noise akin to a growl. "What of my son, Nahar?"

Cassia pressed her ear to the door in hopes of hearing the conversation over the roar of her own blood.

"The prince is alive. He's on his way to Merania as we speak. The young Todrak and your bastard are with him."

Cassia sagged with relief. Derron was alive.

"I want that traitor's spawn questioned," the queen spat. "If they've harmed a hair on my son's head, gods be my witness, I'll bathe Daganver in fire. I want Asharaya found, Nahar. I want her found and I want her dead."

"As you command."

I'll send missives to our men along the coast, Semal said. *Every ship will converge on Eathelin. We'll find her.*

Before Semal could spot her, Cassia hurried away from the door. Asharaya was in Ilahara, and a dragon had returned for that reason alone. What would happen if she were given the chance to raise an army against them? Would more dragons leave the Burning Sea for their beloved Myrassar?

What had happened in Havanya that made Derron fail? He'd reassured Cassia of his loyalty to the family. Even with her probing, he'd made it clear his feelings for the Myrassar wouldn't prevail over his duty. Derron wouldn't betray them.

Someone grabbed Cassia's arm and forced her around the corner. She didn't scream, but Fire simmered beneath her skin.

"It's me," Korban hastened to say before she could summon it.

Cassia tore out of his hold. "Are you out of your mind?"

"You can't marry him."

"Someone could see us." The halls were deserted, though Semal could be headed this way for all Cassia knew, and if not, anyone—a servant, a noble—could see them. Any door could open and spell their doom.

Korban caged her against the wall, arms raised on either side of her. "Is that why you've been acting so strange? You wanted to push me away?"

Cassia nudged him back. "I have bigger things to worry about, Korban. We'll talk when we're not in the middle of a hallway."

She made to leave, but Korban grabbed her wrist. "I know you're a princess and I'm a servant, but you know that what we have isn't just sex. Cassia, I love you, and you love me."

Cassia's heart lodged somewhere between her chest and throat. "You can't say that."

Korban leaned in closer, the magnetism of his furious gray eyes rooting her to the spot. "You say it with every kiss and every touch. Deny it all you want, but I know it's true." He took her hand in his. "I know you don't love the high keeper."

"Of course I don't love him."

"Run away with me."

"What?"

Korban silenced her with a desperate crush of his lips against hers. Cassia's body reacted out of instinct. She drew him closer, tongue sweeping the bridge of his mouth while her hand fisted the fabric of his shirt. Their breaths resonated in the darkening hallway.

Cassia shoved Korban away with a gasp. His mouth was swollen, and hers likely looked as damning. "Now isn't the time. Leave. Before we're seen."

"Tonight. Get rid of Lady Eileen."

"Have you been in my room?"

Korban winked and stole one last kiss. Cassia forced her gaze away from his retreating figure. Fantasies of keeping him in her life would have to end. If the high keeper had nearly bitten his head off for speaking to her, he'd be merciless if he found Korban in her bed.

The sound of hurried footsteps made Cassia's stomach drop.

The princess rounded the corner, but the hall was deserted. "Who's there?"

No answer came, and Cassia breathed in to banish the cold grip of terror that seized her.

It was my imagination.

Or so she hoped.

34

Hours blurred in a monotonous flow, but every second aggravated Mykal's tension. While Raxan Nahar and his merfolk ushered the *No One* toward Merania with a relentless pace, Mykal often turned to the sky. Gone were the traces of the storm from the previous night. Clouds chased one another like cotton rolling in a field of blue.

Some of the merfolk separated from the group on Raxan's orders. Mykal followed them as long as he could, a coil of nerves taking residence in his stomach. He'd bet they'd scout for Asharaya on the same archipelagos he and Kael had singled out with Captain Xoro, before the kiss that still had his knees shaking.

Only hours ago, he'd been kissing Kael, and now he was trapped on this blasted ship, the hostage of fae he didn't trust and forced to the uncomfortable vicinity of a man he loathed. To make matters worse, he'd lost the princess and Derron Argarys was free once more. Derron Argarys, whose lies in their favor were the only reason he and Kael weren't in chains.

Yet.

Mykal squashed any feeling of gratitude with a healthy dose of suspicion. The fact Argarys hadn't betrayed them now didn't mean he wouldn't do it later. Perhaps the usurper prince was waiting for them to reach land. That way he could personally present their heads to his mother and deny the Nahar the pleasure. Or maybe this was a devious conspiracy. Mykal could only guess at the content of the long conversation between Argarys and Raxan following the *No One*'s capture. Mykal might have once been foolish enough to believe Raxan would protect him, if only because of their history. Now, he knew better. The general would always choose the glory of Merania over love or friendship.

Mykal released a tired breath, his eyes heavy from lack of sleep. He wished he put a blade through Derron Argarys when he had the chance or at the very least to go back a few hours and kiss Kael once more.

Raxan Nahar had terrible timing.

He gazed up, hoping and dreading to see the dragon's dark shadow etched against the blue of the sky. Mykal doubted the merfolks' search would bear any fruit. The dragons roamed Ilahara long before the fae and knew the land better than they ever would. If there was one thing Mykal was certain of, it was Asharaya's safety.

What would Asharaya do now that she'd found her dragon?

She could fly back to Havanya. Farther, if she felt daring and adventurous. Maybe she'd go to Adara. From the little he knew of her, Asharaya would be capable of something that rash. After all, she'd made it clear she had no interest in her birthright. Mykal wasn't fooling himself into believing she stuck around for anything but revenge.

Bitterness coated Mykal's tongue, and his thoughts

went, inevitably, to Daganver. He hadn't dared ponder what happened to his family after he and Kael left, but stuck on this ship it was all he could do. If Aerella set a perimeter along the entire coast to imprison them, she had most likely taken measures against Daganver. The thought of his family in danger made shivers rake his spine. For a moment, he flirted with the hope that Asharaya left and that Argarys continued to lie. Without the last Myrassar, there were no charges against him and Kael and no reason to punish Daganver.

Shame heated Mykal's skin soon after. His father knew the risks, and still, he'd sent them to find Asharaya. Mykal couldn't disappoint him. He'd find a way out of Merania, he'd find Asharaya, and he'd find a way back to his family.

The sun had yet to set when the No One entered Merania. Bathed in golden evening light, the city was unlike any in Ilahara. Above the surface, it was barely an island. Large, towering bridges of blue-gray stone connected the mainland to smaller isles. Barnacles grew along the structure in bright coral, green, and gold shades. The palace, which occupied the centermost position, was a lavish display of wealth erected in blue, white, and purple stone. It rose directly from the sea, the façade an intricate and harmonious alternating of gilded balustrades and elegant archways. The archways narrowed toward the top, where domes were fashioned into ivory oyster shapes. The ocean's hues speckled everywhere one looked, summoning the impression of seashells and precious pearls, along with the magnificent bursts of color from the sea creatures and sirens who dwelled beneath the waters.

A few years had passed since Mykal last visited Eathelin's capital. The first time he'd seen it the city's beauty had stunned him into silence, but none of its wonders stole his breath quite like the general who now came to stand at his side. Mykal remembered the secret stroke of Raxan's fingers and the way he'd stood behind him, lifting both their hands to point out the beauties of his home. "Welcome back to Merania," Raxan said.

Mykal didn't acknowledge him and refused to let Raxan catch him remembering their hot and brief time together. At eighteen, Mykal's heart had been too wild to know who or what it wanted. At that time, the Head of Eathelin had been Rasaq Nahar, Andren's father. Though he hadn't been among those to openly oppose Aerella, the former Head hadn't been her most fervent supporter either. He'd been on amicable terms with Mykal's father until he met an untimely end. A stroke, they said, come suspiciously soon after the lord once again refused the Crown's order to have a temple built to Oceana, the Pentagod Creed's goddess of Water and mother of beauty and grace.

The temple had been built once his son, Andren, took his place.

Raxan released a tired breath. "You sure know how to hold a grudge. Myk, what happened with the half-breed was a foolish mistake."

"It's Mykal to you," Mykal said through clenched teeth. "And he has a name."

"He punched me in the face. Isn't that punishment enough?"

"Only your conscience can dictate if you regret assuming there was anything consensual in Kael's conception."

Shame, however fleeting, crossed the man's face. "You know I do." There was a time when Raxan's soft voice would have made Mykal's toes curl in his boots, but now Mykal wondered if the shame and tone weren't part of an act—a means to soften and seduce him. Merfolk and sirens weren't so different, after all. Love was nothing but another hunt.

"A few good fucks and some pretty lies aren't enough to know anything about you." Mykal willed frost into his gaze.

Raxan leaned closer. "I'm not your enemy."

"Nor are you my friend." Mykal moved away. "Therefore, I don't trust you."

He strode to the forecastle deck, where Kael stood beside the bowsprit watching the city. His Do'strath stood like a statue before the sea. Wind weaved through the waves of his pale hair. Hair Mykal had touched.

It was the first time they were alone, or as alone as they could be, since the kiss. Mykal awkwardly stuck his hands in his pockets and then tugged at the bond to alert Kael of his approach. "Is Argarys back in the cabin?"

"He's resting, and Xoro has returned to Solana's bedside." A muscle feathered in Kael's jaw. "Nahar is still playing his old tricks."

A delighted chill frosted Mykal's blood. "It's a shame I seem to have misplaced my appreciation for darker manes."

Kael struggled to hide his amusement. "A shame."

They took one of the smaller waterways leading from the open sea to the palace. The palace loomed ever closer, and from his vantage point, Mykal glimpsed the open gates, where ships sailed in and out.

Guards were placed at either side of the gates. Their lower bodies were below water, while on their upper halves they wore silver and gold breastplates that left their lower abdomen bare. Each of them wielded a lance fashioned into a siren with open arms on the end closest to the sharp blade. The guards crossed their weapons above their hearts at Raxan's passage.

"Welcome back, General Raxan," one said.

The general nodded in greeting. "Close the gates. No one goes in or out."

Outside the palace was all bright colors, but inside darkness enveloped the walls and humidity tainted the air like the interior of a cave. The only light came from the few torches against the walls, those too fashioned into sirens. The eerie blue glow reminded Mykal of the Siren Coves and the thought nauseated him.

"Myk." Kael's eyes flicked to the water. Mykal sidled closer. The blurred shadows of beautiful bodies were visible yet there was no mistaking the colors of their tails. Whether it was sirens or mermaids, Mykal couldn't easily tell, but his hand drifted to the sword at his side as a precaution.

The stream continued on for several miles. At the end was a dark dais made of stone, darker where water lapped against it, on which the Head of Eathelin waited, surrounded by his personal guard. As if summoned from one of Mykal's worst nightmares, Derron Argarys came to stand beside Kael to assess the approaching dais. "Let me do the talking," he whispered.

Mykal tsked.

"Your Highness." Andren Nahar stepped forward as the *No One* came to a halt. His white robe was the same color as his long, straight hair. The blue accents woven across the collar offset the cerulean of his eyes. The Head of Eathelin was no warrior, but his body was lean, lightly muscled, and beautiful. A crown of seashells and seaweed rested upon his head. When Argarys stepped onto the dais, Andren bent low in a graceful bow, his guards following suit. "Welcome to Merania."

"I wish it were on more favorable terms," Argarys said. "Rise."

Mykal schooled his features into neutrality, but he couldn't help the twitch of his eyebrow once the Head finished his groveling and finally acknowledged him. "Lord Mykal, it's good to see you again."

"The feeling isn't mutual, Lord Andren, I assure you." Mykal flicked a challenging gaze to Argarys, who gritted his teeth. "In Daganver, we don't arrest our acquaintances based on mere speculation."

Lord Andren's smile was similar to a shark's. "I've always admired the candor of our northern neighbors." He looked to Raxan, who now stood at his right. "Speculation it may be, but your timing is uncanny, dear friend. I have it on good authority that a raven with disturbing news was dispatched from the Embernest, and not long after you and your companion went missing. When questioned, Lord Darrok refused to answer. Now a dragon has returned to Ilahara, and you were found not far from where it was spotted. I'm not one to believe in coincidences."

Mykal's hands balled into fists. How he wished to wipe the shark's smile off the lord's face. "Odd words from someone who gained plenty from a coincidence."

Beside him, Kael groaned. Raxan's eyes widened a fraction.

Lord Andren's smile vanished.

"Perhaps my father has grown weary of being doubted at every turn," Mykal added after a beat of uncomfortable silence.

Argarys shot him a withering glare. "Lord Mykal and his friend are traveling with me."

"His friend, who is also your brother." Lord Andren surveyed the two silver-blond men. "The resemblance is staggering."

"Half-brother," Argarys corrected, his tone clipped. "And I don't see how it is relevant."

"Don't you?" Lord Andren's amusement returned. His beautiful, cunning smile made Mykal's hackles rise. "It is noble to lie for family."

"Are you calling your prince a liar?" Argarys inquired.

Raxan leaned toward his cousin, taking care to

turn away so none present could read his lips. Mykal straightened his spine. Despite himself, his gaze latched onto the Head of Eathelin. Nahar's expression changed at whatever his cousin murmured. Those uncommonly bright eyes flashed and the shark's smile returned. Warning bells chimed in Mykal's head. Instinct urged him to summon his Ice, though he needed to hold on to reason. A weapon, be it made of iron or Ice, would reveal he had something to hide.

Andren's gaze settled onto Argarys. As Raxan leaned back, the Head of Eathelin widened his arms with an elegant flourish and offered his prince a reverential bow. "I would never doubt your word, Your Highness. I meant no offense," he said, sensuous lips curled at the corner. "Though I must ask, what has become of the last Myrassar?"

"I never found her."

Kael and Mykal dared to acknowledge their surprise only down the bridge connecting their souls. Once again, the chill trickle of Mykal's Ice begged to be unleashed against an unseen threat. He glanced between the Argarys prince and the Head of Eathelin, searching for a rational explanation to this unexpected turn of events. Were this anyone else, Mykal could have believed Argarys had a change of heart for Kael's benefit. He would have struggled with the idea, but he could have tried. But this was Argarys. On her own, Asharaya would have posed a threat to his family's legacy, but now that she was reunited with her dragon, the symbol of her family's power, the crone's prophecy was one step closer to being fulfilled. Were Mykal in Argarys's position, he doubted two weeks spent with a brother he hardly knew would be enough to jeopardize his family's survival.

"The vision was false?" Andren Nahar's shock didn't hinder the maniacal gleam in his eyes, and it rolled over Mykal's suspicion like oil. "But what of the dragon?"

"Asharaya might be aware we're searching for her. If she truly is alive, it's only a matter of time until we find her." Argarys turned to look at the *No One*. The men were gathered on deck, watching the exchange with bated breath. "There is still the matter of the sirens attacking me and destroying my ship, Lord Andren. These fine sailors were chosen for their discretion, not to be dinner."

Raxan nodded. "The humans will be taken care of. We'll provide them with the necessities to repair their vessel and return from whence they came. I'll personally escort you back to Adara."

"There is a young woman in need of a physician," Argarys continued. "She went through a great ordeal."

Lord Andren spread his arms, benevolent. "We'll see that she's given appropriate accommodations."

Argarys looked to Kael and Mykal. "And what of my travel companions?"

Raxan shot his cousin an expectant look. If Mykal didn't know better, he might believe the scoundrel held his breath.

Andren Nahar stared right into Mykal's eyes as he said, "Only the best rooms for our noble guests from Daganver."

35

Shara waited beside Deimok until the *No One* became a speck in the distance and not a moment longer. She had perhaps five or six hours before it would be dark enough to use the Maiden's gifts, and there was much to plan.

"I'm going to need a shirt."

There is a shipwreck on the beach. Perhaps you will find one there.

No sooner had she relieved herself than she trod down the cliff. Now that the Meranians were gone, the birds seemed to have relaxed and chirped a happy tune. Their notes turned shrill whenever Shara nudged a fern leaf too close to their nests. Deimok lumbered quietly by her side. His tension skittered down their soulbond, and it was a surprise after so many years alone with her own emotions and thoughts.

Deimok wanted to fly to Adara. He didn't understand why Shara would risk capture in Merania. Emotions like rage, suspicion, and greed came easiest to a dragon.

Selflessness was reserved for those they deemed worthy of their fiery hearts. But Shara was certain that if Deimok knew Solana and the value of her presence and guidance, and if he knew the Do'strath and how much they'd already risked for the Dragon-Blessed dynasty, he wouldn't turn his back on them. Perhaps Shara could help him understand.

Tell me what happened. He paused, and Shara felt her pulse quicken alongside Deimok's. *After I died.*

Shara grasped the dragon and the ring hanging about her neck, drifting back to that terrible night. "I stayed with you until I heard voices and then I searched for somewhere to hide. It was hard to keep my wits about me after... well, you know." Her voice lowered to a whisper, and her father's ring dug into her skin as she held on tighter. The copper tang of blood seemed to surface from the memory and coated the freshness of the ocean breeze.

Now that she and Deimok were reunited, she felt her family's loss even more keenly. Shara wished her father were here to teach her to wield Fire. She wished she could bicker with Elon about how she was a terrible lady and he a terrible dragon rider. She wished her mother were here to brush her hair at the end of the day and to try teaching her, even if it was hopeless, how to behave like a princess. Shara didn't miss the grandeur of court life, but she missed those simple moments.

She didn't realize tears dripped down her cheeks until Deimok's breath caressed her fingers and his warm scales met her skin. "I found a girl not far from where we fell," she continued. "I don't know who she was. Maybe a servant or a low fae. Some strands of her hair hadn't burned. It was brown like mine. I don't know why I did it, but I thought maybe they would think it was me, so I dropped my hairpin beside her and kept running.

"At some point, I reached the docks. People were running, screaming...no one paid attention to me except one man." Shara couldn't remember much about him. The weeks between the Coup of Fire and her arrival in Havanya blurred, and the face of her savior had been lost in the sea of grief that nearly destroyed her. Some details lingered in her memory—the curve of round, human ears and the unusual purple of the man's hair. "I don't know why he helped me. We were only together for some minutes and I was too shocked to ask questions. He put me on a ship and told me to stay hidden. I did as he said. I stole food and water from the hold when I was alone and hid whenever anyone came down. The ship made port in Havanya, and that's where I met Solana."

Deimok listened as Shara told him of the vrah and the dark goddess they worshipped and of the family she'd found in those incensed hallways coated in blood. Her voice hitched when she spoke of Rami, but instead of hiding from the pain of his loss, Shara pushed through it. Her dragon had already seen too much death, and Shara wouldn't burden him with more. Instead, she told him of how she disliked Rami when they'd been younger and that they'd competed to be the deadliest vrah. She told him of the smile that had won her over growing up and how it irritated her whenever Rami looked through her sketchbooks. The memories brought fresh tears to her eyes, but for the first time, Shara could think about Rami with a smile. She could imagine his face and not the burning body he'd been in his last moments. With Deimok by her side, facing her grief was not as terrifying.

Confusion spiked down the bond when Shara made mention of the Maiden's gifts, so unlike the elemental magic and shifting abilities granted by the Ilah. When Shara had no more words to bridge the fourteen-year gap between them, she felt bare, as if the dragon were seeing her for the first time. Shara wasn't sure Deimok understood all of it, but it warmed her heart that he tried.

You plan to use this Maiden's gifts to save the human and the Do'strath, Deimok said as they reached the beach.

Shara smiled. "That's only part of the plan."

Judging by the amount of rot on the wooden panels, the shipwreck washed ashore upon the golden sand had been there for some time. The vessel was small, and perhaps the property of merchants. A gaping hole in its flank, most likely caused by the impact with the rocks, made the old structure even more fragile. With Deimok's help, Shara hoisted herself onto the battered deck. She sent a silent prayer to the Dragon and the Maiden each time the wood creaked and groaned as she scanned the space in search of human remains. There were none. Nausea gripped Shara's empty stomach. Nothing would remain of the men the *No One* had lost either.

Shara found what must have been the captain's cabin. From a splintered armoire, she extracted a white shirt too large for her build. She tucked it into her leather britches, but the neckline drooped over her shoulder, exposing it. It would have to do.

She returned to the beach and told Deimok her plan.

It is reckless, he protested.

"It's the only plan we have."

I will not let you enter an enemy stronghold on your own.

"You're too big to come along, and if we start raining fire on Merania, we'll only put my friends in more danger than they're already in. My way is better. If everything goes to plan, I'll be in and out before anyone notices."

Deimok made a sound of frustration.

Hours bled together in a flurry of plotting and compromising. It took some time, but Deimok agreed to Shara's plan on two conditions: Shara must let him intervene should things go sour and she must wear a glamour around her eyes to hide the gold.

Both conditions unnerved her. Shara's attention returned time and again to the scars scattered across Deimok's body and her muscles tensed at the memory of Aerella's arrows. Should Derron or Merania's Head plan to use her friends as bait to lure her, they'd expect her dragon. Deimok was strong, but he wasn't invincible, and Shara was unwilling to risk him when she had an alternative. It was crucial that her plan work.

Then there was the matter of the glamour. Shara's repeated failure to conjure one caused shame to rise in a heated column along her neck. The child Deimok had known was precocious and confident when it came to magic, but if her new incapacity irked the dragon, he didn't show it. It wasn't until Shara began viewing the glamour like a painting that she finally grasped its mechanism. Her body was the canvas and her magic the brush. She visualized her face and the rich gold of her eyes and mixed colors to subdue it. The possibilities were endless, but she chose a warm hazel since the browns and greens allowed splotches of gold to peek through. It would be easier to hold for a longer time given its simplicity, yet Shara still felt a constant, slow drain the moment it settled into place.

As she practiced, darkness descended like ink spilled on parchment. The clear blue of the sky darkened into plum, and Shara finally could enact her plan, though its faults struck her now that it was time to set it into motion. She had no weapons outside the five daggers strapped to her belt and the little Fire that had replenished after the siren attack, which she would have to avoid using to conceal her identity. Shara would be alone in unfamiliar territory with no one to guard her back. Should her glamour fade and someone recognize her golden eyes, it was hard to say what would happen.

Shara stroked the hilt of a dagger.

You can still change your mind. Deimok looked at her hand from where he crouched. The speed with which he'd noticed her nervous tick was astounding. Amusement sparkled in his fiery eyes as he waited for her to mount.

Shara narrowed her eyes, her answer being the determined press of her foot against the wing the dragon offered. Her breath caught as she settled between the powerful muscles of Deimok's shoulders. A vibration similar to a purr thrummed against her fingers as she stroked the rough scales of his neck. Exhilaration echoed through the soulbond, both dragon and rider anxious for their first flight in fourteen years. As a child, she'd needed a saddle to ride him, and though having one now would have been preferable, her adult body molded to the dragon as if made for it.

Shara's fingers curled around the red ridges snaking along the back of Deimok's neck. Her muscles tightened for purchase and her heart pounded in her ears. "Bring me the stars," she whispered, and without hesitation, Deimok propelled them off the cliff.

As they plummeted and Deimok lifted into the air, Shara's stomach dropped and then leaped into her throat. Laughter bubbled from her lips as wind whipped her face, and the chilly air embraced her on all sides. The stars quivered at each thrust of Deimok's wings, shying away from Ilahara's mightiest beast and the young woman he'd bound his soul to. Shara's blood turned to molten fire. She was a goddess of the night, the touch of her finger powerful enough to alter constellations. Suspended with her dragon's warmth between her thighs and his powerful muscles flexing beneath her, she was invincible. Untouchable.

For a blissful half-hour, her every woe was far away.

Shara's mind plunged back into her mission at hand when they glimpsed a ship.

Indigo clouds offered cover from indiscreet eyes, and Shara leaned over Deimok's neck as he slowed his flight to silence the sound of his wings. The men on deck seemed like tiny ants scurrying about, though from her altitude it was hard to tell how many they were. From the looks of it, this ship was likely a merchant vessel delivering goods to the city.

Shara's gaze narrowed on the crow's nest as she asked down the bond, *How far from Merania do you reckon we are?*

Deimok suppressed a guttural grumble. *Judging from the ship's speed, I would say several hours. Two, perhaps three.*

That would get her to Merania by sunset. She would have more than enough hours of darkness at her disposal.

We would reach your friends with more haste if I flew you there myself, Deimok argued.

We can't risk you being seen, Shara retorted and drew a dagger from her belt.

She pressed the steel to her palm and cut deep. Blood bloomed crimson on her amber skin. In Havanya, a drop would have been enough, but in Ilahara her body healed too fast. Deimok lurched at the smell of Shara's blood, nostrils flared. Panic seized him for a fleeting moment.

It's all right, Deimok. Shara held out her hand and squeezed her fist. She grimaced through the pain as blood dripped into the open space.

Darkness unfurled like a rip in the fabric of the sky.

Her pulse quickened in response to Deimok's surprise.

I know what I'm doing, Shara reassured him. *I'll be fine.*

Be careful, Asharaya.

Shara leaned forward to kiss his scales. *Same to you.*

Before he could change his mind, she leaned into the darkness and let herself fall.

Wind roared in her ears, and Shara bit down on her lip to keep from screaming, blood coating her tongue. The pull of gravity and the spike of fear that came with it lasted only a handful of seconds. Once her body faded into the void, she felt suspended in time and space. Colors bled away and the world narrowed into shadows. Shara could make out the ship's shape reflected on the water's surface, the men moving along the deck, and the dark lines cast by the rigging and the masts.

A man's shadow elongated against the wood of the crow's nest.

Shara drifted toward it, her weightless body like a leaf dragged along by a stream's current.

An invisible hand braced the dagger's hilt as the shadow shifted. The man to whom it belonged turned his back to her, unaware of the predator lurking in the dark.

Shara sprung from the darkness. Before the man could raise an alarm, her bloodied hand clasped his mouth and her blade slit his neck from side to side. Blood gurgled from the wound. Drops of it spurted back against Shara's face. He grasped her arm, fighting with his last breaths to claw his way to freedom. As he spasmed, Shara noticed the pointed tip of his ears.

Let him live, he will heal, a voice like her mother's said.

If she listened, and the fae healed before the ship reached Merania, she would be discovered.

He's fae. He's one of us, Asharaya. These are your people, one sounding like her father pressed on.

Shara clenched her teeth and plunged her dagger into the man's heart.

His body stilled instantly, and Shara eased him to the ground. He had no weapons on him. This man hadn't expected a threat so close to their destination, away from the open sea and the clutches of pirates and sirens alike. He'd only been doing his job.

He was innocent, unlike the countless lives she'd taken in the Maiden's name.

She crouched to stay out of view as blood pooled around the dead body and spread toward her. The man's eyes were still wide in shock, and she felt their judgment.

It was necessary, she reminded herself. The quickest way to enter Merania was to hide on a ship headed into the city. Her friends and her sister needed her.

Shara cradled her knees to her chest.

It had to be done.

36

Afters the surprise encounter with Korban in the hallway, Cassia ran back to her room, where Eileen still slept. Hands trembling, the princess shook her friend awake to tell her everything she'd overheard from the queen's quarters. A dragon had flown close to Merania, and Derron was on his way there on a ship with Mykal Todrak and his friend.

Arkael. Her half-brother.

Cassia had seen him only once, on Eileen's sixteenth birthday, yet his face remained seared in her memory. He and Derron shared the same sharp, handsome face and a warrior's lithe build, but the freckles, the blue eyes, and the fuller lips didn't belong to the Argarys. They belonged to a human woman, somewhere in the North. A woman who must have been beautiful.

A woman who'd suffered her wretched father's urges.

Eileen's bright smile cast aside thoughts of Arkael. "Derron is back in Ilahara."

"Did you not hear what I said? He failed."

"But he's back. Aren't you happy?"

"Yes, I'm happy, but that's not the point." Cassia straightened away from the bed and stared incredulously at her friend. "Derron wouldn't betray us," she said with more vehemence than she'd intended, rejecting the doubt slithering through her heart. "His affections for the Myrassar are a thing of the past. We are what matters—his family."

Eileen arched a brow. "Your point?"

"My point is that if he failed in his task, then something must have gotten in his way. Or someone."

Eileen's expression turned somber. "My brother?"

Cassia crossed her arms and nodded. "Nahar said Derron was alive, but nothing more. He might be injured, or they might have tortured him."

"Mykal wouldn't."

"You don't know your brother."

Eileen flinched. She stood and kept her gaze downcast as she shouldered past Cassia and stormed into the living room.

"Eileen." Cassia snatched the book from the foot of the bed and raced after her. She extended it as a peace offering. "It's only the truth."

Eileen stopped her trembling lip by clenching her jaw. Ice hardened her sorrowful eyes. "The truth hurts, Cassia, and you wield it like a blade."

"I didn't mean to."

Eileen yanked the book from her hands and avoided Cassia's confused gaze as she strode to the door. She gripped the handle, voice steady as she said, "I know it in my heart that Derron is safe, and it's not my wishful thinking or my love speaking for me." She spun to face Cassia, eyes shining fiercely in the light. "I might not know my brother, but he's my blood. He's a Todrak, and we're not animals."

Unsure of what to say, Cassia remained quiet and stared after her friend as she left her quarters. Lately, she was often at a loss for words with Eileen. Their problems began the moment the seer prophesized Asharaya Myrassar's return. Eileen was defensive, sometimes distant, and her attitude reminded them both that they were friends because Eileen was a hostage.

Because Eileen's family was dangerous.

When she felt like she was going mad in the hollow silence of her quarters, Cassia withdrew to the gardens. She was alone, but it would have been the same if courtiers had surrounded her. Loneliness sank its roots inside her, festering. Derron was away, Eileen grew more impatient by the day, and her mother wouldn't listen. Cassia's only solace was Korban, a forbidden fruit she'd have to give up before his recklessness got him into trouble.

She sat at a bench nearby a bush of white roses. The flower reminded her of blissful days in Tyrra, a time in which she'd known true happiness. When he'd discovered her fondness for roses, Johan ordered a rose garden planted in Heartstar, the seat of power in Tyrra. His home.

Your mother will be annoyed with me if you keep spoiling me like this, my lord.

It doesn't matter. The look in your eyes is worth every nuisance.

She's the Head of Tyrra.

And you're the queen of my heart.

Cassia lifted her fingers to her lips, tracing the shape of her smile. She leaned closer to one of the roses, eyes closed as she breathed in its sweet scent. "I wish things had been different, my love," she whispered.

The stars had come out when she decided to return to her chambers, but no sooner had she stepped inside than someone knocked on the door. A servant waited outside, head bent in deference. "My apologies, Your Highness, but I was told to give you this," she said, handing a note to the princess.

Cassia accepted it with a nod, which the girl recognized as a silent dismissal. The note was written in Vaemor's neat scrawl.

I wish to speak with you.

Father.

Perfect. Her night had taken a turn for the worse.

Crumpling her father's note, Cassia trod a path to the king's quarters. His was the only hallway of the castle not painted white but instead a blue gradient meant to honor the Meranian heritage of the king's line. The colors interacted the same way the sea and the sun did and created the illusion of walking along the coast as Cassia strode by. The king's devotion to his region of origin was perhaps the only pure emotion she'd ever seen him display.

The princess knocked on her father's door, squaring her shoulders as she always did when forced to face him. Thoughts of the beautiful woman in the North came unbidden whenever she stood in Vaemor's presence. In those moments, she struggled to be in the same room and breathe the same air as the king, wishing she could remove any trace of her father from her blood.

A human man ushered her inside. Tall, stern, and elegant, the king stood from his seat behind the desk when the servant announced his daughter. Moonlight shone in his silver-blond hair. Cassia frowned at the surprise drawn on his face. "Leave us," he ordered, and the servant took his leave without a word. "Sit, please."

Cassia obeyed, but not without a dramatic flair as she sat on the divan. With their carefully decorated rugs covering every visible inch of stone, the king's chambers weren't unlike the queen's in their opulence, though they were a tad bit smaller. The door to the sleeping quarters was open and the bed looked untouched—a rarity for the king.

An odd hopefulness lit the king's face, but Vaemor kept his distance. Cassia chose to ignore it and went straight to the point. "Since I'm here, I might as well tell you I know Derron is in Merania. I wish to speak to him."

"You were eavesdropping." A conflicting measure of admonishment and amusement resonated in the king's tone, as if he couldn't make up his mind as to what to feel or show her. "How much did you hear?"

"I heard enough." Cassia leaned back in her seat, arms crossed. "I would speak to him myself but..." She vaguely gestured to herself. "No Song." Her gift was Fire and she was glad of it. The Song made her think of her father and his entitlement in using it all those years ago, manipulating the human woman into thinking she desired his attentions.

Cassia shuddered.

"There's a blanket on the armrest if you're cold," the king said.

"Let me speak to Derron."

Vaemor's shoulders sagged. He grabbed a glass pitcher from a side table and then walked back to his desk, pouring water into the basin he kept there. Cassia walked to his side and stared into the water. She wouldn't see anything, but still she looked, foolishly waiting for her brother's face to appear.

Vaemor leaned away from the basin. "I can't feel him."

"Try harder."

"He's not nearby any source of water, Cassia."

The princess swore under her breath, pacing away from the basin.

"I'm sorry."

Cassia whirled on her father, teeth bared. "I don't need your apologies. I need to speak to my brother."

Derron alone could banish the worry and doubts

strangling her. Ever since the day the queen tasked him with Asharaya's murder, Cassia knew something horrible was going to happen. Alone, the twins faced trials they would have been better equipped to tackle together. Their mother had bartered Cassia's future for the crown while Derron fought their enemies in a foreign land. Worse, Derron had come face to face with the demons of his past and perhaps succumbed to them despite his promise. What if Asharaya lived because Derron had shown mercy? Cassia would have her chance to vanquish any suspicion once her brother returned, but until that happened the uncertainty would always be there. Patience had never been Cassia's strong suit.

Vaemor's fingers curled as if to stop himself from attempting any reassuring gesture. Cassia didn't care for the hurt in his silver eyes. She and her brother had turned their backs on their father long ago. If not for the so-called friends he invited into his chambers, the king would be alone.

"Why did you want to see me?" At the king's confused frown, Cassia produced the crumpled note still palmed in her fist. "This is your handwriting, is it not?"

Vaemor took the note, shaking his head as he read its contents. "I never wrote this."

Cassia's heart sank like a stone in a dark well. "You didn't?" Vaemor had no reason to lie about a note, which meant someone had lured her from her room.

Only one person could forge the queen's handwriting, and that of the king if need be.

"Semal," she breathed.

Cassia stormed out of her father's rooms, heedless of Vaemor's calls. Fire burned in the sconces along the walls. The halls were quiet, and the few servants minding their chores walked on quiet feet so as not to disturb the restful sleep of the fae. The sound of Cassia's hurried steps echoed in the silence. Those who still milled about turned to look at her with curious frowns. She was vaguely aware of another set of footsteps behind her—her father's.

The princess's steps slowed when she reached her corridor. A sliver of light shot across the floor from the open door of her room. She was certain she'd closed it when she left, and it couldn't have been Korban since he would have taken the tunnels.

Vaemor stopped behind her and grabbed her arm. "Cassia."

She twisted free of his grip, opening the door wider and stepping inside. Pillows were tossed carelessly on her couch, and the silver curtains were drawn to let in light. Crumpled parchments littered the wastebasket by her desk from futile efforts to write down an apology for Eileen.

Everything was exactly as Cassia had left it.

A copper tang tainted the air and froze her feet to the spot. Bile rose in her throat and caused her heart to sink even lower.

Blood.

Cassia didn't feel her feet drag her to the bedroom nor did she feel her breath rush out of her through parted lips. It was as if her body belonged to someone else and she was stuck beneath their skin, forced to witness her worst nightmare come to life.

Korban had been waiting for her as promised.

He lay in her bed. Cassia wished it would at least look like he was sleeping, but his eyes were open wide, lost into nothingness. A dull sheen already muted their luster. Blood spurted from a red line crossing his neck from side to side, spilling over his shirt and the white sheets. His rigid hands were in an awkward position as if he'd tried to pry his attacker's hands away before his throat was slit. And by someone who knew he'd be in her room. Because Korban had been reckless. Because they hadn't been careful. Because they'd been seen.

Vaemor came to stand by her side, his hand suspended in midair before he brought it to her shoulder. Cassia was stunned into stillness, oblivious to his touch.

Blood bloomed on Korban's shirt above his chest. Cassia gently lifted it and tore it open. Her stomach heaved at the sight of his ruined chest. Burn marks marred his skin. She couldn't make sense of them at first, but the longer she stared at the lines of his charred flesh, the more she understood their pattern. The burns arranged into letters and the letters into words.

A message burned onto her lover's skin.

Hide your heart.

The princess dropped to her knees and held the frays of her lover's shirt in closed fists. Her eyes roved from his ruined body to his open throat to his beautiful face stuck in an expression of horror. Korban had fought to stay alive, but it hadn't been enough.

Semal's message might have lured Cassia from her room, but this was her mother's doing. The queen's love for dramatics unfolded in the hurt inflicted on Cassia's beloved and her machinations were unveiled in the way he'd been put on display for her to find, right down to the door left ajar.

"P-please..." Cassia grabbed his hand and pressed it to her trembling lips. She couldn't accept what was right before her eyes. Her vision blurred with hot, stinging tears. "Korban, please." A sob broke out. Mere hours ago, he'd told her he loved her. "Please don't be dead."

The truth was Korban would no longer smile. There would be no more stolen glances in a crowded hall or midnight rendezvous in her room. There'd be no sneaking in the hidden tunnels. No more heat pooling in her core as he undressed her or giggles as he said something preposterous to get her back into bed.

Sorrow poured out of Cassia's cleaving chest as she gripped her lover. She cried and threw herself over his body, seeking comfort from him one last time. That comfort wouldn't come. Her heart pounded to the point of pain, her ears rang, and her throat burned. She'd never felt so much at once, not even at her happiest.

"Cassia." Vaemor made to pry her from Korban, but she bared her teeth and her grip tightened. Shadows danced in the room. Her father's face shone brightly in the light of the candle on her bedside table. The flame reached high, and then stretched toward Cassia. "You must calm down, daughter. I know it hurts, but you have to let him go."

Cassia came undone in a shattering scream. Flames burst from every pore. Fire consumed Korban within seconds and spread with alarming quickness to the bed they'd shared. It caught onto the carpet, the furniture, and the drapes. A maelstrom of red surrounded Cassia in her grief.

Vaemor stumbled away from the inferno she'd created. He tried to approach her, but the flames forced him back. The king called for help as he rushed from the room.

Cassia let free an agonized scream. She wished the fire would devour her and burn down the entire castle with everyone in it. Shouts came from outside as the flames reached the hall.

Tears and smoke fogged her vision. Cassia blindly made to grab what remained of the human who loved her, but his ashes were lost amid the ruin she'd caused.

There was nothing left of Korban.

Nothing at all.

37

Night fell over Merania as the merchant ship entered the city's waters. A chilly wind blew from the north and dragged along gray clouds, which dimmed the moon's silver light. Shara hugged her knees to her chest, breath misting as she exhaled. Her fingers were numb, and her limbs weary after hours spent crouched in the close confines of the crow's nest. The fae's blood soaked into her leather pants and froze the blood in her veins.

The disappointed echo of her parents' voices and the shocked expression forever chiseled into the stranger's face had been her constant and unwanted companions. Shara repeated her friends' names in the quiet of her thoughts—*Solana, Mykal, Kael*—to remember the reason she was here and to find peace for the innocent life she'd taken. Each drop of blood soaking her clothes also seeped through skin and bone, leaving a permanent stain on her soul.

It had to be done. Had Aerella said the same on the

night of the Coup of Fire?

The thought haunted Shara during the empty hours of her voyage. The steady beat of Deimok's heart through the soulbond and the silent prayer of her friends' names were all that kept her anchored to her task.

Merania spread before her like a beguiling painting on an artist's canvas. It was unlike anything Shara had ever seen, with its myriad of waterways and colors. The barnacles growing along the bridges glowed and the bright colors danced like living flames. The palace at the heart of the city glinted with hundreds of lights like flickering stars reflected in the ocean.

Despite her body's protests, Shara peeked over the edge of the nest to take it in. Merania couldn't have been more different from Havanya, yet the city rising from the water dragged her back to the place that had been her refuge. She replaced the shimmering palace with the bright red Keep and the fresh smells of clean water with the putrid odors she'd grown accustomed to on the Human Continent. Shara pictured the Vrahiid's kindly face and his steady gaze as he put a blade into her hand. *You will be the justice men fear*, he'd said.

Shara brushed a thumb across a dagger, her mentor's voice drowning out all other noise.

The ship docked in a harbor a short way east of the palace. From her vantage point, Shara followed the vessels circling the waterways around the palace and the shadows of merfolk who swam toward its gates. She twirled the blade between her fingers as she perused her surroundings. The vessels moored alongside were empty, their goods either stacked on the wooden landing or being unloaded from the hold. Crates were being carried off the gangplank by groups of men—low fae, judging by the pointed tips of their ears and their unremarkable clothing. Thoughts of the gray-eyed boy from Solana's stories and the countless others like him occupied the forefront of Shara's mind. She edged forward, searching for rounded ears. If there were human servants in Merania, it seemed they didn't labor in this harbor.

Movement from the vessel captured Shara's attention. Flanked by two of his men, the captain—or the fae Shara assumed was the captain—walked down the gangplank. A fae stepped forward from the landing, arms across his chest.

"You're late," he said. His soft voice was reminiscent of Derron's tone when he used his magic, though if these were truly low fae then the man wouldn't have the gift of the Song. Perhaps it was typical of Meranians to have every word sound like a lover's murmur.

"Apologies." The captain removed his battered tricorn hat. Unlike the other man, his voice was rough and harsh on the consonants, like a less refined version of Mykal's accent. "You must know the queen set perimeters along the coast and inspections are even more thorough for ships coming in and out of Daganver. It was out of our control."

The other man waved off the apology. "No matter, you're here now, and with these cloaks, I'll no longer have to listen to a Nahar whine about the cold." The hairs at the back of Shara's neck stood on end at the name. "I doubt you'll have as many problems with the return trip. Our Head's got himself some guests of honor."

"Guests of honor?"

The other nodded. "Rumor has it a dragon was sighted in the early hours flying over siren waters."

"A dragon? But no one's seen a dragon for years. Not since…"

Once again, the other nodded gravely. "And now the general's returned with none other than the prince and Mykal Todrak in tow."

"The prince and Mykal Todrak?"

Shara sucked in a breath. It was nothing she hadn't already suspected, but she couldn't help the pang of fear hollowing her chest. Were her friends safe? Was she too late?

"Have you turned into a parrot? Stop repeating everything I say."

"Are you sure of this, mate? First, a dragon returns, and then the prince and Mykal Todrak sail together?"

"It's true, I tell you. It seems Lord Andren is planning a feast in their honor before the prince sets sail for Adara."

"Sounds like fiction to me."

"Don't believe me? We'll see who's telling fiction after I return from the palace."

As the men said their farewells, Shara sliced her palm and stepped into the darkness pooling at her feet. She identified the captain and his men, and then followed the retreating forms of the low fae who returned to a smaller ship than the one she'd hidden on until now. Some of the men loaded the last of the cargo into its hold, and Shara glided in after them. Judging from the conversation she'd overheard, they would be headed to the palace to deliver some cloaks. Unbeknownst to them, they would be delivering Shara as well.

The shadows became harder to tell apart in the scarcely lit space. Unable to rely on sound while using the Maiden's gift, she waited until the darkness contorted and betrayed the ship's movement to forsake her cover. Shara bumped face-first into a crate and held out her hands to steady the small stack before it could topple over. She scrunched her nose against the sharp pain and a curse slipped between her lips. It took a few moments for her eyes to adjust to the dark space, but the heavy air and the way she crammed between the crates betrayed the tightness of her accommodations. This smaller vessel was likely meant for the sole purpose of delivering goods into the palace.

I still believe my plan was better, Deimok chimed down the bond with a sound akin to a chuckle at her distress.

Shara rolled her eyes.

The journey to the palace was short, but it felt like a lifetime cooped up as she was between the crates. No sooner had the vessel anchored at its new port than Shara drew new blood from her palm and slipped into the cover of darkness. Light flooded the hold a few minutes later. Several men stepped inside to unload the cargo. Shara followed, a wolf prowling in their shadows. It wouldn't be practical to linger in the darkness for long. While the Maiden's gift kept her concealed, it also hindered her other senses. She would need them to find her way in this unfamiliar environment and save her friends. For now, the men were the easiest way to access the palace. The fae at the harbor mentioned cloaks intended for the Nahar—hence, the nobility. If she found the nobility, she would likely find Mykal and Kael, so long as they were guests and not prisoners.

They reached a new area, one where the shadows skittered about. Servants, perhaps, tasked with distributing goods to their intended owners. Shara glided to what seemed to be the shadow of a stack of crates. She sent a silent prayer to the Maiden and the Dragon that it would be enough to conceal her before stepping out of the darkness. Noise rattled her mind—the thump of crates being set on the floor, the patter of slippers over smooth tiles, the commanding tone of a woman who directed servants to this lord or that lady. Each of them had the pointed ears of the fae, and once again Shara found no trace of human labor.

Shara crouched behind the crates and cast a precursory glance at the room. Though large, the area was scarcely adorned. Large bay windows were the room's main source of illumination. Sewing supplies, cutlery, and an array of decadent serving trays littered the wooden desks cast against the white-and-blue walls.

The lid of one of the crates in front of Shara was askew. A quick peek inside revealed cloaks made of dapple-gray fur, the same carried in armfuls by the servants who hurried from the room.

"Those need to be taken to Lady Maira," the woman instructed one of the servants.

Shara made quick work of the belt of daggers at her hip and reached into the crate. Even her heart had aligned to the frantic pace set by the woman-commander. The cloak was far too heavy to have any practical use, but the fur's warmth radiated through her fingers at the slightest touch. Shara threw her belt across her arm and covered it with a cloak. Her plan was hazardous, but with a bit of luck, everyone would be too busy to notice an unfamiliar face. Once she gathered a small stack of cloaks, most of her front was hidden from view, along with the blood splattered on her shirt and the weapons she carried.

Shara scurried to line up after the servants headed for the door. A victorious smile sprang up on her lips as she neared the threshold despite her racing heart.

"You, there."

Shara stopped, a shiver raking down her spine. The daggers were too far from her reach, trapped by the weight of the cloaks slung over her arm. As she turned to face the fae woman, she kept her gaze downcast and stoked the flicker of Fire at her core. Though weak, the flame warmed at her summons like a cat arching beneath its master's hand.

"Don't drag those on the floor," the woman reproached. "They're worth more than you earn with a month's wage."

Relief coursed through Shara, though she fought against the instinctive slump of her shoulders.

Shara followed the other servants down the hallway. Pastel shades of coral, green, and blue coated the high walls, and every corner and archway was lined with white marble. Candles hid behind golden ceramic shells and paintings adorned the walls, each one depicting a different scene from Merania's history. One showed sirens circling a shipwreck at the bottom of the ocean, indicating a time when the creatures were the only rulers of the sea. Another rendered a vicious fight between sirens and fae, commemorating one of the many moments of bloodshed that characterized the Siren Wars. Another still depicted the wedding between a fae and a siren—Vembren Nahar and Sahariel, whose love ended the conflict. That had been one of Maenar Elvik's most successful lessons.

Shara followed the servants up a winding staircase of white and gold. From what she'd spied of Merania's palace, the building was wider than it was tall. Shara suspected that the majority of the palace extended below water and the surface floors were devoted to guests. Lavish fragrances tickled her nose and grew stronger as they ascended. The servants stopped at the first landing, which broke into various sections of wide, intersecting hallways.

Shara peeked into each one in search of guards. She was estranged from the ways of Ilahara, but the presence of guards would likely signify illustrious guests—or prisoners. Shara counted four intersections before she spotted two guards flanking either side of a door at the end of a hallway. Their chests were bare in the Meranian fashion, and each held a spear. Shara's senses tingled in alert. None of the men had mentioned other nobles aside from the prince and Mykal, which increased the chances of one of them occupying the room.

Use the shadows, a voice which sounded like the Maiden's lilted, but her gifts could alert the servants or the guards. Besides, Shara couldn't be certain she was right about the identity of the room's occupant, and she couldn't find out while lurking in the dark.

Muscles tensed, Shara glanced at the row of servants. She counted three breaths as she waited for one of them to break the line. Several did, but none ventured toward the guards. She could almost hear Mykal's voice ring in her ears and advise her to caution. If an important guest resided in those chambers, why had no one instructed the servants to deliver them a cloak? Powerful people used expensive gifts to woo one another into partnerships. Shara had seen it firsthand in the Lioness's Establishment.

With a steeling breath, Shara turned for the room. The guards stood straighter the moment she left the line, their attentive gazes sweeping over her.

"Are those for the prince?" one guard asked with an undercurrent of amusement as she approached.

If Mykal were here, he'd be screaming conspiracy louder than a dragon's roar. Had it been luck that she'd found the Argarys prince so easily? Pushing down the queasy feeling knotting her stomach, Shara nodded.

"I don't reckon seeing you around before. Are you new?" the other asked.

"Stop that," his companion reprimanded with a short laugh. "You'll have to come back later, sweetheart. The prince has his hands full."

Shara cursed wordlessly. She wished she could wipe away the smug smile on one guard's face and carve the eyes out of the second. His lingering gaze made her feel as if she were covered in grime. "The prince is expecting me," she said slowly to make sure her Havanian accent wouldn't betray her.

A moment passed. Then another. The two guards shared a knowing look and wolfish smiles. Shara fisted her hands beneath the cloaks.

"Very well," the first guard said with a nod. He opened

the door.

"When the prince is done with her, I'll pay her a visit, too," she heard the other guard say as the door clicked shut.

Shara grimaced. "Pigs," she muttered under her breath and dropped the cloaks unceremoniously on the ground.

She fastened the belt of daggers at her waist and entered a living room colored in light shades of green and coral. A couch rested against the wall, big enough to accommodate two people. The tea on the small table in front of it remained untouched. The lack of vapor rising from the cup indicated it had been sitting there for a while. Moonlight spilled inside from the open balcony, and a midnight breeze carried with it the salty scent of the ocean. It reminded Shara unnervingly of the prince lurking somewhere within this room.

Shara felt like she'd walked right into the lion's den. Derron would know where in the palace the Meranians kept Solana and the Do'strath. If he'd lied to keep them safe, did that make him her ally? Had he done it for Kael's benefit?

Why was he protecting them?

Shara clutched the hilt of one of her daggers. She couldn't know where Derron stood now that he was free and protected by his mother's allies.

Careful of any noise she made, she padded to the bedroom. The only source of light came from a second balcony. A large wrought iron bed occupied the space immediately to her right. A young woman lounged naked on rose sheets. Swirls of silver paint colored her pale skin. It covered her legs and belly, following the curve of her breast and whirling around the peaked hill of her nipples until it rose up her throat in dizzying spirals. The color was resplendent in the pale light of the moon. Her hair was the same light green of the walls and held half up by a silver pin. Shara's attention narrowed on the rounded curve of her ears.

Human. This woman was human.

The two women stared at one another in a moment of shocked silence, Shara immobilized by the sight of a human in Derron's bed and the woman staring wide-eyed at the stranger in the bloodstained shirt. At the human's quick breath, Shara anticipated the sound of her scream and sprung.

Shara's hand silenced the woman's muffled cry before she could sound an alarm. She forced the woman's back against her chest and wound her arm around her neck, applying enough pressure to incapacitate.

The human went limp in her arms, and Shara eased her back on the bed. She brushed fingertips against the woman's pulse point. The tightness in her stomach receded at the gentle beat. This close, she noticed there were starfish, pearls, and seashells drawn into the intricate designs on the woman's body, the same one engraved in the iron bed frame. From an artist's perspective, it was a beautiful composition, but Shara's skin crawled. A human's body had been decorated in the same manner as a piece of furniture as if she were a doll or a pet to be used when its masters fancied. No wonder she saw no humans in the harbor. What use did merfolk have of servants who couldn't serve them below water, where they dwelled the majority of the time?

Shara bit down on her lower lip. Her insides were rattled, but outside she was steel. She prowled closer to the bathing room. A fresh scent wafted to her, enveloping her in its clean fragrance. A twinge of envy overcame her. Weeks had passed since she'd had a proper bath and she refused to acknowledge how terribly she must smell in comparison.

A sliver of golden light beamed into the main chamber

from the door left ajar. Shara nudged it open further, hand lingering in close proximity of her daggers as she chanced a glance inside.

Derron stood with his back to her as he reached for a towel. Water trickled along his bare skin as if desperate to cling to his body a moment longer. Shara's gaze followed the drops as they wriggled from his wet hair onto his broad shoulders, his muscular arms, his sculptured back, and lower still to the firm muscles of his buttocks. He was like a work of art, though Shara doubted any mortal artist could have created something so proportionate. It was unfair that so much beauty should belong to a single man.

Warmth flooded her face and her eyes widened as they followed the patchwork of burn marks marring Derron's back. Scars scattered along its surface from his shoulders to the end of his spine. Their sizes varied, and the red lines had long since faded to pale pink. That the marks were there at all meant they'd been caused by magic—otherwise, they would have healed.

Alerted by her sudden breath, Derron looked over his shoulder. "I told you I don't want your services." Though the glamour around Shara's eyes held, it took him a single glance to recognize her. His muscles went rigid, and the air between them thickened. They stared at one another, unmoving.

Shara charged first.

She barreled into him, crashing them both into the wall. The water on his skin seeped through the fabric of her shirt. With one hand, she covered his mouth to keep him from speaking. With the other, she pressed the tip of her blade to his throat.

Shara's speeding pulse betrayed her nerves. She'd seen Derron use his Song in Havanya without a single word. She could only hope that, should he choose to use it, her magic would warn her of his intrusion and give her enough time to counter. "One peep, and I'll slit your throat."

Derron hesitated a moment before he nodded. Shara drew her hand away slowly and took a careful step back. For a moment, her traitorous eyes slipped below his waistline.

Derron took advantage of her distraction. He grabbed her wrist and locked his foot around her ankle in one fluid movement. Shara plummeted to the ground, her back hitting the smooth marble of the checkered floor. Air swooshed out of her, and stars dotted her vision. Derron was on her before she could get her bearings. His body pinned her to the ground as he held her dagger to her throat.

The scent of sea moss and ocean breeze lifted from his skin, fresh and heady at once. Shara couldn't help the flush of heat racing up to her cheeks, so at odds with the cold flow of the blood in her veins. "Go on then, do it," she challenged in a shaky breath. "Make your mother proud."

Derron gritted his teeth, applying more pressure to the dagger. Shara refused to succumb to fear. If this was her last breath, she would meet it with grace, and she wouldn't make it easy on him. She relinquished her hold on the glamour, and let the gold drown out the hazel. Derron's silver gaze remained steady on hers, yet she felt his hand tremble.

"We should start doing this when we're both dressed," he whispered. His breath brushing against her lips sent traitorous shivers down Shara's spine. She hadn't been this close to a naked man since Rami, and that her body should react to the nearness of a man who had tried to kill her twice was nonsensical.

Derron dropped the dagger as he straightened and heaved a great sigh.

Shara furrowed her brow as she lifted herself onto her elbows. "Why do you keep hesitating?" Derron scoffed, but

Shara pressed on as he grabbed the towel and wound it around his hips. "You attempted to kill me in Havanya, and when you failed you pursued me. Yet you've hesitated at every opportunity." Her frown deepened. "When you could have let me die by other means, you saved me. Don't you want me dead?" She stood and took a step toward him. "Am I or am I not your enemy?"

"One would think you'd be happy you're still breathing."

"You're evading my question."

"What do you want me to say, Shara?" She flinched at the sound of her name on Derron's lips. "That I'm a shit killer? That I'm a failure as a prince, a son, a brother? That I lost my nerve?"

"What happened to your back?"

Derron seemed taken aback by her question. "Another lesson I didn't learn." He moved past her and into the main chamber. Shara followed in time to see him looking at his bed, where the human was still unconscious.

"Your mother gave you those scars." Who else could have dared to raise a hand to Aerella's son? The stiffening of Derron's back was confirmation enough. Bile rose in Shara's throat. How old had Derron been when Aerella inflicted those wounds? What crime could he have committed to deserve such treatment?

Before she could think it through, Shara lifted shaking fingers to Derron's back and grazed a smooth scar along his spine. Derron stilled, sucking in a breath as he turned to face her.

Shara dropped her still outstretched hand.

"I don't see why you should concern yourself with my scars," he said.

They were close enough for Shara to spy the flecks of blue in his silver eyes. Her throat was dry when she swallowed. "We were friends once."

Derron's gaze lingered on her a moment longer, the

silence charged with tension. He seemed on the verge of saying something, then thought better of it, and he stepped back to put some distance between them.

"How can you serve her after all she's done?" Shara asked.

"You shouldn't have come here."

"Where else should I be? My sister is here, as are Mykal and Kael. I don't abandon my friends."

"The best you can do for Arkael and Todrak is to forget about them. The only thing saving them from execution is the fact that they weren't found with you."

"And the fact that you didn't mention their involvement with me," Shara added.

Derron ignored her. "As for your sister, she's been seen to by a physician. She's alive but spent."

Shara clutched her chest, nearly collapsing with relief. "Do you know where they've taken her?"

Derron nodded. "I'll take you to her."

38

Once Derron dressed, he sent the guards outside his door away with an excuse. Shara couldn't make out the soft words spoken by the prince, but she heard one of the men snicker and felt tempted to lodge a dagger between his eyes. The human woman was still unconscious in Derron's bed. In the time she waited, Shara tucked her under the covers so she wouldn't wake naked. A part of her knew it was foolish. The woman was a prostitute, and modesty had likely been trained out of her long before she'd ended up in the prince's bed. Yet after the fright Shara had given her, the least she could do was make sure the woman woke up to the comfort of a blanket. Even Derron had shown Shara that small kindness on the night of Rami's death.

When it seemed like a reasonable time had passed for the coast to be clear, Shara emerged from the bed chamber and glared at Derron by the door.

"I haven't made allusions if it's any comfort," he said.

It wasn't, but there was no reason to discuss the matter

further. Shara walked over to the cloak she'd dropped on her way into the room and hid her belt of daggers beneath its folds. She would need it as an excuse to enter Solana's room. "Men think what they think."

"At least it'll avoid questions."

"Just take me to Solana."

Derron nodded. "Come."

Shara didn't have to follow him far. Derron led her to the next hallway, and Shara immediately spotted a guard stationed outside one of the doors. Shara kept her head low and her pace steady, but all she wanted was to drop the heavy cloak and run to her sister.

"Let me speak to the guard," Derron whispered low enough for only her to hear. "You keep your mouth shut until you enter the room."

"Why is there only one guard?"

Derron raised a brow. "Why should there be more?"

Because you've seen what Solana can do. Shara pressed her lips together to keep the thought to herself. The cautious part of her that had taken to speaking with Mykal's voice returned. With the Maiden's darkness at hand, one guard was hardly an obstacle for Solana, so unless her sister's condition was so severe that Andren Nahar didn't feel the need to station any more men at her door, this was a trap. "Will Solana be all right?" Shara asked Derron instead.

"What did I tell you about keeping your mouth shut?" A smile hid in the corner of Derron's lips. "You'll see for yourself."

They had almost reached the door. Shara looked to Derron one last time. "I suppose I should thank you. If Andren Nahar had someone look at a human stranger, it wasn't out of the goodness of his heart."

"Strong words for someone you don't know."

"I don't have to know him. I've seen enough of this

place to know his kind." Shara only had to think of the human currently sleeping in the prince's bed, who was simply another embellishment in this beautiful palace. Even though she didn't say the words aloud, Derron turned away as if ashamed. It wasn't his fault humans in Merania were treated as pets, or that somewhere in Ilahara they were likely used and abused in other ways, but he was the prince and he'd done nothing to help them. "The boy I remember would change things."

"The boy you remember is gone."

Shara lowered her voice as they approached the door. "I saw scars, Derron, not ashes."

"Your Highness." The guard saluted the prince, bringing his hand to his chest. He didn't spare a glance in Shara's direction.

"This young woman will take care of the human's needs. Should she be in need of anything, make sure you provide it." Derron said.

Shara's hands became clammy with sweat beneath the cloak as she listened to the exchange. It was the first time she saw Derron in his role of prince, and he played the part well. She was reminded of her father, who could exude authority even with the kindest words. The thought stung more than she cared to admit.

The guard nodded and opened the door for Shara. For a moment, she feared more guards would rush out and seize her, and she tensed. But none came.

As Shara took a step toward the door, she felt the brush of Derron's fingers against her side, the touch concealed by the cloak's folds. "Farewell."

Shara listened to the sound of his retreating steps, her heart suddenly heavier than before. Derron had said goodbye, which meant he didn't plan to see her again. He expected her to return to Havanya, and perhaps Shara would have—once. But she was no longer certain she was the same person she'd been two weeks ago. She was still Shara, but with everything that had happened in the last weeks, she was also rediscovering pieces of Asharaya within herself. The divide between her two identities was no longer as wide as it had been.

Vengeance called to her, and not only for her family but also for Deimok. And for Mykal, whose life had changed on that dreadful night, too. Whether there was something of her friend left in Derron or not, their paths would cross again, and they'd be enemies either way.

Shara opened the door and entered a room similar to Derron's. She treaded lightly to the bedroom, heart lodged somewhere between her chest and her throat. If Solana didn't wake, if the Maiden had taken more than she could give, Shara wasn't sure she'd have the strength to survive another loss.

Xoro sat on the side of the bed, his hand covering Solana's. Shara knocked on the doorframe to alert him of her presence. "It's me," she said before he could inquire.

"Shara?"

At the sound of her sister's voice, Shara dropped the cloak and stopped only to grab her belt of daggers before hurrying into the room. She walked around Xoro's big frame to find Solana sitting against the pillows. Her brown skin was paler than she'd ever seen it, but her sister was awake. The white gown she'd been dressed in gave Solana the appearance of a phantom. Relief washed over Shara like fresh summer rain, and she didn't think as she threw herself onto the bed and wrapped her sister in an embrace. "You're okay."

Solana laughed, but she was unable to hide her flinch.

Shara jerked away. "Sorry."

"How did you get here?" Xoro asked. "The Meranians are looking for you and your dragon." Awe crept into his voice when he mentioned Deimok. "You shouldn't be here."

"Xoro's right," Solana said. "It isn't safe for you."

"And leave you here?" Shara's lips thinned in a stubborn line. "You must have hit your head harder than I thought, Lana."

Solana may have been tired, but her gentle smile was as beautiful as ever. She took Shara's hand, squeezing as tight as she was able. "I love you, sister. I'm sorry."

Shara shook her head. "We'll talk later. We don't have much time." If Andren Nahar and his people were indeed looking for her and Deimok, the longer they stayed in Merania, the more dangerous it became. She had no doubt in her dragon's ability to hide, but she wouldn't put him at risk longer than necessary. She turned to Xoro. "The Do'strath?"

The click of the main door, followed by the sound of an unfamiliar voice, interrupted them. "Your suspicion wounds me, Mykal. How can you doubt that we're treating your human friend? You're absurd."

"You don't show trust by having us tailed by your guards." Mykal's irritation was palpable in his tone. "We just want to verify that she's all right."

Shara and Xoro had only the time to spring to their feet before the men entered the chamber. Mykal and Kael stood on either side of a tall, dark-haired man. Two guards were behind them, one being the man previously stationed outside the door. Kael's and Mykal's mouths hung open at the sight of her, but the third man overshadowed their surprise. His attention narrowed on Shara's face, and too late she realized what he saw there. The golden eyes of the Myrassar, and the amber skin of Queen Jaemys. Shara had removed her glamour in Derron's room, and she'd forgotten to conjure it back. Recognition sparked in the man's blue eyes, and Shara grabbed one of her blades.

"You're Princess Asharaya."

Kael slammed him face-first into the doorframe. The

man crumpled to the floor, a smear of blood in his wake. The element of surprise played in their favor. Shara lunged toward one of the guards while Mykal tackled the other. Shara struck her opponent in the face with the hilt of her dagger, rendering him unconscious before he could swing his spear. Mykal wrestled the other man on the floor, holding him in a chokehold until the man's body went limp.

Shara walked over to Mykal and helped him back to his feet. "What are you doing here?" Mykal asked. "It's dangerous."

"I'm saving you."

A flash of heat started at the back of Shara's neck and spread toward her cheeks at the softening of the Do'strath's expressions. They, too, had likely expected her to run back to Havanya and escape the past that had found her and the violence that came with it.

They hadn't believed she would come back for them.

Shara pointed to the black-haired fae unconscious on the floor. "Who's that?"

Mykal cleared his throat, eyes glistening. "That vermin is General Raxan Nahar, the Head's cousin." He brushed past her to the window. "Well, then, how do we escape?" He looked out the balcony, scanning the skies. "Where's your dragon?"

"Are you mad? If I let Deimok anywhere near the palace, he'd be seen." Shara crossed her arms. "It would defeat the whole point of sneaking here unnoticed."

Mykal tilted his head back and released a groan of the long-suffering. "Can you magic us out of here the same way Solana did with the ship?"

Solana reached for Xoro's hand, and he helped her onto her feet. "I could do it."

"No," Shara and Kael said together.

Solana's dumbfounded gaze turned to Kael as did

Mykal's. "You're too weak," he explained.

Shara agreed. "I won't let you risk yourself like that." She addressed Mykal next. "I'm not like Solana. I can't carry all of us at the same time."

"You must have some plan. How were you planning on getting us out of here?" Mykal asked.

"The same way I came in."

Mykal clapped his hands. "Lovely. We're all going to die."

Shara rolled her eyes, though warmth spread through her chest. Weeks ago, she never would have thought to find friends in the fae who had come for her or that she'd grow so fond of Mykal's pessimism and Kael's quiet strength.

"Nahar had our weapons confiscated before showing us to our rooms," Kael said, tone grave. "Myk and I could combine our powers if it came to a fight, but fighting the sirens took more out of us than we'd anticipated. We're not at full strength."

"How's your Fire?" Mykal asked Shara.

Shara reached for it, but her Fire was still a sputtering flame. "Not well."

Mykal looked like he wanted to throttle her. "We warned you not to use too much."

"If we're lucky, we won't need magic to escape." And Shara prayed her luck would hold as she turned to Solana. Xoro helped her stand, but her sister was unsteady on her feet. "Can you walk?"

"No, but I'll run."

Mykal placed a hand on his Do'strath's shoulder. The touch seemed to ground Mykal, and he stared at each of them with new resolve. The camaraderie binding them was an invisible thread, but Shara felt it settle inside her heart with vigor. The people in this room were a piece of a mosaic that made up her soul—the sister who'd saved her when the world was dark, the fae who'd gifted her friendship, the pirate who'd risked it all to bring her home. Shara allowed herself a moment to take in their faces and sent a silent vow into the world that she'd protect them with all her might should the need arise. "The guards will be low fae, but there may still be some high fae hidden in their midst and they'll have their Song," Mykal said. "Stay alert."

As Kael reached for Solana to help Xoro support her, Shara opened the door a sliver and peeked outside. A servant closed the door of one of the rooms down the hall, and Shara listened in on the hushed sound of her hummed tune as she padded to the stairs. Once she was gone, the hallway was deserted, and no sounds alerted Shara to the contrary.

Shara signaled for the others to follow as she eased open the door. They kept close to the pastel walls as they stole down the hall, with Solana, Kael, and Xoro at her back and Mykal guarding the rear. Shara memorized the route she'd taken, but the Do'strath moved as if familiar with the palace, hastening their pace.

Her stomach dropped to her feet at every intersection they passed. Hope sprang up in her whenever she found each hallway empty, but the cold touch of steel from the hilt of her dagger reminded her to stay focused.

Is everything all right, Asharaya? Deimok's voice rumbled down the soulbond.

I found them, Shara answered as she peeked into the next intersection. If doubt were an insect, she'd stomp it down without remorse. Instead, the feeling slithered unwelcomed into her thoughts. The prince resided on this floor, but no guards patrolled it to ensure his safety. The servants slipped in and out of rooms, but no sounds came from them as if they were uninhabited.

One last intersection separated them from the stairs. Shara's heart sped, pulsing blood into her ears. She wanted to scream at her own thoughts and run for the safety of the stairs and the refuge of the servant's quarters. Once they reached those, freedom was within their grasp.

Gaze fixed on the stairs and head throbbing in tune with the drumming of her own heart, Shara didn't notice her pace had quickened until Mykal tugged at her shirt. Startled, Shara flinched and stumbled. Her boot squeaked against the tile floor, and in the dead silence of the hall, it echoed like the gong of a bell.

A spear shot out of the last intersection, missing her by a breadth.

Shara barely heard Mykal's muffled curse. Dread coursed through her as a dozen guards poured from the adjacent hallway, a barrier of flesh and steel between her and the stairs. Two others filed out after the guards, unhurried as they positioned themselves in front of their lines. One was a man with white hair and a shark's smile, but it was to the other that Shara's gaze slid and held. Twin swords with blue jay pommels were strapped to his back, hands curled into fists at his sides. Unreadable silver eyes looked straight at her, and the blue jays glinted as if laughing in scorn.

Dread morphed into a stone weighing down her chest and made it hard to breathe.

"Derron," Kael gasped.

39

A sharaya, is something amiss?
Deimok, they know I'm here.

Derron's gaze didn't stray from Shara. His throat bobbed, unnoticeable if she hadn't been staring back with the same intensity. She'd expected his betrayal—he was an Argarys—yet it stung now that she faced it. He had made her hope for a trace of the boy he once was, despite his earlier attempts on her life.

The boy you remember is gone.

Shara hated the quake in her knees and the way she kept searching for signs of regret on his face.

Mykal and Kael flanked her sides. The cold touch of Mykal's Ice seeped through the leather of her pants as it frosted his fingers. Though Shara didn't turn, she sensed Solana's presence at her back. "We're surrounded," her sister whispered.

Shara peeked over her shoulder. Raxan Nahar, the black-haired man Kael attacked in the room, had regained consciousness and now led a few dozen men at their backs.

They were trapped.

The man with the white hair chuckled, sensual and amicable at once. The sound reverberated through Shara and chilled her bones. "Well, well, if it isn't Asharaya Myrassar. We've been expecting you." He made a half bow, meant as a mockery rather than a show of respect. "Andren Nahar."

"Charmed," Shara said with the same amount of sarcasm dripping from his tone.

"I didn't think you would return, but the prince believed you'd come for your friends." He looked at Derron, who didn't smile. "He said we'd only have to plant clues of their stay in the palace throughout the city to lure you here."

The men at the port. They were servants following their Head's orders. That she'd heard of Mykal and Kael from them wasn't blind luck—if not from them, then she'd have found out through other means. Derron had orchestrated every event so that she'd learn they were guests, not prisoners. So that she'd find them without difficulty. Her blood curdled.

"You set me a trap."

Andren Nahar laughed. "Yes," he answered, even though her gaze burned holes into Derron, who stared back unflinching if not for the regular tightening of his fists. "To catch you, Asharaya, and those who support you." The Head of Eathelin's smile was nothing short of malicious as he looked at Mykal. "Two birds with one stone, one could say. Quite brilliant."

Mykal bared his teeth.

"Talking on our behalf was just a show?" Kael wasn't good at hiding the emotion from his voice.

"We needed incontrovertible proof of your treason, or the Daganverans could have said Her Majesty, Queen Aerella, had framed you to dispose of the Todrak," Andren

Nahar rattled on. "That kind of unrest leads to civil war. But with the Head of Eathelin, his general, and palace guards to support the prince's claims? No one would deny the truth of it."

"I wasn't talking to you," Kael snapped. Derron continued to ignore him. "You saved me on that ship. What was the point? Did it mean nothing?"

Finally, Derron looked to his brother. Silver eyes met blue, and regret seemed to flash in the prince's eyes. Shara didn't know if it was true, or if she'd conjured the emotion. The truth was she didn't know who Derron was. "Seize them."

The guards moved in unison at their prince's command, spears poised to attack. Solana grabbed a dagger from Shara's belt while Shara unsheathed the one she'd been clutching.

Mykal thrust his hand forward. Daggers of Ice found their mark in one guard's neck and in another's shoulder. The first went down with a wet gasp. Blood gurgled from his open mouth. The other shouted in agony but hesitated only a moment before he continued his charge.

Shara sprang from behind Mykal. She flung out her arm as she ducked, and her blade drew a red line through the man's calf. He fell on his knee, but his grip on the spear remained firm. Shara swiveled out of the weapon's range. A flash of blue arched before her eyes as an Ice sword collided in the spot between the guard's neck and shoulder. The weapon splintered at the impact. Blood spurted from the gash, spraying both Shara and Mykal. His eyes glowed blue as they met the golden ones of the Myrassar.

"Thanks," they said in unison.

A meaningful look was all they could exchange before they charged back into the melee. Guards surrounded them. Kael sent out whips of Fire, which caught some in the legs and limited the number of guards charging for Solana and Xoro. Her sister slashed at those who got too close, but her breaths were heavy from strain and sweat broke in beads on her brow. Shara attacked whenever she was close enough to inflict damage, her daggers an extension of her body. The guards fought to incapacitate and not kill, but Shara had no such qualms. She scoured for weakness, and steel cut through every unguarded flank. Where her blades struck, death followed.

The fizz of Kael's Fire whip rang over the clamor of steel. A line of red cut a path through the guards, creating an opening between Shara and Derron.

Shara tightened her grip on the hilt of her bloodied daggers.

A distant cry gave the fighters pause. The sound belonged to no human or fae. Seconds ticked past, and the whisper of unsheathed steel and the scuffle of feet were the only sounds. Enemies and friends looked to one other with bated breath.

An ear-splitting roar, closer this time, shook the foundations of the floor beneath their feet. The wall came crashing down, and Shara spun in time to catch a black blur among the debris.

Deimok had come.

The men cried out, crushed by the crumbling structure. Deimok dragged others with his hind paws in his flight. The dragon braced for impact and smashed through every wall standing in his way. Everything—the hallway, the rooms beyond it, the balconies—collapsed.

The palace quaked around them.

Shara stepped back and grabbed Solana with one hand and Mykal with the other. "Hold on," she shouted. Mykal held onto Kael's shoulder and pulled him back as the floor vibrated. Where Deimok flew, the ground shook, coming undone under the weight of debris. The hole grew larger as more of the foundation caved in. General Nahar ordered his men to move back, but some weren't fast enough. They plummeted into the chasm, crushed by the landslide of rocks and pillars raining down on them.

Deimok made a wide turn and raced back toward the castle. General Nahar shouted orders to his archers, and the men aimed their arrows on the dragon charging in their direction.

Deimok, Shara's terrified plea shot down the bond. *Turn back.*

At General Nahar's command, the archers released their arrows. Shara's scream clawed at her throat. She slashed at the fae standing in her way, starting forward as if she could stop the arrows with nothing but the force of her will.

Arrows whizzed into the gaping hole where the wall had been. Deimok veered sharply to the left, and the arrows flew past him. The dragon's panic cut Shara's breath short. The memory of pain pierced her mind. The men's screams overlapped with those from the dreadful night of the Coup of Fire, and the sound of Andren Nahar's order to seize her and the others muted. Shara's focus was on her hand and the arc it made as she reached out. A volcano erupted within her. The tiny flicker of her magic rose in a pillar of destruction, coaxed to life by fear and determination. Exhaustion burned away as the same Fire that had killed Rami now answered her call to save Deimok.

A column of Fire spiraled from Shara's palm. It blasted through the line of men, scorching at least three of those holding the bows. Shara bellowed as she rotated, widening her Fire's range to include more of the Meranians. The screams of the dying and Deimok's triumphant roar filled the air.

Around her, Mykal and Kael fought the Meranians. Sometime during the fight, Xoro had disarmed one of the guards and now used the weapon to defend Solana, who fought back-to-back with her lover.

Someone barreled into Shara and knocked her over the chasm's edge. She wasn't sure which of her friends called her name. Pain speared through her back when she hit the mountain of debris that had formed at the bottom of the hole. Shara rolled down, and someone not too far from her grunted as they tumbled to the floor. Her blistered wrists caught the worst of the impact. Shara screamed at the agony traveling over her body, momentarily blinded by it.

Asharaya, Deimok called, panicked.

Shara rolled onto her back, drawing in a strangled breath. *I'm okay.*

They were in the lower level. The servant's quarters were empty but for the corpses of the guards. Not too far from her laid Derron, bloodied and blistered, twin swords still strapped to his back. Breathing heavily, he turned to her. Their gazes met, and for a moment neither of them moved. He'd thrown himself at Shara to stop her from roasting the men who were hurting Deimok and risked his own neck in the process.

Shara tasted blood in her mouth, and she spat it in Derron's direction. She must have bitten herself during the fall. "You're fucking insane."

"You had to be stopped."

"I won't let you kill him." Shara rose on unsteady feet, fighting against the barking throb of her body. Derron also rose and was similarly unbalanced. "Your family has taken enough," she said.

Sometime during her fall, she'd lost her dagger, but she grabbed the two strapped to her belt. Rage gave her the necessary strength to rush at Derron. He ducked before she could slice his throat, unsheathing his double swords. It was an uneven fight, but she was tired of the Argarys besting her.

Derron made to slice her middle, and she jumped

back. Pain was forgotten as adrenaline and magic kicked in. With only two daggers as weapons, she had to rely on speed. Shara danced a careful breadth away from Derron's strikes. Derron hacked with his swords, slicing the air. The prince's swords were as deadly as they'd been in Havanya's market, though his movements weren't as precise. His left leg had taken the brunt of the fall, but with magic healing him, the slight limp would be only a short-lived advantage for Shara.

Shara twisted away from Derron's swords. Drawing on the blood coating her skin, she slipped into the darkness at her feet. She emerged a moment later from a shadow beside Derron. He spun in her direction, wide-eyed. As he made to attack, Shara struck with her dagger, fast as a viper. Her blade sank into his right hand. Derron's scream silenced the sound of his sword clattering to the floor. Shara lunged for it and rolled back on her feet once the blade was in her grasp.

The weapon was heavier than her sword, clearly crafted with Derron's body and strength in mind. She imagined it felt light as a feather in his hands, as natural an extension as her daggers were to her.

Derron panted through the pain. Blood dripped from his torn hand. He pointed his other sword at Shara, eyes simmering.

"You wanted us to face off in a fair fight," Shara said as the two circled one another, swords at the ready. "Looks like you got your wish."

Derron wasn't wearing any armor. If she found the right opening, she could put a swift end to this fight. She aimed for his neck. Derron, however, didn't leave himself open to attacks. He parried each of her strikes without losing ground. Their blades sang in a perfect duet.

Shara feigned an attack on Derron's chest. Then she dropped low and swung for his legs. Derron jumped back, but Shara persisted in her onslaught. Derron rushed to meet her blow. Their swords clashed, his strength having the better of her speed. Shara stumbled back and crashed into the wall. Her blade pushing against Derron's was the only barrier between their bodies.

"That was quite the performance you pulled off in your room," she snarled through her teeth. "What did I expect from an Argarys? You excel at stabbing your friends in the back. Your mother would be proud."

Tremors wracked Derron's body, and he bared his teeth.

"I used to think you were the most valiant of Elon's friends. You were kind and honest. Honorable." And Shara had loved him, in the way a child could love. Her eyes stung, but she continued, relentless. "You were right. The boy I knew is gone. I'm glad Elon isn't here to see the man he became."

Derron screamed his fury and backed away, raising his sword.

Shara stepped into a pocket of darkness before the blade could touch her. This time, she struck from above, falling onto him. Derron toppled to the ground. Shara pinned him down. She immobilized his arm with her knee to prevent him from using his sword and pressed hers to his neck.

"You don't choose your family," Derron said in a broken voice. A shimmer of tears swam through his eyes. Perhaps she hadn't been wrong. Perhaps the boy she remembered was still in there, buried beneath a patchwork of scars.

That didn't change what he'd done.

She forced the blade harder against his neck, drawing a bead of blood. "You're wrong."

Solana's scream startled Shara and she whirled toward the chasm. She looked up to see Xoro's limp body come rushing down toward her. Shara extended her hand as if she could freeze him in midair or catch his fall, but the pirate crashed to the floor with a deafening thud. The crunch of his head hitting the ground was a nail piercing Shara's heart, and Solana's desperate cry the anvil sinking it deeper inside.

"Kill me and be done with it," Derron hissed.

Shara spun back to him, his face distorted through the tears clouding her vision. He had caused this. If he hadn't betrayed them, if he'd tried to be better than his wretched mother, none of this would have happened. Shara's hand shook. There was no version of her plans in which Derron survived. Whether she killed him in front of Aerella or struck him down on opposite sides of a battlefield, his life would end either way.

"Do it," Derron whispered. His throat bobbed as he swallowed.

Do it. Shara couldn't remember Aerella's voice, but the smooth tone in her thoughts conjured her silver hair and eyes and the bloodstained train of her dress. The hidden laughter in the voice taunted her to take the killing blow.

But Shara was not like Aerella. Derron had been her friend, and the weeks of forced proximity on the *No One* made those memories of Asharaya's past occupy more space in her mind than they should have. In those weeks, Derron had rescued her from her dream when he could have let her own nightmares consume her. He'd helped them save the crew from the siren's Song even when Shara no longer held him at knifepoint. He'd been ready to die with her when the sirens surrounded them.

Shara's hand shook, and the pressure on Derron's neck eased.

Asharaya, Deimok's voice shot down the soulbond. *Tell your friends to reach you. I am coming.*

Instead of slicing Derron's throat, Shara smacked him on the side of the head with enough force to incapacitate him. She would have time to regret it after her friends were safe.

Shara scrambled from the prince's side and ran to Xoro. Blood spread from his head, but it wasn't the fall that had killed him. Xoro had been stabbed. A hole pierced his belly and blood seeped through his clothes.

Shara wished there was time to mourn Xoro properly, but that would have to come later. She shut his eyes and whispered a prayer to the Maiden that she judge him fairly. Then she looked up at the chasm and called to the Do'strath. She couldn't be sure they were still alive, but she had to hope.

A small weight lifted from Shara's chest when Kael appeared over the gaping hole in the ceiling. He held Solana as he slid down the rocks, her sister frozen in shock. Mykal followed immediately after. No sooner had they touched the ground than it shook again with the weight of another wall coming down. This time Deimok tore through the floor, headed straight for them.

"Arrows!" one of the Nahar ordered.

Shara called out and gestured her friends toward the dragon.

Kael helped Solana onto Deimok's back. She cried as she tried to reach for her lover. Arrows shot past them. One struck Deimok's tail. The dragon let out a roar, more of panic than pain. He whipped his tail and struck the wall.

"Go," Kael said to Shara. He helped Mykal climb after her. A wound on Mykal's leg made it hard to mount the dragon without assistance.

Once Kael climbed behind Mykal, Deimok lifted with a powerful thrust of his hind legs. The Nahar called for order, but the castle crumbled around them. Deimok breathed Fire to stop the Meranians from firing more arrows as he flew toward the opening he'd created. To freedom.

Metal pierced the air, and someone grunted behind

Shara.

"Kael!" Mykal shouted.

Shara looked over her shoulder with a sound halfway between a gasp and a scream. Kael fell over the side, an arrow embedded in his shoulder. As he plummeted toward the hole, Kael reached out for the ledge, barely grasping on as guards rushed him. Mykal made to throw himself after Kael, but Shara held him back by his shirt, grip tightening as he tried to wrest free.

Deimok, stop. We have to go back.

Asharaya...

More arrows fired toward them, this time from below. Guards stood on boats and rose from the water. They fired at the dragon, shooting arrow after arrow without mercy. Shara moved to shield Solana with her body. Deimok veered so the majority of the arrows jumped off the tough scales armoring the majority of his chest, but still he roared as one found his wing.

The dragon rained Fire upon them.

"Shara, please," Mykal cried. "I can't leave him."

An arrow narrowly missed Deimok's throat. It wiped away Shara's hesitation, hardening her heart, though tears lined her cheeks.

Guards swarmed Kael, and it was the last thing Shara saw before she urged Deimok to escape.

40

Shara didn't know where else to go. Muscle memory led her to the island that had been her and Deimok's refuge. It wouldn't be safe for long. The Nahar were looking for them, and sooner or later they'd find this island. She needed some time to collect her thoughts. Her mind swarmed, and she was unable to focus.

Going back for her friends was a decision Shara didn't regret, but she could find no peace while the mistakes she'd made followed her like ghouls. She'd expected some sort of trap, yet when Derron dangled the possibility of being on their side, she'd wanted to believe him. Shara walked right into his deception, feeling the weight of the lie but choosing to remain blind, all because she hadn't let go of a boy who no longer existed. She should have killed him. Instead, she showed mercy, a mistake that came at a high cost. Kael was in enemy hands. And Xoro was dead. Another name to add to the list of friends lost to Asharaya Myrassar.

No sooner had Deimok touched land than Mykal leaped from his back, tromping away as if he couldn't stand to be near her. "Myk," she called, to no avail. Mykal didn't deign her a glance. Shara rubbed her temples, the blood marring her fingers scorching against her skin.

"Go talk to him," Solana said, voice raw from crying. Shara squeezed her sister's hands. If only she could take away Solana's grief and remove the tears making her brown eyes glisten. If only there were time to wrap her in an embrace and give her strength if not comfort. "Don't let this rift between you fester. You need him, Shara, and he needs you."

Shara's grip on Solana's hand tightened. "You need me, too."

Solana swallowed hard. A tear lined her cheek as she looked out toward the blackened horizon. "There is nothing you can do for me." She removed her hand from Shara's. "Xoro is...he's gone. But Kael can still be saved."

Shara leaned forward to kiss Solana's forehead. She could give Solana this time alone to grieve, but she'd be there to comfort her in any moment that came after. Family had gotten Shara through the aftermath of the Coup of Fire. Friendship was the lifeline that would get her through losing Rami. It didn't erase the pain or wipe away what happened, but it helped. Family and friendship were the pillars that made life worthwhile.

Shara brushed her fingers along Deimok's neck. *How's your wing?*

Healing, Deimok said, reassuring her though his voice sounded tired. *I am sorry, Asharaya. I have failed you.*

You've done no such thing.

Shara kissed her dragon's scales and made her way to where Mykal stood by the ledge. His gaze was lost to the sea in the direction of Merania. "Forgive me," she whispered. "I thought I could get us all out unscathed. I overestimated myself."

"It doesn't matter," Mykal said, though his voice suggested otherwise. The space between them was colder than the Ice that flowed in his veins.

"They would have killed Deimok." It was no excuse, but if anyone could understand the fear and primordial need to keep her dragon safe, it was Mykal. The same instinct urged him to protect Kael. The same bond now multiplied his worry and fear tenfold. "Can you feel him?" Shara asked after a beat of silence.

"He's alive," Mykal whispered, hand on his chest. "I abandoned him. He's my Do'strath and I left him."

Shara grabbed his arm and forced him to look at her. Something in her chest shattered at the broken look in Mykal's eyes and the fear contorting his handsome face. She squeezed his arm. "You can't blame yourself for something you couldn't control. You didn't fire that arrow, and you couldn't throw yourself after him. It would have gotten you both killed."

"So, it's best to let him die alone?" Mykal wrenched free of her grasp. "I made an oath to him, Shara. Through blood and fire."

"Listen to me," Shara begged. "No one is going to kill Kael. As things are, he's leverage. They'll use him to turn you against me, do you understand?"

Mykal closed his eyes, every muscle of his body taut. "I can't lose him."

"You won't." Shara stroked his cheek with the back of her fingers. When he looked at her again, the shadow of determination she'd grown to admire darkened his brown eyes. It coursed through her and set her mind in motion. "We're going to help your family, and we'll rally our allies. If it's a war Aerella wants, we'll bring it to her."

"Does that mean you'll fight for your throne?"

"It means I'll fight for my friends." Shara pulled Mykal

into a fierce hug. "We're getting him back, Myk."

Mykal embraced her with the same fervor, and Shara's gaze strayed to her dragon. His approval rippled down their bond. The red in his eyes blazed in the dark as if a fire raged behind them. Together, they turned south. Somewhere past the horizon was their home, the golden castle on the cliff that had seen Asharaya born and then broken. Away from it, she'd honed herself into a blade.

Now it was time to be a flame.

Pronunciation Guide and Glossary

Characters:

Aerella Argarys: Eh-reh-llah Ar-gah-ris
Andren Nahar: An-dren Na-har
Arkael/Kael: Ar-kell/Kell
Asharaya Myrassar/Shara: Ah-sha-rah-ee-ah
Mee-rah-ssar/Sha-rah
Baramun: Bah-rah-moon
Cassia Argarys: Cas-see-ah Ar-gah-ris
Darrok Todrak: Da-rrok To-drak
Deimok: Day-mok
Derron Argarys: De-rron Ar-gah-ris
Dougas: Doo-gus
Eileen Todrak: Ayl-een To-drak
Elon Myrassar: El-on Mee-rah-ssar
Gailen Myrassar: Gayl-en Mee-rah-ssar
Imiri Vynatis: Ee-mee-ree Vee-nah-tis

Jaemys Myrassar: Jay-miss Mee-rah-ssar
Johan Vynatis: Yo-han Vee-nah-tis
Korban: Kor-ben
Luna Todrak: Loo-nuh To-drak
Mykal Todrak: Mee-kal To-drak
Rami: Rah-mee
Raxan Nahar: Rak-san Na-har
Semal Leneris: Seh-mal Leh-neh-ris
Solana Spirre: So-lah-nah Spear
Vaemor Argarys: Veh-mor Ar-gah-ris
Xoro: Ksoh-roh

Places:

Adara: Ah-dah-ruh
Daganver: Dah-gan-ver
Eathelin: Eh-theh-leen
Havanya: Hah-vah-nee-uh
Ilahara: Ee-lah-ha-rah
Lur: Loor
Makkan: Mah-kan
Merania: Mur-ah-nee-uh
Tyrra: Tee-ruh

Other words:

Ashari: Ah-shah-ree (I am here)
Do'strath: Doh-strath (Soulbound warrior)
Dragaelan: Drah-gay-lan (Friend or beloved)
Drakasi: Drah-kah-see
Maenar/Maenari: Meh-nar/Meh-nah-ree (Scholar)
Vrahiid: Vrah-heed

Acknowledgments

Between the flash of a beautiful fire-wielding wraith living in our minds and the physical book *Ilahara* has become today, this has been a journey years in the making and the list of people to thank is long.

To Ren, the witness of our fangirl moments and desperate breakdowns. Thank you for always supporting your crazy sisters and their love of words and for providing the much-needed insights on fight sequences, armors, and weapons that your gaming experience grants you. We couldn't ask for a better younger giant brother.

To Kiche, the most dramatic dog queen the world has ever known. We can tell by your confused little face that you don't understand why your humans spend so much time on the strange device called a computer, but we wouldn't exchange your bossy interruptions and your loyal companionship during editing time for anything in this world.

To our parents, for shaping us into the women we are

today and for your counsel and loving support.

To Gabriella Bujdóso, whose art and vision for this story has turned it into more than we could have ever done on our own. Thank you for your friendship and talent. You'll forever be our dragon fairy godmother.

To Sharon Salonen, editor extraordinaire. Your passion for our book has motivated us in more ways than we'll ever be able to put into words. Thank you for believing in us, for challenging us, and for helping shape *Ilahara* into something we're incredibly proud of.

To Susan Brooks and the team at Literary Wanderlust. When we thought the querying trenches would keep us hostage forever, you opened your doors and gave us a loving home. Thank you for all that you do for us writers and for giving us a voice in the important decisions regarding our book's future. You are magic, and we're thankful to be a part of your vision.

We wouldn't have gotten through writing (and editing!) this book without the support of our closest friends. A giant hug and endless gratitude to:

Our Italian sassy pants and crazy cat lady, Maria Rosaria. Siamo fuori dal bosco!

Jess (@starlitlibrary), thank you for the writing advice and for being the most passionate, loving, cookie-making auntie to the Do'strath.

Our owl, Marina (@marey.reads), thank you for your support and enthusiasm.

The most wonderful and supportive group of ladies #bookstagram has ever seen: Giota (@giota_the_reader), Thais (@tata.lifepages), Vanessa (@ve_xo), Ambrine (@the_riddle_reader). Thank you for the laughs, the rants and for being your strong and capable selves.

Carmen (@kimcarlika). Your friendship has been one of the best gifts. Thank you for cheering us on and for uplifting our works with your talent. Your designs are incomparable and your Ilahara chapter header will forever be tattooed on Chiara's face.

Aleksandra (@acedimski). Where do we even begin with you? You've been with us since Ilahara was only an idea. You've read every version and know every doubt and joy this story has instilled in us. Thank you for collecting our tears during the querying hell. Thank you for motivating us day after day and for believing in us when we struggled to believe in ourselves. Thank you for the long hours plotting covers. For your vision. For the map! Just...thank you. This book will always be yours as much as ours.

The High Ladies of Fae Crate, Meagan and Brittany, and their team of badass ladies. Thank you for believing in us from the very start and for giving us a magical purple crate to help our story reach more readers.

A special thank you to the wonderful Ilahara Beta Dragons we haven't mentioned yet: Joyly (@queenof_midnight), Alex (@captain.valour), Anna (@rattletheshelves), Christine (@arcana.imperii), Lisa (@littlemeadowreads), Meeghan (@meeghanreads) and Mena (@darkdecembers).

A group hug to our writer friends, with whom we've shared the joys and woes of the writing and publishing journey: C.J. Rafaké, Tyffany Hackett, Becky Moynihan, Hanna Sandvig, Swearingen Durham. You're all superstars.

All our love and gratitude to the #bookstagram community. Thank you for being such a supportive space, for your excitement about our book baby, and for being the most amazing community the world has ever known.

And lastly, to you. Yes, you. Thank you for giving Ilahara a chance. Thank you for giving two girls with a passion for writing stories a chance. We hope that you've lost yourself within the pages of this book and that you've laughed and cried as much as we have while writing it.

Thank you, from the bottom of our hearts. Through

blood and fire.

About the Authors

C. M. Karys is the author name of two Italian sisters, Chiara and Maria Elena. Their love of reading and writing started in reading classes with their American teachers in elementary school. As young girls, their love of fantasy was fueled by obsessive Disney marathons and the Harry Potter series; they have added Game of Thrones to that list. When Chiara and Maria Elena are not hunched over a notebook jotting down ideas for stories or hiding away in their writing cave they can be found on Instagram discussing books with the online community. They currently live in Naples with their family and their dog queen, Kiche.

Follow Chiara and Maria Elena on Twitter and Instagram @_ckarys and @_mkarys.

CPSIA information can be obtained
at www.ICGtesting.com
Printed in the USA
BVHW071108161121
621753BV00005B/117

9 781942 856832